Egret's Cove

a Webb Sawyer Mystery

by

Douglas Quinn

Other Books by Douglas Quinn

Webb Sawyer Mysteries

Blue Heron Marsh
Pelican Point
Swan's Landing

The Ellis Family Books/Suspense

The Catalan Gambit
The Spanish Game
The Capablanca Variation: The End Game

The Ancestor Series/Historical Fiction

Cornelius The Orphan
Samuel The Pioneer

Mystery Suspense Anthology

Four of a Kind

Children's Book Series

The Adventures of Quinn Higgins: Boy Detective
—The Case of the Missing Homework
—The Case of Bigfoot on the Loose
—The Case of the Haunted House
—The Case of Blackbeard's Treasure
—The Case of the Lost U-Boat
—The Case of the Gray Ghost's Belt Buckle

The Adventures of Summer McPhee of Ocracoke Island
—The Midnight Skulker
—Kilroy Was Here!
—The Pink Lady

Charles and Hero (Fantasy)
—Charles of Colshire Castle
—Isle of Mists
—The Dreadmen

Little Books for Little Readers

—Gracie The Undercover Beagle
and her Sidekick Boston Blackie—The Egg Thief

—Solstice The Determined Beagle
The Long Journey Home

Egret's Cove
a Webb Sawyer Mystery
by Douglas Quinn

ISBN 13: 978-1511994347 / EAN-10: 1511994347

Published by AAS White Heron Press
1623 Soundneck Road, Elizabeth City, NC 27909

Printed in the U.S.A.

Cover Art by Donna Higgins Colson
Cover Design by Kim Colson

Thanks to

Donna Higgins Colson

and Brenda Kay Wynn

for the

readings and good advice

This one is

for

Big D

I wish you were
still around to read it

"Amicus certus in re incerta cernitur."

— Quintus Ennius (circa 239-169 BCE)

Prologue

Does madness end where reality begins?
Or does reality begin where madness ends?

WHEN MASON LANE wrote, he was never sure whether he lived in the real world or in the fantasy world he was creating. When he was younger, it was video and online fantasy games that drew him in. Until his mother gave away all of his equipment.

After his mother died, he used money from her estate to purchase another state-of-the-art game station and computer. It was then he realized that gaming was no longer satisfying. That was when he turned to writing. He did use the computer to write because writing everything in longhand was too frustrating. He just couldn't write as fast as his mind set out the scenes and the dialogue.

When he wrote, he felt as if his fingers worked the keyboard independently of his mind. He would sit down at the computer, conjure up the scene, then later, sometimes five or ten minutes, sometimes hours, he found he had written several pages. It was like magic.

Elizabeth Traynor stood in front of Dr. Alejandro Soto's desk. She gave him the hand-written paper. "This morning's production," she said.

Dr. Soto read what Mason Lane had written. "Hmm. Interesting. This is the first time he's talked about himself and his mother, rather than just one of his fantasy scenes."

"And his writing," she added.

"I still find it interesting that in his scenes he uses his own name as the main character. And here," tapping the page, "writes about himself in the third person."

"And that he believes he is writing it on a computer."

"This is great stuff for my book," Soto said. "Great stuff."

"So I should keep him on the increased dose of alprazolam."

"I think so, Miss Traynor. As far as his writing is concerned, he's not near as lucid on the lower doses."

"Odd isn't it?"

"In what way?"

"That a higher dose will help him focus on his writing."

Dr. Soto laughed. "He's a special case, Nurse Traynor. Too complex for you to understand. That's why I'm the doctor and you're the nurse," shooing her away with the back of his hand.

Red-faced, Elizabeth Traynor left his office. From that day on, she made it a point to deliver Mason Lane's papers whenever Dr. Alejandro Soto wasn't there. Two days later, she delivered the following bit of writing from Mason Lane.

Mason Lane had sent a message by raptor. Now he watched as the raven-haired beauty, seated upon the neck of her red dragon, came flying across the arid plain. When she and her mount neared the castle, they swooped down and landed in the huge courtyard, just inside of the gate.

As soon as the girl dismounted, Mason ordered the guards to feed and water the reptile, then took her by the hand. They went immediately to his quarters. Mason quickly undressed and laid back in his massive bed. He watched the girl as she slowly undressed, bit by bit revealing familiar parts of her body. When both breasts were exposed, he became erect.

"This is where he stopped writing," Elizabeth Traynor said after Dr. Soto had tracked her down in one of the patient halls. Soto had been sweating and she could tell he was agitated.

"How can I analyze his motives if this is all I have!" from Soto.

"I can't make him write. He writes when and as much he feels like."

Soto glared at her. "Maybe you should bare your breasts for him."

"What?"

"See if that will stimulate him to continue where he left off."

"Are you crazy, Dr. Soto?" Then, before she knew what had happened, Alejandro Soto's left hand shot out and closed around her throat. Startled, she dropped the clipboard she'd been holding and it bounced twice before it came to rest on the highly polished black and white tile floor.

"You like your job here, Miss Traynor?" Her eyes had gone Orphan Annie round, her mouth opening and shutting like a fish out of water. "Won't be able to take care of your mother if you lose it, will you?" Soto's eyes pierced her like a rapier. He let go and pushed her away.

Elizabeth threw her hands to her throat and gasped for breath.

Dr. Soto started to walk away, then turned and said, "Don't you ever call me crazy, bitch!" When she didn't answer, he shouted, "You fucking understand?"

She nodded and croaked out a "yes."

"And I want anything from him delivered in person," he ordered. "I don't like to find them on my desk without being able to question you. You understand me?"

Again, she nodded.

The words, "Insubordinate bitch," trailed behind him as he stalked down the hall.

Mason Lane sent off his work of fiction to the Fantasy Magazine fiction contest. When the submission made the cut as judged by the magazine staff, the top ten would be personally selected by his favorite author. Mason didn't want to mention the author's name because he knew someone was reading what he wrote. He knew his minders would try and sabotage his chances if they were made aware of his judge.

As for the story, Mason didn't think in terms of whether or not his story would make the cut. He knew it would. And he also knew that it would be selected over the other nine. When he won he would not only be published in the most prestigious magazine in the genre, but he would receive a $5,000 publication fee. He would be the special guest of his favorite author at the next World Fantasy Convention.

Now all Mason Lane had to do was wait for the letter from the magazine, announcing him as the winner.

"Where is the rest of it?" Soto demanded.

"As I told you before, sir, he only writes when he feels like it. He may be writing more in his head and not putting it on paper." Elizabeth Traynor's voice trembled. She'd never liked Dr. Soto. Now she was afraid of him.

Soto's phone rang and, as he picked it up, he waved her out with the parting shot, "Encourage him to write more." She was thankful he didn't mention baring her breasts as an incentive. She'd been expecting him to accompany her to Mason Lane's room and force her to do so.

Mason Lane didn't write another word while he waited for a reply from Fantasy Magazine. Why were they taking so long? And he was sick of that idiotic shrink who called himself Dr. Soto. In his mind, Mason Lane called him Dr. Dodo. And what was with his nurse, the Traynor woman? Did she really think that taking off her blouse and bra was going to make Mason Lane write more than he wanted? She did have a nice set, though, and Mason Lane didn't bother to look away.

"I'm beginning to lose interest, Miss Traynor," Dr. Soto said. "I'm ordering you to go back to his room and convince him to write. Tell him that we won't feed him until he fucking writes! You understand me?"

"Sir, we can't do that. It's against—"

Soto stood up and came around his desk. "Against what, Miss Traynor?" Elizabeth shrunk back. "You listen to me, bitch" he said, shaking his bony finger at her, "You do whatever you need to do to get him to write more. Get naked if you have to."

Elizabeth Traynor began to cry. "Don't make me do that, sir." She'd been mortified when she'd had to bare her breasts for the little twerp. Whether she needed the job or not, she was ready to just walk out of there and never come back. There was only so much she could take from this bastard.

Where is my letter from Fantasy Magazine? It doesn't take that long to sort out the wheat from the chaff and realize I'm their winner. I'm beginning to get angry now.

ANGRY!

#

"Good morning, staff," looking to his left and right.

The other four doctors returned the "Good morning" to Dr. Avery Janowitz, the chief of staff for the Harrow-Martin Psychiatric Hospital.

The five of them sat in white, high-back leather chairs around a U-shaped wood conference table. The drapes were drawn on the plate glass windows behind the three men and two women, exposing a deep rolling lawn with the Appalachian Mountains on the horizon. Beneath the windows, three pots of coffee were on a serving table: a bold, a mild and a decaf. There was also a substantial selection of donuts and Danish pastries. Everyone had made their selections and was ready to begin.

"This morning we will begin with the case of Elizabeth Traynor. Her files are in front of you; however, I would like to start with the video. If you will, Miss Chamberlain."

Samantha Chamberlain, who was standing by at a desk in the corner, punched some commands on the computer keyboard and, soon, the video began. When it ended, Dr. Charlise Acton said, "Interesting. I take it she's a multiple."

"Seems that way," from Dr. Janowitz. "It is interesting that she doesn't bother to change her voice when she takes the part of Dr. Alejandro Soto or Mason Lane, particularly since they are both males."

"And that she uses her own name for the nurse character. Something we need to explore," from Acton.

"It is also curious that when playing the part of Mason Lane, she pretends she is writing while she verbalizes the text," Dr. James Anderson offered.

"She certainly has an active imagination," said Dr. Jane Courtland.

"And well spoken," from Acton.

"How long has she been here?" from Dr. Perry.

"Only a week," from Janowitz. "We wanted to get something to work with before we began the sessions." Agreement cascaded around the table. "Her story is in the file, but I'll give you a brief account before we begin discussion on her treatment."

Dr. Janowitz told them that Elizabeth Traynor had always been a troubled child. When she was sixteen, her mother died. There was never a father in the picture. She had a good relationship with her grandparents, who she visited every summer, but after they passed, with her mother gone, she ran away before she could be placed in the foster care system during the last two years she was eligible.

Eventually, she found her way to an aunt on her father's side. According to the aunt, while there, Elizabeth lost herself in video games and online gaming. She fancied herself a writer, and spent a lot of time writing stories that were never published, and hanging around fantasy conventions.

"The aunt said that she became so withdrawn into her fantasy worlds that she couldn't take care of herself and, in fact, became a burden. In addition, the aunt said she'd become afraid of her, although she could never quite articulate exactly why."

“Maybe the aunt was looking for a graceful way to extract herself from Elizabeth’s care,” Acton suggested.

“Highly possible,” said Dr. Janowitz. “Fortunately for us, the aunt had the financial resources to buy her way out of the problem, which is why Elizabeth is now here.” He shrugged. “Now, I suggest that while you finish your pastries, go ahead and take the time to read through the file. Then we will begin our discussion about how to proceed.”

Chapter 1

DURING MY ARMY days, the man I worked for in The Hague, Colonel, now General, Brad Tillman, once showed me a quote about friendship that has stuck with me over the years. Oddly enough, it was attributed to an advertising executive by the name of Lois Wyse. It stated, "A good friend is a connection to life, a tie to the past, a road to the future, the key to sanity in an insane world." I remembered it because it more closely fit my view of the matter than anything else I'd seen or read.

My father, on the other hand, had a much narrower view of friendship. "Most people you know or meet," he told me, "don't deserve to be called a friend. They barely deserve to be placed into the category of an acquaintance." I'll never forget his reply when I reminded him that if he was acquainted with someone, all that meant was that he knew them, nothing more. He said, "You never really know someone until you can get into their mind, and if you ever do that, the chances are you won't like what you'll find."

Dad and I have—had, as he has since passed—a different take on the meaning of the word "friendship." I agreed with Dad in one respect—the word "friend" is thrown around rather loosely by most people. Me? I don't think I have too many friends. Mine fall into different categories. There are my few close friends, who I see and interact with frequently, those who are good friends who I don't see as often because of geographic restraints, and those with whom I'm not particularly close, but who I'd do a favor for, if asked.

Dad was straight-forward about it. He said, "If you aren't willing to step in front of them and take a bullet, they ain't no friend."

My ideas on friendship had more to do with loyalty than whether or not I'd take a bullet for them. Brad Tillman was a friend who was loyal to me, even though I was a lowly sergeant. If it wasn't for him, I'd be spending the rest of my life, or at least a good chunk of it, busting rocks at Leavenworth. He got me the lesser of two evils; a stint in the U. S. Army looney bin in Fayetteville, 'cause I must have been crazy for shooting a Serbian prisoner of war in the face with a 350 magnum.

But that's another story—one I'm tired of telling.

As for friends, I'm not sure where I place Nan Ftorek. Of course we're friends. Close friends. When you're in bed together getting hot and sweaty, you're real close . . . and real friendly. No. Nan is in a special category all by herself. What category that actually is, I'm still contemplating.

Old friends are the best. And by old, I mean long time. I've known Blythe Parsons since the fifth grade at the Weeksville School. That's the old Weeksville School, where everyone from the Weeksville area, first through the twelfth grade, attended. They since built a new one, just for kids up through the fifth grade. The rest all have to travel so long by school bus that it's almost like workers who make the daily work commute from the Elizabeth City area up to Tidewater, Virginia.

Blythe Parsons was born with spina bifida, a neural tube defect that caused the failure of her spine to close properly. Even though Blythe had surgery shortly after birth, the nerve damage was permanent, causing paralysis in the lower limbs. Because of the inability to use them, Blythe's legs from the knees down had atrophied and were maybe half the normal length, with no muscle tone, although she had sensation down to her knees.

The thing about Blythe was that ever since I'd known her, she was always upbeat. She never played the "feel sorry for me" card. I've always admired her. We became friends when one insensitive lout made some awful remarks about her condition and I beat the living crap out of him. The five-day suspension from school was worth it.

I thought about all of this as I traveled south down highway 12 from my stilt home at Blue Heron Marsh, located in the waters off the Nags Head-to-Manteo causeway.

Blythe, who I called Bly, had invited me down for some fishing in the Pamlico Sound, pronounced Pimlico by the locals. Blythe didn't let her handicap get in the way of enjoying life. She liked to fish and she had a twenty-foot blue and white Boston Whaler tied up at a pier behind her house. She'd named it *Lady Bryn,* after one of her book characters. She also had a lift apparatus installed on the pier to get her in and out of the boat.

Blythe was a fantasy writer. She began writing after her parents died. She'd never said, but I guess it kept her mind off the fact that she was suddenly on her own in the world and had to find a way to survive. She was not only talented but lucky. The work of most writers, even good ones, never see the light of day.

She'd started writing short stories and even won a Hugo Award for best short fiction. After that, she had no problem finding a publisher for her first novel *Lady Bryn and The Red Dragon – Book One of The Chronicles of Nnyw,* for which she won another Hugo, this time for Best First Fantasy Novel. Her second *Chronicles of Nnyw* novel, *The Elvens of Ackersly* made the Science Fiction and Fantasy Best Seller's List and was one of three featured novels on the Sci-Fi/Fantasy Book Club new issues. Her most recent book, *The High Kings of Kull,* was still topping the fantasy best seller's list and had been in the top ten overall best selling fiction for over six months.

Blythe was currently working on the first book of a new series. Her publisher had wanted to continue on with the *Chronicles of Nnyw,* offering her a three-book contract for books four, five and six. She said no, she was ready to move on to new worlds and new characters. When they balked at her plan, she threatened to go to another publisher. They caved and gave her a high, five-figure contract for the first book of the new series based on a one-page story idea. In the world of fantasy fiction, Blythe Parsons was a force to be reckoned with.

By the time I hit the Bonner Bridge over the Oregon Inlet, my thoughts had turned to fishing. Before I picked up Trusty Rusty, my dad's 1986 faded, powder blue Ford Ranger pick-up, which was still running after 245,000 miles—frequent oil changes and tune-ups helped keep the engine alive and cranking—I'd stopped in at Brant Cloninger's Whalebone Junction Bait and Tackle Shop on the causeway.

Brant was a long-time friend who let me use his docks to moor my boats when I made runs back and forth to the house. He also allowed me to park Trusty Rusty at the far end of his lot, since stilt homes out in the marshes don't have driveways and car ports.

Even though I had a pretty good armory of lines, lures and leaders, I always like to see if Brant has anything he'd like me to test. If he does, I get it free and he gets my unbiased report. When I'd told him our main target was red drum, his eyebrows raised. I'd shot the breeze with his son Adam, while Brant went in back to look for whatever had lit him up.

Red drum, known as channel bass, also called old drum because they can live up to fifty years of age, are best fished with a chunk of mullet on your line—according to old timers, anyway. I thought Brant would bring out some fancy artificial lure that was the best/latest/fanciest hot-out-of-the-catalogue wonder bait. I figured it would even include a secret odor and taste that was irresistible to red drum, so help the Gods of Fishing. Instead, he came out with a thirteen foot rod, tough enough to handle heavy terminal tackle with a reel larger than any I'd experienced for sound fishing; one that could handle several hundred yards of fifty-pound test line. "It has the best drag system I've ever seen," Brant said, ending his spiel.

"If I catch anything with it, do you want the whole fish, or will you settle for a dozen filets?" I asked, joking.

"A whole fish would be a little much, don't you think? The filets would be good if you can spare them." He was serious. I laughed and said a dozen filets would be his if I was so lucky as to land a good one.

Brant had gone on to tell me that dark nights, heavy tackle and oyster beds were the secret to catching the "old ones," but I would leave that up to Bly because, believe it or not, for this fish she had a lot more experience than I. And for a small girl in a wheelchair, that's really something.

The storm surges and shifting currents from last year's passing hurricanes, tropical storms and nor'-easters had caused major shifts in the channels used by the North Carolina Ferry System's boats that hauled traffic back and forth between the southern end of Hatteras Island and the northern end of Ocracoke Island. For several months, people traveling by car to Ocracoke had to go all the way around the mainland to either Swan Quarter or Cedar

Island and take the ferry to Ocracoke Village. In the meantime, new channels had to be dredged further out into the sound. Once they were ready, it added an extra twenty to thirty minutes to the trip. I didn't care. I had plenty of time.

Bly wasn't expecting me until sometime after three pm. I presumed that meant we'd be heading out early the next morning. Then again, maybe she was on to the dark nights theory that Brant had mentioned, although she had said something about buying me dinner at Howard's Pub on Highway 12, so maybe not. In any event it was a three day excursion with free accommodations in Bly's guest room, so I wasn't in any hurry if she wasn't. She'd even said she would stock up on snickerdoodle, my favorite coffee, and Grolsch, my *only* favorite beer.

I had wondered if my friend and lover, Nan Ftorek, would be jealous of my spending overnights at another woman's house, but she knew all about my and Bly's brother- sister-like relationship. In Nan's smarty-panties way she'd said, "The only two pussies you love and feed are both right here at Blue Heron Marsh, waiting for you to bring back the goodies."

Goodies!

While I was away, Nan was staying at my place, cat-sitting my four-legged child, Basil, who would probably sit in the window the whole time, waiting and watching for my return.

* * *

With the new route, the ferries were running late and even though it was June, traffic was already beginning to build. I had to wait over fifty minutes because the first ferry back in filled up just before the car in front of me was ready to go aboard. I'd yawned, leaned my head back and dozed until the horn from the next incoming boat jarred me back to the land of the living.

An hour and five minutes later we arrived at the docks at the northern end of the island. It was a twelve mile trip to the village but, as I was in no hurry, several miles down the road I pulled in at the corrals where they kept Ocracoke's wild ponies, hoping to spend a few quiet moments watching them.

The Banker ponies, as the locals called them, were supposedly abandoned on the Outer Banks by sixteenth and seventeenth century shipwrecked European explorers, but who knows the real story. I'd read that these animals, which are smaller and more compact than standard horses, even had different vertebrae and rib structures.

However, there wasn't a pony in sight. *What the hell*!

I was dying for a cup of snickerdoodle and angry at myself for leaving behind the thermos I'd specially prepared. I knew I'd have to count on Bly for the correct blend. From past experience I knew that no one else in the village had a clue what snickerdoodle was, even the one and only coffee shop on Back Road.

Putting that out of my mind, I decided to walk across Highway 12 and up the boardwalk to the ocean side. I was horrified to see that the high white dunes had been completely washed away and, in fact, the walkway ended abruptly, boarded across so that unconscious hikers wouldn't fall of the edge. Since the horses and the beach there were big tourist attractions, I was surprised it hadn't already been repaired. And where were the damned horses?

Damn fools in Raleigh. If it didn't put any money in their and their friends' pockets, they weren't interested. I laughed at my own political-based ranting thought. My father always said, "It don't do no good to get yourself worked up about what they're doing in Raleigh, no matter what party is in. They're all in it for themselves." Maybe he was right, I don't know. Whatever their occupation, narrow-minded, greedy, short-sighted, racially bi-ased, misogynystic blowhards were hard for me to ignore.

No ponies. No coffee. No dunes. My mood had turned sullen.

Now anxious, annoyed and aggravated, I caught up with and pushed Trusty Rusty past several slow pokes who had gotten off the ferry after me. If I had a cell phone, I'd've called Bly and said, "I'm ten minutes out. Brew the coffee and have a hot mug waiting."

Annoyed that I was too difficult, if not impossible to get in touch with, Bly had once sent me a cell phone along with one year's worth of service. Some of my friends call me a technophobe. I'm not really. I do have a laptop computer, which I use to do certain types of research. But as for Facebook, Twitter and all that social media crap, forget it. And cell phones? I live out on the marsh for a reason. I enjoy peace and quiet, and the idea that anyone at any time of the day and night can intrude upon that irks me to no end. I had a friend use Bly's cell phone for target practice, then mailed Bly a check for what I presumed she'd paid for the phone and the service. She'd never asked about it or mentioned it again. Now that's a true friend.

Okay. So I could wait for the coffee to brew or go straight for the beer. I was contemplating this important decision when I entered the town limits. Rather than go all the way down Highway 12 to British Cemetery Road, I turned right at Sarah's Snack Shack and cut over to Back Road, where I turned left. This cut out the ferry traffic which, by now, was fighting for the few parking slots available along Silver Lake Harbor.

As I passed the Ocracoke Coffee Station, I had a brief thought about stopping and . . . I kept going. At the end of Back Road, I turned right on British

Cemetery Road. Shortly, I passed the tiny plot of land that housed the odd little cemetery with the same name as the road. An interesting story.

The short version is, there is a memorial plaque with all the names of the Brits who died after their ship, the *HMS Bedfordshire,* was torpedoed by a German U-boat. Four men who washed up on shore were buried in what was now known as the British Cemetery. The cemetery is officially British territory and considered forever part of England.

A few minutes later, I pulled underneath Bly's stilt house. The house sat on a corner lot. Actually, it was on two lots. The west side of her property faced the Pamlico Sound, the north side, which was the back of the house, faced a small bay where her boat was moored. The house was built on eight, six-by-six posts.

From the outside it was a modest looking home on stilts. To the right was an attached carport that housed Bly's specially converted silver Chrysler Town and Country van. A concrete ramp led up to the carport, allowing the van to be parked five feet above the ground. In Ocracoke Village, particularly right next to the water, this made sense. I'd heard about cars floating away from flooding during major storms.

I exited Trusty Rusty and headed toward the elevator that allowed guests access to the house.

There was an intercom with a button, a doorbell, so to speak, for guests to announce their presence. Before I pushed it I listened. Bly had hearing like a cave bat and usually was right there to greet her guests, especially when she expected their arrival. I heard nothing, so I pressed the button.

While I waited, I walked past the elevator so I could get a better look out toward her pier.

Huh?

No boat there.

Odd. Very odd.

I went back and buzzed again.

Waiting.

Nothing.

Had she forgotten I was coming? I didn't think so. It wasn't like her to forget anything. Had she taken the boat out for a test run and wasn't back yet? Was I early?

I didn't wear a watch, so I returned to the truck, inserted the key and turned the key to on without cranking over the engine. It was 2:47 pm. I was a little early. I returned beneath the house, walked to the back, pulled myself up onto the boardwalk and walked out onto the pier. The arm of the device she used to maneuver her and her wheelchair in and out of the boat was still out over the water. I stood there for several minutes, looking out into the sound. I saw a boat heading northwest, away from the village, but it didn't look like hers.

"Huh!"

I went around to the garage. There was a gated ramp that led up to a walkway between the house and the garage. Actually there were two gates, one at the bottom of the ramp, and one at the top. As I remembered, both had remote controlled coded locks. Both gates were shut, but I tried the handle on the lower one anyway.

Locked.

I stood there for a while thinking about whether I should just hang around the boardwalk and wait, or check out the garage and house. I decided to wait. Bly liked her privacy and just because we were friends I didn't want to take advantage.

After what I guessed was about half an hour, my impatience got the better of me. I vaulted the lower gate, then the top one. I remembered the garage had no windows, so I couldn't see inside. I tried the door. Locked.

Reluctantly, I walked down the boarded walk onto the covered open deck that overlooked the bay. I knew the railed-in porch wrapped around the west side of the house to a covered glassed-in porch that had a hot tub at the far end. Except for the larger doubled-pane window to her study, all the windows had blinds that were closed. The room that Bly called the study was where she did her writing. I looked inside. It was empty and everything seemed in place. I tried the door handle. It was locked. I continued to the hot tub porch, as I called it, and tried that door. Also locked. Except for the elevator, all Bly's direct entrances to the house were on the back.

"Damn!"

Should I continue waiting or should I find a phone and call her? I opted to go find a phone.

Normally, I wasn't a worrier, but as I backed out from beneath her house I began to get a bad feeling.

Hopefully, the phone call would put that to rest.

Chapter 2

AS IT TURNED out, the phone call didn't put my bad feelings to rest. It only exacerbated my uneasiness.

I really didn't know where to find a public phone. After wandering around Silver Lake for a while, I finally pulled into the last parking space available in a small lot surrounded by a general store, an ice cream bar and a charter boat rental place.

The ice cream place was crowded, so I walked down the short boardwalk to the boat charter place, figuring if that didn't work, I'd try the general store next. When I entered through the open door, the girl in the charter office looked up and smiled. She appeared to be mid twenties with sun-bleached, shoulder length blonde hair, cobalt blue eyes and a pretty face. If she'd been fifty pounds lighter, she'd have been a knockout.

"Afternoon," I said, putting on a forced smile and exuding as much charm as I could dredge up. "Lost my cell in the water," I lied, "and have an urgent phone call to make. Could you direct me to the nearest public phone?"

"Make you a deal," she said, without hesitation.

"Always up for a good deal," I answered, holding on to the smile.

"You can use this," patting the phone on her small, messy desk, "if you will stay here until I get back. Gotta run over to the store and get something."

"Sure," I said. "Won't get you in trouble though, will it?"

She laughed. "Mr. Meads is out on a charter to Portsmouth Island and won't be back until five, so who's to know?"

"Gotcha," I said.

"Just don't touch or look at nothin'," she said, then laughed. "Not that there's anything to see."

I laughed back and watched her head for the door. She had on a pair of shorts that were about two sizes too small. Why do Reubenesque girls do that? While I was contemplating her exit profile, she turned around and said, "You're not calling outside the country are you?"

I shook my head. "Not unless we're outside the country here." It sounded stupid, but that's what came out of my mouth. She giggled, then went on her errand.

I picked up the land line and punched in Bly's cell number. It rang only once, then went straight to voice mail. Not knowing what else to do, I left a convoluted message, trying not to sound overly concerned. I waited for a while, trying to decide what to do next. I got up to leave, then realized I'd promised the girl who's name I didn't know that I'd stay there until she returned. I tried Bly's phone again. Same thing. One ring, then straight to voice mail.

I wandered over to a bulletin board crowded with charter schedules, maps and a variety of business cards and notices for everything from accountants to wave riders for sale. While looking without seeing, my mind cluttered with scenarios I didn't want to contemplate, none of them good, the girl's voice broke my worrying with, "Get your call made?"

I turned. She had already gone to her desk, looking it over, making sure everything was in place.

"Yeah," I lied. It was easier than engaging in a conversation why I hadn't and "oh, that's too bad," or whatever. "Thanks, I appreciate it." I forced another smile, giving her a half-assed wave as I exited the door.

One of the things that had popped into my mind was that Bly had taken the boat out on a test run and ran into engine trouble . . . or, thought she'd filled up the tank and ran out of gas. If so, I needed to call the Coast Guard and convince them to do a search.

First, though, I decided to go back to her house and see if, by any chance, she'd returned, which would leave me feeling foolish and happy all at the same time. If she still wasn't there, before I did anything else I'd check with the neighbors. See if they knew or saw anything.

I hated uncertainty.

I was back under her house in less than seven minutes, two of those just trying to turn left onto Highway 12. Still no boat in sight. Again, I walked under the house and climbed up on the boardwalk that led out to the pier. I took another stroll onto her dock, looking around, trying to determine if there was anything amiss. Everything looked as it should, except for the *Lady Bryn* not being there. The arm of the loading device out over the water bothered me, but my mind convinced me that maybe it was left there because she was making a quick trip and didn't want to bother waiting for it to move back and forth.

Even so, I was torn between rechecking the house to see if I'd missed something during my first walk around on her deck, or go canvas the neighbors. I decided to check neighbors first. In the Army, canvassing neighborhoods and interviewing the people who lived in them was one of my specialties.

During my time in The Hague under Colonel Tillman, I was assigned to do field investigations of suspected terrorist cells in the northwestern area of Europe, but primarily in Holland, Belgium and Denmark. Most of that was footwork, knocking on doors and asking "innocent" questions, posing as an insurance salesman, insurance investigator or whatever Tillman thought was my best cover for the assignment. I'd been a star in language school.

For whatever reason, people like to talk to me. Back then I was a lot more friendly and affable than I am now. Not to say that I'm a sullen and grumpy person, although at times I can be. Events in Serbia brought out some long-suppressed hostility inside me that I'd never before had. At least that's what the Army shrink told me. At the time and for some time afterwards, I thought he was full of shit. I finally decided maybe he was correct after all, even though I could never figure out just what that buried hostility might be. It was a burden I was still trying to deal with.

Doing something eased my anxiety. Since Bly's house was at the end of the street, I began with the first house on the left, the north side, deciding to work my way up the short block, then back down the other side. There were only two other houses on either side of the road, none directly across from hers.

The first place, like the rest of them on the street, was also a stilt house, this one built in the shotgun style. There were no vehicles in the driveway or under the house, but I went up the stairs anyway and knocked on the door. As I expected, there was no one home, although it did look as though someone was currently residing there. I'd come back later.

Same with the next house. No one home, but this place looked as if it hadn't been occupied for some time, although I saw a bike thrown on the ground behind the house, apparently left behind. Across the street, an elderly man who had no problem talking to me, introduced himself as Bud

Flannigan from Altoona, Pennsylvania and invited me in. Before I accepted his invitation, I asked, "Do you know Miss Parsons?" but he ignored me and gestured for me to follow him, asking, "Would you like a Bombay and tonic? It's almost tea time, ya know," chuckling as he said it. I politely declined, but followed him through the Spartan great room into a small kitchen, where he proceeded to finish fixing himself his gin and tonic. Apparently, I'd interrupted his libatious preparations.

"Sure you don't want one?" he asked again.

"No thanks."

"Juice?"

"Nope."

"Water?"

The man was so deliberate and so goddamned slow fixing his drink, it was all I could do not to grab the stirrer he'd precisely placed on a folded napkin and mix the damn drink for him. But, mouth closed, I sucked air though my nostrils and shook my head.

Finally, he finished his cocktail and nodded for me to follow him, which I did. Out to his back deck. He sat down at one of two chairs around a small glass-top table. I took the only other seat, opposite his. He looked at me waiting for my question.

It was the same one he hadn't answered before. "You know Miss Parsons, the lady in the wheelchair at the end of the street?"

"Seen her, but don't know her," he replied.

"Have you seen her today?" He thought for a long while, took two sips of his B&T, then said he hadn't. "When was the last time you saw her?"

Again he spent some time contemplating and sipping before, finally, he said, "I think it was last fall."

"Last fall?"

He took another sip. "Last time I came down. Stayed until just before Christmas. Had to get home to see the grandchildren over the holidays, you know."

"Right," I replied, exasperated. "So, how long you been here this time?"

"Hmm." He pondered, mulled and sipped. "Was Sunday around 8:15 pm."

"This past Sunday?"

"Would have been Monday, but got the last ferry down here. Thought I was going to miss it and have to stay overnight in Hatteras. Had to do that once before, but—"

I held up my hand, palm toward him, interrupting his rambling. "Sorry to interrupt you Mr.

Flannigan." He looked at me, as if trying to record where he had stopped his story so he could resume when I finished being rude. "So, you haven't seen Miss Parsons at all since you arrived here?"

"Hmm," looking up toward the sky. "Nope. Can't say I have. But you never know when—"

I stood up, interrupting his next thought. "Well, thank you, sir, for your help." If I carried business cards or, as they called them in my grandfather's day, calling cards, I would have left one, just in case, but I didn't have any. More than likely, it would have been a useless gesture. I'd just check back if I felt the need. I hoped I didn't. He didn't bother getting up to see me to the door, which was just fine by me.

Just as I was closing the man from Altoona's front door, from the top of the landing I saw a silver Honda Civic pull out from the sandy driveway of the house next door. I could see a woman in the driver's seat.

"Crap!"

I waved both arms like I was in New York City trying to hail a cab. As she was going by, I yelled, hoping she heard me, even thought it looked as if the windows were closed. Just because I drove around with my windows down because my air conditioning blew like Frosty with emphysema, didn't mean everyone else did. Apparently, the woman didn't see me, or did and didn't want to stop. Probably thought I was Flannigan and didn't want to be trapped in a long-winded conversation.

Should I run for Trusty Rusty and try to follow, or go knock on the door and hope someone else was still home? I opted for the knock on the door. If that didn't pan out, I'd come back in an hour or so and try again.

Where Bly's three other neighbors' homes all had unpainted, weather-worn wood siding, the Civic woman's place was painted lime green, with a pink front door and window trim. I thought it looked silly, but each to his or her own. My dad used to say, "Some people wouldn't know good taste if it was served to them in a five-star restaurant." He meant it in a universal way, encompassing food, art, music, decorative matters. Whatever. Dad was a meat and potatoes, Norman Rockwell, Frank Sinatra, tan siding with dark brown trim kinda guy.

As I climbed the steps to the front deck I heard loud music from deep inside. Even though I knew it was useless, I gave five hard, deliberate raps on the door. As expected, I received no response. Just for the hell of it, I tried the handle. It was locked. Probably a good thing, or I'd been tempted to go inside, then have to explain to the police why I frightened a poor teenager, who I imaged was in a back bedroom lip-synching in front of a full-length mirror.

I decided to go back to Bly's and snoop around some more. Maybe later I could catch one of the two remaining neighbors at home, or back home, in the case of the Civic woman.

As I crossed the street and headed back to Bly's house, I wondered if the Coast Guard was like the police, unable or unwilling to take action of a possible missing person until twenty-four or forty-eight hours went by. I wasn't willing to wait that long. I had to keep moving forward . . . doing something.

"Maybe she'll show up soon and all my angst will be blown out the window," I mumbled to myself.

Chapter 3

I PEERED IN the only window where I could see inside. Earlier, when I looked in, it was more of a quick scan around Bly's study which, as I mentioned before, is her writing room. This time I actually studied the study.

To my right, her computer workstation was built into the corner. From it, she had views of the sound and the bay. Everything looked in its place. I scanned the room. To my left, against the wall, was a supply cabinet. Closed up. Nothing on top of it. Bly was a well-organized and neat person. I ran my eyes across the open bookshelves on the back wall. Everything was as I remembered it.

Bly liked art and had some really nice pieces in her great room, her bedroom and the guest room.

However, the only thing in here study were pictures of her parents, which hung over the supply cabinet. When I asked why she didn't have anything else on the walls in there, she said, "I don't like distractions when I write. If I want to see something beautiful, I just look out my windows."

She had a good point.

Out of habit, I tried the study door again, then the door to the side porch. As before, still locked. I wondered which one might be easier to pick, but I wasn't ready to do a break in just yet. If I was overreacting and she suddenly returned home, she wouldn't be happy with me if she caught me doing a B&E and snooping around. I went back to the study window and stood there thinking about what I should do.

While looking at her computer desk, my eyebrows furled. Something was not quite right. But what? I started at the left side of the desk, my eyes moving from front to back, then back to front, like a police detective at a crime scene, walking a grid with my eyes. When I reached the desktop computer, I studied the computer screen, then the CPU, which Bly kept under the monitor, then the keyboard. I started to move on when I stopped.

"Huh!"

The power on/off button. It was lit up. At first I'd missed it because the monitor's screen was in sleep mode. Bly never left her computer on when she wasn't inside the house. I knew this because she'd once gone into the village without turning it off, and a sudden electrical storm came up. An errant lightning strike took out her motherboard. Since then, she was freakishly meticulous about turning it off when going out; even when she was home, at the first sound of thunder, no matter how distant, off it went.

Seeing the computer still on sent a chill up and down my spine.

Then, another thought hit me. Suppose she let someone inside, then they did something to her and stole her boat. That would mean she was still here. In who knows what condition. Injured or immobilized.

Or . . . .

That did it. I had to get inside. Then, I remembered she had an alarm system. What to do? If she was inside, I was pretty sure it wouldn't be on, but wasn't entirely sure.

Another scenario. If she was sleeping and woke up and saw that her boat was missing, maybe she called the sheriff. Maybe he'd been out, then she went to his office to fill out a report. Maybe. But if her boat was stolen and she'd rushed to the sheriff's office, would she leave without turning off the computer or setting the alarm system? In too much of a hurry? Not likely.

The worst scenario was that she'd been kidnapped and the kidnapper or kidnappers took her and the boat. Was it a ransom situation? If so, why weren't sheriff's deputies crawling all over the place? Unless, the kidnapper hadn't sent any demands yet. And who would he send it to? Her parents were deceased. She had no siblings. Would he be brazen enough to demand money from her publisher? And if so, what would they do? Call the F.B.I.? Maybe that's why there were no sheriff's deputies around. The matter was grinding through bureaucratic channels. The nearest regional F.B.I. office I knew of was in Elizabeth City, so it would take time for any of their agents to get to Ocracoke.

While all these crazy scenarios ran through my mind, I had a quick thought about breaking into the garage to see if her van was in there, but quickly realized that the alarm system also extended into that structure.

What to do?

Fuck it. If I broke in and the alarm went off, the sheriff would come. There or not, if Bly had been victimized, that would be a good thing. If she wasn't there, I'd probably be arrested, or at least held for questioning, and I'd have their attention. I could deal with that.

I took off my t-shirt, wrapped it around my right hand, made a fist and punched through the glass pane closest to the door handle. I held my breath. No alarm. I knocked out the remaining shards of glass still stuck in the molding, then reached in with my left hand, found both the lock latch and, reaching higher up, the dead bolt, and unlocked them. The door opened in. Still no alarm.

I stepped inside. I immediately went over to the computer and touched the space bar on the keyboard. A second later, the screen lit up. On it was an unfinished manuscript page, ending at what looked like the middle of a narrative paragraph.

"This isn't good," I mumbled.

Bly had an unusual floor plan, one that suited her needs to easily navigate from one place to the other without too many doors or obstacles. The study opened into a short hallway between the wall dividing the back of the house from the front of the house. On the left of the hallway was a specially equipped bathroom with an entrance off her sleeping area. I say sleeping area because it was more an open space than a room. I held my breath until I reached the end of the hall where I could see her bed. I stopped and looked around. No one was there and nothing seemed amiss.

I looked in the bathroom. Nothing, On the other side of the bed was a walk-in closet. I looked inside. Everything looked normal.

The one door that allowed passage between the back of the house and the front was ajar. I opened it slowly, peeked my head through and looked into the great room. To my immediate right was a handmade oak dining table with five chairs, one at the far end and two on each side. Bly hadn't set a chair on the end closest to the back wall because she said it obstructed her traveling space. Beyond the table was a modest sized kitchen with a custom built low-top island to accommodate Bly in her wheelchair. What cabinetry she had was built more as a bookcase. It was on the floor for easy access. Between the storage space in the island and in the cabinet, there was plenty of room for Bly's needs. She wasn't big on entertaining.

To the left of the kitchen was the elevator, enclosed on all sides so only the door showed. I walked around the island and back to the far end of the table and stood there looking at the other end of the great room. It was sparsely furnished. She had a medium brown cloth-covered couch set in front of a large double-pane window that looked out the front of the house onto the end of the street. The couch wrapped around the far wall enough to seat one extra person. In front of the couch was a custom made coffee table with a blue and white marble top shaped like a kidney.

On the wall above the short end of the couch hung a wood collage by John Tucker. Tucker is a local artist whose work, inspired by the well-known contemporary Native American Indian artist George Morrison. I remembered Bly telling me she'd heard about Tucker and went into his studio and bought it right off his wall.

At the end of the couch was a small round glass-topped end table with a Tiffany lamp on top. Across from the couch, a huge plasma TV was built into the wall. The gods of fate and destiny had balanced the scales for her. Between her inheritance and what she made from her writing, Bly had done well for herself, financially.

The only room remaining to check out was the guest room, where I'd slept on my previous visit. I took a deep breath and went to the door, which was closed. I opened it and went straight inside. The head of the double bed was set against the common wall with the great room. There were small night stands on each side of the bed. I walked around and looked at the other side of the bed. Nothing. Like Bly's bed, this one was built on a platform that housed drawers for storage, so there was nothing to look under. The only thing left was the closet and the guest bathroom.

The closet was totally empty, as it was when I'd been there before, only for the use of a guest or guests. Besides me, I don't think she ever had a guest stay in there. Not to say that she didn't have a guest in her own bed, but that was her business, not mine. The bathroom was cleaner than a five-star hotel and ready for use. Nothing behind the bathtub curtain, either.

What the hell is going on?

I returned to the great room and sat on the end of the couch near the expensive multicolored lampshade Bly had inherited from her parents. It was set on a hand-carved wooden lilac tree trunk, the trunk continuing onto the wood base. I had no clue what the wood was and, if Bly had told me, I didn't remember.

I sat there staring into space, left arm across the back of the sofa, fingers of my right hand drumming the arm rest, trying to gather my thoughts. I realized I hadn't checked the hot tub porch. A bad image dropped into my mind. I pushed myself off the couch and went to the back of the house through Bly's study. I spent a moment rummaging through a desk drawer and found a large paper clip, then went outside, straight to the hot tub porch. In the Army, I'd learned to pick locks with a variety of available items, including paper clips—

not something the average soldier learned. In several seconds, I had the door open. I went straight for the hot tub. I'd envisioned it full of water with a body underneath. It was empty. I breathed a sigh of relief.

Back in Bly's study, I stopped one more time to look around. The computer screen was still lit up—I guessed it was on a thirty minute cycle. I pulled over her one visitor's chair, sat down, and looked at what she'd been writing, in case that might yield a clue. The only thing odd was that she'd finished a paragraph and had written the first two words of the next one, stopping there, as if she'd been interrupted. I thought about it for a moment. If she had been surprised, I doubted it would have been from somebody already inside the house. They would either have been on the back deck looking in, or knocking on the door or window. Anyone coming up onto her back deck would have had to do some climbing onto boardwalks and over gates and, if so, wouldn't be someone who was supposed to be there. If that was the case, and if she didn't know them, she probably would have called the sheriff. She certainly wouldn't have let them in. And there was no sign of a forced entry—except for mine.

If someone had entered her house, it would have to have been via the elevator. Someone had rung, she'd connected with them on the speaker system, and they somehow had talked their way inside. She didn't have a video system. When I'd asked her why, she'd said the minimal threat level didn't justify the cost. Maybe she'd been wrong.

As I got up to leave the study, I noticed a crumpled up piece of paper on the floor under her computer desk. I bent over and picked it up, then opened it up. It was blank. As I've said, Bly is a neat and orderly person and would never throw anything on the floor. Unless . . . . I looked under the desk for a trash can, then realized the one she had was on the outside of the desk against the left side. And, in any event, why would she throw away a blank piece of paper?

I unfolded the paper and smoothed it out to see if there was some hidden message on it. I checked both sides. Nothing. I laid it on the computer desk, then looked over the rest of the room, including inside the trash can, which was empty. Nothing else caught my attention.

I returned to the front of the house and went over to the elevator. I knew Bly had a code to lock and unlock it but didn't know what the code was. I pressed the button to open the door anyway. To my surprise, it slid open. I stepped inside and looked around. The doors closed and I took the elevator down. When it opened again, I set the doors to remain open, stepped out under the house and looked around.

I saw no sense looking for footprints. She'd graveled the parking area. I went back inside the elevator and rode back up. When the doors opened, I stepped back into the great room. Then it hit me. Why was the elevator not locked? Bly would never leave it that way. I remembered back to my visit. Even after I'd rode it up and was inside her house, she'd locked it behind us.

I would have locked it then and there, but I needed the code for that. If I'd known it was open and usable, I wouldn't have broken the pane in the back door.

The elevator was the third thing inside the house that didn't seem right; the first two being the crumpled paper on the floor and the alarm not being set. I did another sweep of the house just to make sure I hadn't missed anything. In her bedroom, I even checked the elaborate ceiling track installation that moved her from the bed to the bathroom and back without her ever having to get off the bed and in and out of her chair just to use the toilet or take a shower or bath. Nothing seemed out of place with that.

Back in her study, looking out at the dock, the fourth thing out of whack hit me. It was the equipment built into the pier with an arm that would lift her, chair and all, in and out of the boat. I'm not sure why it hadn't dawned me before. Earlier I had noticed that the device was still hanging out over the dock where her boat would have been. While that might seem normal to most people, Bly liked everything in its proper place. I wasn't positive, but was pretty sure that once, when we'd taken out the boat, she'd sent the device back via remote to its dock position. Then, when we'd returned, she'd called it back to exit the boat. I doubt she'd leave it over the water without a good reason.

Then again, maybe she did leave it there on purpose. Just as she'd left the crumpled up paper on the floor under her desk—on purpose. Just as she'd left the alarm system off—on purpose. Just as she'd left the elevator open—on purpose.

They were messages.

She hadn't left her house of her own accord.

Now, all I had to do was convince the local sheriff's office that Blythe Parsons had certainly been taken away by someone and that not only should an investigation be started immediately, but the Coast Guard should be notified to conduct a search as soon as possible.

A minute later, I was in my truck heading back to Highway 12.

Chapter 4

THE SHERIFF'S OFFICE was a small, fairly new, brick building located on Highway 12 at the north edge of town. I'd passed it on the way in and remembered it from the last time I'd been down to Ocracoke. There were only two vehicles in the parking lot. One, a black, late model Ford F-150 and a police cruiser. I parked next to the cruiser and walked inside.

There were only two people inside. The one at the front desk was a short, pudgy woman with goggle-like glasses resting at the tip of her nose. Her nameplate said she was Eloise Terwilliger. There was a man at the back of the room clicking away at a desktop computer.

"May I help you?" Terwilliger asked, eyes roaming up and down, followed by a big smile.

"I'd like to speak to the sheriff," I said. I saw the man in back look toward us and nodded to him, as if I knew him.

When Terwilliger turned to look back at the man, he got up from his desk and walked toward us. I presumed he was the sheriff, although he could have been a deputy. He was a good looking man, tall with a full, well trimmed moustache.

"May I help you, sir?" he asked.

"Are you the sheriff."

He nodded. "Randy Caswell." He had on cowboy boots. I doubted they were regulation wear with his sheriff's uniform. Hopefully, that meant he wasn't a total by-the-book tight-ass.

"I want to report a possible abduction."

Eloise Terwilliger drew an audible breath and whispered, "A child?"

Caswell nodded me back toward his desk and I followed. As I walked around the woman, I looked at her and touched her on the shoulder, whispering, "Not a child." I wanted her in my corner if I had to interact with her again. She mumbled something as I left her behind.

The sheriff ushered me to a chair next to his desk and I sat down. "And your name is?"

"Webb Sawyer. I'm from Nags Head just off the causeway. I live in a stilt home on Blue Heron Marsh."

"Webb Sawyer?" he repeated. I nodded. "Nags Head?"

"Right. Blue Heron Marsh. Everyone's favorite recluse," wanting to get to the business of Blythe Parsons, but playing the game so when I told him my problem he'd be on my side. I felt like a fucking crab sidling up to my prey.

"You wouldn't happen to be the army guy who whacked that Serbian asshole?" voice lower so his secretary or receptionist or whatever Terwilliger was couldn't hear.

I just couldn't seem to get away from my vigilante justice in the Balkans. "Yep," was all I said in reply, wondering if I should have lied to him, hoping I hadn't just dug a hole I couldn't climb out of.

"You did the world a favor," he said. I didn't reply. Then he asked, "You Randy Fearing's friend?"

"You know Randy?"

"Met him not long ago at a law enforcement seminar. Were talking about that bad guy in

Perquimans County who turned out to be a serial killer. Mentioned your name. Something about you solving a whole shitload of murders. Said you and he went to school together."

I just nodded.

"So what's this about an abduction?" he asked. His voice was somewhere between friendly and annoyed that I'd interrupted him. I wasn't sure which way he was leaning.

I told him everything, beginning with the invitation to come down to Ocracoke for a fishing excursion with Blythe Parsons, what I'd found at her house, and my canvas of the neighborhood.

"She that writer in the wheelchair?" I nodded. "How'd you get inside the house?" he asked. I told him about the elevator being unlocked. I didn't mention my breaking and entering first. I didn't want to ruin the mood.

"No blood anywhere?" he asked.

"No, but—"

Caswell held up a hand, "Yeah, I know, that doesn't mean something isn't wrong. Usually, we wait 48 hours on missing persons cases unless there is evidence of foul play, but it seems you have cause to be concerned, so let's go take a look."

From up front, Eloise Terwilliger asked, “Weren’t you about to go home, feed the cat and get some dinner?” I could call—”

Annoyed at her inserting herself into his business, Caswell growled, ”The damn cat won’t starve to death if it gets fed an hour late.” Then, as we walked out he said to her, “Contact Deputy Campers and tell him where I’m going. If he’s not back before you leave, forward incoming calls to my cell.”

“Yes, sir,” she whined.

I followed Sheriff Caswell’s cruiser down Highway 12 and out British Cemetery Road, making the last left before the road ended, a right onto Bly’s dead-end road and down to her house. Caswell let me pass and pulled his cruiser in behind, blocking me in. I didn’t know if that was on purpose or just habit.

I waited for him at the elevator, then pushed the button. The elevator was programmed to return into the house, so we waited as it came back down and the door opened.

“After you,” he said.

We rode up and exited into the great room. The first thing Caswell said was, “I see what you mean about her not being here and leaving access to the house through the elevator." He stood there for a moment, turning his head, eyes taking in the room like a hawk scanning for its prey. "She really designed this place to fit her own needs, didn't she."

"Yes she did."

"You say you went through the front of the house and didn't find anything unusual?"

"Except for the elevator," I said.

"Show me the back of the house."

He followed me through the only door that led in back. He moved to my right and stood there looking at everything. "What's that door?" nodding to the right.

"Walk in closet."

"You checked that, too, I presume."

"Didn't look through the clothes, though. Didn't think this situation called for it, but probably wouldn't hurt to look."

"Later," he said.

That was a good sign. As I saw it, it meant he was getting with the program. He walked to the left of her bed and looked up at the tracking system, then followed it into the bathroom. "Never seen anything like that," he said.

I opened the blinds to the bedroom window and gestured out toward the pier. "Boat gone and the device for getting her on the boat is still out over the water." He came around and looked. "Like I said, she never does that. She always sends it back to the original position." I was almost positive that was her practice, but didn't want to sound unsure and muddy the water.

"And you're positive about that?" he asked, as if reading my mind.

"I asked her. She told me," I lied. "She's very meticulous about how she does things." Then I said, "We should get the Coast Guard in on this as soon as possible." Time was passing and I was becoming more and more on edge about Bly's well-being.

"First things first," Caswell replied, then, "And you're sure she didn't just forget you were coming, or blow you off for someone else?"

I turned and glared at him.

Caswell held his hands up in front of him, "Okay, I didn't mean any offense. Had to ask."

"Look sheriff, Blythe Parsons and I have been friends since childhood. And just friends. I have a woman I'm involved with and, in fact, she's staying at my place and cat-sitting while I'm here."

Caswell chuckled. "So you're a cat guy, too, huh?"

"Having a dog in a house out in the marshes doesn't make much sense, does it?"

"I suppose," he said, wandering toward the hallway that led to Bly's study. I followed behind. Immediately upon entering the room, his eyes went to the door and the broken pane of glass. "You didn't say anything about this," moving over to the door, his hand automatically touching the butt of his weapon.

"I, uh, forgot to mention that's how I initially got inside."

He looked around at me. "Forgot to mention?"

"Look, sheriff. Something wasn't right and I had to get inside and check things out. I didn't discover the elevator was unlocked until later."

"And you didn't think to call my office?" I could tell he wasn't pleased about this turn of events.

"I don't do cell phones," I said. "And she doesn't have a land line." He looked at me, wrinkles forming on his forehead. "Besides, if I would have called or driven over, I wouldn't have had anything except the missing boat and the device on the pier in the wrong position. You and I both know how far I would have gotten with you on that."

Caswell shook his head. "Randy Fearing must really enjoy having you as his friend, loose in the community." I wasn't sure if he was serious or just giving me a rash of shit.

“He always backs me up,” I said, in my own defense, even though the sheriff was right. There were times I had exasperated my good friend.

“Against the police?” the sheriff asked, a smirk on his face.

“They haven’t always been as cooperative as you,” I replied.

Caswell gave me a half snort. “We’ll see how that goes. In the meantime, I think you better get someone over here and fix that before someone else waltzes in here where they’re not supposed to be.”

I didn’t mention that I had no way of securing the elevator without the code. “That’s the other thing, sheriff,” I said. He waited for my latest observation. “As I already told you, she didn’t have her alarm system on. She never, ever, leaves the house without turning it on. In fact, when she’s sleeping, even when she’s home but not going to be in her office here for an extended period of time, she turns it on.”

“And obviously, it didn’t go off when you broke in.”

“No, and I didn’t actually break in. At least not in the criminal sense.”

Caswell looked at me for a long time before saying, “I guess she’s lucky she has you for a friend, because otherwise, we wouldn’t be standing here debating the definition of a B&E." Before I could answer, he asked, "What else? You said something about trash on the floor and a computer still on." He looked at the blank screen, which was in sleep mode.

I slipped past him and went to the computer desk, pointing at the piece of paper I had smoothed out and left lying there.

"That's the crumpled piece of trash?"

"I picked it up and smoothed it out to see if there was anything of importance written on it. It was there on the floor." I pointed under the desk where I'd found it.

He looked past me. "Nothing on it. Should have left it where it was."

"And hope like hell there was nothing important on it, I guess."

"Don't be a smart ass, Sawyer."

"Just saying . . . ."

"Tell me about the computer again," Caswell requested.

I hit the space bar and the screen lit up. He stared down at it, reading what he could see of her writing. While he did that, once again I ran through what I knew of Bly's habits regarding her computer, including her fear of not only losing another motherboard, but having her hard drive wiped out. "There's no way in hell she would have gone out and just left this thing running. No way in hell," I repeated.

I waited for him to respond. Finally, he said, "Let's go look at the dock."

We went out onto the deck and found our way down to the boardwalk and the dock, scaling the gates between the levels on the way. "I see what you mean about security," Caswell said on the way out onto the dock.

The sheriff walked up and down the dock several times, eyes everywhere. Then he stopped and studied the contraption that was used to hoist Bly over to the boat. He ran his eyes along it all the way out to where the arm and the small platform for her wheelchair hung out over the water.

I waited while he contemplated.

Finally, he turned to me and said, "I think you may be right, Sawyer. Something fishy going on here." Then he pulled out his cell and made a call. He said to whoever answered, "This is Randy. Get in touch with Coast Guard rescue and have them call me on my cell." There was a short pause and he said, "Yes, right now," and hung up.

Caswell looked at me with a look of consternation on his face. Expecting a plan of action, I said, “What?”

“I don't know about you Sawyer, but my cat's hungry and I'm hungry. What are we going to do about it?”

Chapter 5

I'D OFFERED TO pay for dinner and suggested Howard's, which is where Bly and I intended to go; but, as with most places this time of year with the tourists pouring in, he said it was too noisy and public. He suggested I follow him over to his place, that he had something available and easy to fix we could have and that there was plenty for two. Besides, he needed to feed the cat.

I felt as if there was something else we should be doing to find Bly, but there really wasn't anything. Caswell said he'd send Deputy Campers, who had the most training in forensics, over to her house in the morning. "But don't expect C.S.I. here. Pulling a decent print might be the best we can do, if there is anything to find." He also reminded me that, since I'd already compromised the scene, even that would be a long shot. I reminded him that we wouldn't even be talking about it if I hadn't. He'd pursed his lips and only grunted and nodded in agreement.

The sheriff's cat was a female tabby named Pixie. She was all over him when we arrived. He took care of her food dish right away.

"When my wife left me for a man who had what she called a 'regular job.' she took our daughter and left the cat."

Randy Caswell lived in a small cottage on the east side of Silver Lake Harbor on a sandy lane called, of all things, Sandy Lane. While it wasn't on stilts, it was on a rise of sand I presumed was once a dune. The place was neat and clean, which surprised me. I was neat but, except for my kitchen and bathroom, which I was kinda anal about, not so much on the cleaning part. Nan was always after me about changing my bed sheets more often, particularly after we sweated them up.

I presumed the sheriff's place had two bedrooms in back. The front of the house had, as most of the cottages in town, a great room in front that comprised the living room, kitchen, and an area off the kitchen for a dining table and chairs. The furniture was modest and functional. There weren't many pictures on the wall and those that hung there were either prints of local scenes or photographs of, I presumed, friends and family. One was a photo of himself and a teenaged girl.

"That your daughter?" I asked. I sat in the living room while he heated up some pre-cooked meals in his microwave. Growing up, we'd always called them TV dinners. I'd had a choice of boneless fried chicken or Salisbury steak, both with mashed potatoes and a vegetable.

Randy looked over his shoulder at the photo I was studying. "Yep, that's Talitha. We call her Tally. She's almost sixteen."

"Pretty girl."

The microwave signaled the one meal was done. He took it out and put in the other one. Pixie finished eating and stalked off to the back of the house, probably in search of her litter box.

"Takes after her mother." The tone in his voice made me think that he hadn't been happy about them leaving—either of them. "I see her for the month of July, then over the Christmas holidays for five days, then during spring break."

"Better than I had it with my son."

"You have a son?" Then he laughed. "That's my police training. The perp tells me something and I repeat it as a question, as if I'm interested, trying to get him talking." When he saw my uneasy smile, he said, "Just yanking your chain, Sawyer."

I gave a half-laugh and replied, "I only let people who call me Webb or Sarge yank my chain." Some of my friends still call me Sarge, from my Army days.

"Maybe we can go to first names once this business is over. For now, let's stick to Sawyer and Sheriff, just so people take this business with Miss Parsons serious. And so I can yank your chain," he added with a wry smile.

"I presume that means you take it as serious as I do," I said.

"You know the old saying, 'If it quacks like a duck and looks—'" His cell phone ringing interrupted his quote. "Caswell," he said into the speaker. After a few moments of listening, he growled, "Well, isn't that just ducky."

I guessed he had ducks on his mind.

"What's the other thing." More listening. Then, "Sounds like the next few days are going to be a barrel of laughs."

After he clicked off, I said, "I take it that wasn't the Coast Guard."

He shook his head. "They'll have someone call me within the hour. That was just more shit hitting the fan."

I smirked. "You do like your metaphors don't you? Or is it similes? I'm a smart guy but I was never an A student in English."

"A smart-ass at the very least," he said.

Ignoring his banter, I asked,"What's going on? If you can tell me."

"Let's talk while we eat," he said.

I had the chicken. He took the Salisbury steak and reheated coffee already in the brewer. He'd offered to brew some fresh for me, but I gladly opted for water. I didn't feel like getting into my peculiarities about coffee. Not right then, anyway.

"You live near Wanchese," the sheriff said. "You ever hear of a guy named Wiley Jenkins?"

"Yeah, I know who he is. Does boat repairs there. Never had him work on either of mine, though. I've heard talk that he has a shady reputation." I didn't want to tell Caswell that not only did I know Jenkins, but got involved with him when my friend Dave "The Wave" Meekins got in a jam with a very bad man. As it turned out, Jenkins had actually killed a Miami gangster by the name of Nick Panetta in order to save Dave's ass. Jenkins had done it for Dave, not me. Made it look like an accident. Panetta was an evil man and the world is a better place without him. Even so, it wasn't something I could talk about. Ever. Even thinking about it made me uncomfortable.

Caswell tried to peer into my soul, as if he suspected I knew more than I was telling. "Ever hear of a boat called *The Pink Lady*?"

"Doesn't ring any bells," I said, shaking my head. "This boat somehow connected to Jenkins?"

"Got a call from the Dare County Sheriff. Says a boat by that name was in Jenkins' boat yard for repairs. Suspects a drug delivery."

"They didn't find a reason to go aboard and check?"

"One of Moon's deputies saw it there. You know Sheriff Moon?" I shook my head. "At any rate, the deputy went into the yard and told Jenkins he wanted to look aboard. Jenkins told him to get a warrant."

"And?"

"They got a warrant, but it wasn't until the next day. By that time the boat was gone."

"No idea who was on the boat?"

"Boat's registered out of Naples, Florida to a man named Jed McMannus, but whether he was aboard or not, or anybody else for that matter, we don't know."

"What's that got to do with you. They think he might be coming here?"

Caswell chuckled. "No thinking about it. The owner of McShane's just called the office and said the boat just pulled into Silver Lake Harbor a half hour ago."

"So you had one Irishman watching out for another one," I laughed.

Caswell moved his head back and forth. "Huh! Hadn't thought of that. Is kinda funny, I guess," but he wasn't laughing. "Problem is, for the time being, it ties up my only available deputy."

"Campers?"

"Right. Campers. Billy Henderson is over on the mainland on a family emergency and won't be back for a couple of days. In the meantime, we need to keep an eye on this *Pink Lady*. See if we can catch whoever is aboard in an illegal act while they're here."

"So—" Again, I was interrupted by the sheriff's cell phone chirping.

"Caswell." There was a short pause. "Oh, Captain Harkswell, thanks for your prompt response to our call. Here's the situation." I presumed that Harkswell was from the Coast Guard because the sheriff then went on to give the caller a detailed briefing on the situation with Blythe Parsons. After Caswell finished, he listened, then said, "I can't say for sure if it's foul play, but at the very least she may have run into trouble out on the Pamlico Sound." He listened again, then said, "The woman has a solid reputation in the community and, because of her infirmity, doesn't take risks. Plus, as I said, she had an appointment with a close friend, which she missed." A Pause. "No we can't. I don't have the staff or the boats available." Then, "Not yet, but—" Interrupted. "No, I understand." More Listening. Longer this time. "I knew there was something brewing, but hadn't had time for the latest update on it. Always something to keep things interesting." A short pause. "I appreciate it, Captain."

After Caswell hung up, he looked at me and said, "There's only three hours of sunlight left today," he said to me. "They can have a chopper in the air and over the sound in half an hour and hope for the best. Since it's not a distress call, if they run out of time tonight, they will resume at daybreak."

"I don't understand. They do night searches all the time."

"Sawyer, I'm sorry." I could tell by the tone of his voice that a sales job was coming. "Unless there's an imminent danger or threat to life, they can't commit total resources."

"But there is—"

Caswell held up a finger. "Not until I say there is, and I can't say so yet. And I'm certainly not going to lie my way to get help with the Coast Guard, or the next time, when it's a real situation, I won't get the time of day."

"This is real, goddamm it!"

"They're sending choppers up. That's more than I had hoped for, so let's just accept that and move forward with the investigation. I'll try to work something out around this *Pink Lady* business. In the meantime, I'll call up to Hatteras and Buxton and see if I can borrow somebody to help out."

I couldn't eat anything else and, like a kid, pushed the plastic tray of half-eaten chicken and sides to the center of the table.

"Look, I know you're frustrated, but we'll find a way to get on top of it tomorrow. In the meantime, there's another problem that may be heading our way."

"You want to deputize me. If you're already spread thin, maybe I can help out. At least I'll feel like I'm doing something with . . . whatever," shrugging my shoulders.

Caswell laughed. "From what your friend Fearing said, you're a pretty resourceful man, all right. But do you really think you can stop a hurricane?"

Chapter 6

ABOUT AN HOUR and a half of sunlight remained when I left Randy Caswell's house. He returned to the office. With instructions from Caswell not to go back to Bly's place until they processed it, which, hopefully, would be sometime tomorrow, I headed back to her street to see if the two neighbors I had yet to speak with were home.

When I told the sheriff that I would find a motel room to stay for the night, he'd said, "Good luck with that. It's June. It's the weekend. The tourists have everything tied up. You can stay here." He had a furnished second bedroom for when his daughter came to visit. Reluctantly, I agreed. He'd told me where to find the spare key in case I returned before he did.

In addition to what had happened to Bly, I was worried about the news of a weather problem. For the moment, the sky was Royal Dutch blue with interspersed groupings of cotton ball clouds, showing no hint of the impending onslaught coming up from the Bahamas. Randy hadn't gone online to look at the tracking from NOAA, the National Oceanic and Atmospheric Administration, but said that Deputy Campers told him we would begin to get a hint of weather tomorrow evening from the system they were now calling Tropical Storm Angela. Whether the house was already processed by Deputy Campers or not, I planned to get Bly's glass door pane fixed before tomorrow ended.

June tropical storms and hurricanes hitting the Outer Banks were a rarity. I was overseas on special assignment doing some intelligence work in Liberia when, in June of 1996, Arthur formed as a tropical depression over the Grand Bahamas, then headed north, making landfall near Cape Lookout, southwest of Ocracoke. Even though it turned northeast, out into the Atlantic Ocean, it caused high winds and surge flooding in Ocracoke Village. I don't know what might have happened if it had hit here head on. Maybe we would pull some luck with Angela and, like Arthur, it would turn east before it reached us.

If things weren't already complicated, the storm made the prospects for tracking down Bly more difficult. I was sure the Coast Guard would push their search as long as possible. All I could hope is that they would find her before the storm drove them back to base. Even so, I was not going to stop my own search until I found her alive and safe.

The house on the right just before Bly's was now occupied. A red, late model Chevy Suburban with a rack on the roof was parked in the driveway. The driveway of the house just across the street, where the woman in the Honda Civic lived, was empty. I parked at the end of the road near Bly's, then walked back. I came up the stairs to the deck of the red Suburban's house when a man came out the front door. He was startled to see me and almost stumbled toward me, as if he'd caught the toe of one of his black and white sneakers on an uneven board.

I gave him a short-armed wave and, before he could say anything, said, "Sorry to have surprised you, sir. Just wonder if you could help me with something."

Embarrassed, the man who looked like a tall, skinny version of Mr. Peepers, a geeky-looking early TV sitcom character with horned rim glasses of the early 1950s I remembered from 1970 reruns, regained his composure, sputtered a bit, then said, "If I'm able."

Mr. Peepers stood at the top of the stairs, blocking my way, so I stopped halfway up the steps. It was disconcerting having to crane my neck to look up at him to speak, a fact about which the man either had no clue or sympathy. I figured it was the former. "The lady next door," I said, gesturing toward Bly's house. The man looked in that direction, as if expecting to see something. "Have you seen her recently?"

"Uh, no. Can't say that I have. We just got in an hour ago," shrugging.

"You mean from out of town?" He nodded. "On vacation?" Again, he nodded. "So you don't own the place." He shook his head. "Well okay then," I said. "Sorry to have bothered you." and turned to find my way back down the stairs.

"Is there some problem?"

Suddenly he was nosey. "Nope," I lied. "Just hoped to catch her in." I figured if this guy was around tomorrow when the sheriff's department showed up, he'd be right there, living up to the name I'd given him. I left him with, "Enjoy your vacation," then walked away. Maybe the boom-box kid would still be there. I could feel Mr. Peepers' eyes on me, wondering who I was and what I was doing.

I'd just stepped into the street when I heard a vehicle coming. I stopped and looked. It was the woman in the Civic. I took several steps back and waved as she turned into her driveway, hoping she'd take me for a neighbor rather than just any old stranger wandering the streets.

When she got out of the car she gave me that do-I-know-you look. She was a short rotund woman with close cropped, sun-bleached blonde-going-gray hair, Pince Nez sunglasses, and a round face that reminded me of my mother's sister, Aunt Tabitha.

Instead of introducing myself and trying to give her a whole explanation of why I was standing on her property, I said, "Quick question for you." My first thought was of an apple pie in the oven and an in-progress quilt on the arm of the sofa kind of lady. Then she opened her mouth.

"Yeah, well I got groceries ready to melt, so make it short and quick." Her voice was like tires on loose gravel.

I guess she took me for a home repair guy trying to drum up some business. My thoughts of affability and glibness swirled down the toilet. Instead, I gave her my investigator's voice. "Sheriff Caswell asked me to check with the neighbors about the lady at the end of the street," I said.

The woman looked over at Bly's house. "Really?" not questioning my insinuated authority. "What'd she do?"

Instead of answering, I said, "Can we talk inside? I'll help with the groceries." I figured she was one of these people who probably knew everything that was going on up and down her street. In private she'd tell me everything she knew and there might even be something of interest inside her gossip.

"Well," looking me up and down. "Okay then." She looked across the street at the guy who I presumed was still watching us. Not that it really mattered to me, but I could see the hamster cranking the wheel in her head. We had secret business to talk about and didn't want the snoopy outsiders to know what was going on in our community.

She went over and clicked open the trunk. "Just grab somethin'. In the trunk, I mean," laughing uproariously. It was like a cross between a howler monkey with laryngitis and a dying hyena. Dad used to say, "It takes all sorts to make up the world, son. And it's not always easy to tell who the good sorts are and who the bad sorts are, so keep an open mind, but stay suspicious." At the time I thought it was a hell of a way to think, but since then I've learned it was a wise way to deal with all the "sorts" of people who have crossed my path.

I followed the woman, who had yet to identify herself (then again, neither had I), up the stairs to the deck. She had on tight stretchy shorts. It was like watching two loaves of bread having a dispute over the limited territory they'd been forced to occupy together. It wasn't a pretty sight. Before she reached the screen door, it opened. Standing there was a teenage girl, well on her way to emulating her mother's physique.

The girl looked about fifteen or sixteen. She had fuchsia hair, cut short at the back, top and right side. An electric blue streak of longer hair hung on the left. In addition, she had heavy black makeup around her eyes, and full lips sporting black lipstick. She wore a rainbow color tie-dye shirt and loose fitting hot-pink shorts. It was like she couldn't decide whether she was a punk-rocker, a Goth queen, a hippy or a go-go dancer.

Strange!

When her mother asked Jenine, who I presumed was her daughter, to bring in the rest of the groceries because she had to discuss some important business with, "Detective . . . ah —"

"Sawyer," I filled in.

"Detective Sawyer," she repeated, letting the title float there in her mind, such as it was.

My next surprise was when Jenine answered with, "Sure, Mom. No problem. Hope you got those salt and vinegar chips I like." She talked like a California Valley Girl. My only guess was that the girl, confused as to her place in the world, was still looking.

Again, as Dad said, "It takes all sorts . . . ."

"So, what'd she do?" the mother asked.

"Well, Mrs. . . . ?"

"Wahab," she said. "Tamblin Wahab. But you can call me Tammy."

I smiled. "Well, Tammy, she didn't do anything. It seems she's gone missing."

"Really?"

I nodded.

"Missing?"

"Seems like it. I'm asking— "

She cut me off with, "You sure she just didn't have like a business trip with one of her big New York publishers?"

"So you know that she's an author," more a statement than a question.

Tammy laughed, the dead hyena side of her hybrid voice standing out. "Everyone knows she's a famous writer."

"You know her personally?"

"Only to wave. Sometimes when she's driving her van. Sometimes when she's riding in that motorized chair of hers. She gets around pretty good for a crippled person."

"I think people in wheelchairs prefer the term disabled person," I said, trying not to show my annoyance.

About then, Jenine was back up on the deck with two hands full of plastic bags full of groceries. "You talking about Miss Parsons?" she asked.

Before I could reply, Tammy cut in with, "Yeah, and guess what?" waiting for an answer. Her daughter only raised her eyebrows. "Someone's kidnapped her and is holding her for ransom."

The daughter looked at me through her mascara encircled eyes, that were dark periwinkle. I'd never seen eyes that color and almost asked her if she was wearing tinted contacts, but didn't.

"Ah, we don't really know if she was kidnapped. Someone had an important appointment with her at her home and she wasn't there and hasn't been seen since. At this time, we're just concerned," I said, trying to remain calm when I said it.

"Don't you worry about it, Jenine. This is grown up business," her mother blurted out, a smug look on her face.

Jenine just shrugged, then went to the dining room table, unloaded the bags on it, then went back out onto the deck to go down and get the next load. I started to ask her mother something, when Jenine stopped and came back to the screen door, pointing across the way to Bly's house. "Boat's gone. Maybe she forgot about her appointment or is just late getting back from a boat trip or something, you know." The Valley Girl speak was annoying, but at least the girl was observant, maybe even intelligent —compared to her mother, that is. Mrs. Wahab rolled her eyes, dismissing her daughter's observation.

"We're following up on that, too," I said. "In the meantime," turning to Tammy Wahab, "we'd like to know if you've seen any unusual activity at her house, or maybe anyone on the street watching her house. Or even someone on the street who seemed as if they didn't belong here."

Tammy half laughed, half cackled. "The only ones who come down this dead end road are people who live here, or guests of people who live here, renters, like the guy across the street." She shrugged, then added, "Sometimes tourists riding around come down here and turn around and leave. You know, just exploring."

"Would you call the sheriff's office if you think of something that might be helpful?"

"You got a card?" she asked.

"I'm on loan from another county," I lied. "Best if you just call Sheriff Caswell."

"You don't have to run right off, do you?" Tammy asked with hope-filled eyes.

"Sorry, ma'am, but yes I do."

As I reached the bottom of the stairs, I noticed two things. Mr. Peepers had finally given up on what I was up to and had gone back inside. The other thing was that Jenine was standing at the back of her mother's Civic, trunk open, as if she was waiting for me.

Chapter 7

WITHOUT WAITING FOR her to say anything, I asked the teenager, "You see anything you think I should know about?"

"Probably," she said. I waited. "Besides tourists driving cars in and out of here, sometimes there are bike riders, you know. Sometimes even a golf cart. Tourists joy riding. I guess you know they're renting those out now, too."

"Right. I've seen 'em. Too bad they don't make all the tourists park their cars on the edge of town and use bikes or golf carts to get around. Be a lot quieter and more pleasant for the locals if they did," I observed.

"Or make 'em walk," she laughed. Actually, it was more like a giggle. Thankfully, it wasn't anything like her mother's.

"You said maybe you saw something?"

"Oh, yeah. Well, like I said, tourists ride their bikes down here. Like wanting to see where each road goes and all, you know."

I nodded.

"But only once, you know."

Again I nodded, waiting for something of interest.

"Well, there was this guy came down here maybe four or five times, maybe even six. So no way he was lost or just joy riding, you know?"

"When was he here? What days?"

"Last time I saw him was yesterday. It was just the one time yesterday. The other times he was down here more than once." She tapped her right index finger to her forehead, as if trying to coax out the memory. "Three days ago was the first time I saw him." Eyes looking at the sky. "I think. Pretty sure, anyway. Then again the day before yesterday. Twice each day. I was sitting at my drawing board at my window," she pointed to the last window at the side of the house facing the end of the street. "I make up anime characters. Draw them, you know."

Another new dimension in her search for herself? I guess she was waiting for a response, so I just said, "Uh-huh."

"So I stare out the window a lot, especially if something distracts me." I nodded again. Seemed like the best way to keep the story going. "So, I see this guy ride his bike to the end of the street, then circle back and ride into the yard across from us. No one was in the house then, you know?" Nod. "I could just barely see him and had to put my face up against the window. He parked his bike up against the bushes, then got off and walked to the back of the lot. Then he disappeared. So I walked out to the front of the house and stood at the front door. After a while, he returned to his bike and rode off."

I waited for more, decided that was it, then asked, "Which time was that?"

"What do you mean?" she asked, scrunching her eyebrows.

"I mean, was that the first time you saw him? Two three days ago, I think you said."

"It was . . . ," tapping her forehead again, "the second time the first day I saw him. The first time he just rode to the end of the street and then rode away, so it didn't register with me until the second time, you know?"

"What about the next day? When did he come?"

"You mean the time of day?"

"Whatever you remember."

She shrugged. "Once in the morning and then again early in the evening. I don't remember the exact times. Hmm. Late morning, I think. The first time I saw him that day I was in the kitchen, getting myself a soda and chips."

"Salt and vinegar?" I said, a half smile on my face.

"Right!" she said, pointing at me.

"You're in the kitchen and you saw him do what?"

"Actually, the first time I just noticed the bike there, against the bushes. So I kept watching, you know. I watched for a while, but didn't see him, so I went back to my room. When I came out later, the bike was gone."

"Hmm. Didn't you say you saw him twice that day?"

"Yeah, you're right. I did. I saw him later that night. Just as it was getting dark. He rode to the end of the street then turned around and left. But I did notice he was looking her house over."

"You think he was definitely interested in Miss Parson's house?"

"Oh, for sure. But I just figured it was some fan who wanted to get a look at her."

Tammy's gravelly voice interrupted from above. "Jenine! You bringing the rest of those groceries up here or what?"

"I'm coming, Mom!" Jenine yelled back.

"And you leave that detective alone. He's got important business to attend to." Jenine just waved her off and started grabbing grocery bags out of the trunk.

"Just one more quick question," I said.

"Sure."

"That last day you saw him, the day before yesterday was it?" She nodded. "What was he doing?"

She went into the tapping the forehead mode again. Finally, she said, "You know, I think he just did a ride by. Then I didn't see him again." She grabbed the last bag out of the trunk, then added, "I mean, he could have been by other times and I didn't see him." She shrugged.

"Give me a quick description and I'll get out of your hair," *for now*, I thought.

Jenine looked up at the front of the house. I glanced up but didn't see her mother. "Not real big. Had on shorts and a . . . white short sleeve shirt.

Kinda baggy on him. Tan shorts. Sneakers, don't remember the color, and a dark blue baseball cap pulled down low over his eyes."

I could see she was becoming uncomfortable, standing there with her arms straight down, several grocery bags in each hand.

"You get a look at his face or how old he might be? Or even how much he might weigh?"

She shook her head. "Not really. Was slight built, but—" Again the shrug. Then, "Gotta run. Hope Miss Parsons is okay, you know."

"Yeah, Jenine. I know." The girl was not only smarter than her mother, but she had a spark of empathy for others.

I stopped for a beer at McShane's on Silver Lake Harbor. They didn't have Grolsch. They did have Heineken. As they say, close but no cigar, but— I got an order of wedge fries with it and drank from the bottle, washing down the fries laced with malt vinegar and dipped in a mix of ketchup and yellow mustard.

I sat up at the bar and scanned the harbor for the target of Sheriff Caswell's investigation, the boat he called *The Pink Lady*. It was at the end of the dock, two piers down. The harbor lights shown off the pink hull, which stood out like Tammy's shorts on her pudgy backside. Why would a drug runner have a pink boat? I scanned the docks for one of Caswell's deputies, but if one was there, I didn't spot him.

When I pulled into his yard there were no lights on the sheriff's house. I found the key in the phoney birdhouse with no opening for birds and a small door with a knob to pull it open. The key hung on a nail inside.

Inside the house, Caswell had left a bottle of Johnny Walker Red Label Scotch on the dining table with a note that said, "Help yourself!" A clean tumbler held down the note. Personally, I was a Jack Daniels Tennessee Whiskey man but, as the night had worn on my mood had soured and the scotch beckoned. I poured two fingers and downed it neat. Then poured another.

Caswell wasn't home when I dumped my suitcase and dopp kit in an empty corner of the room, took my shoes off and, clothes on, fell on top of the covers.

I dreamed that I was out over the Pamlico Sound in a Coast Guard helicopter, searching for Bly. Someone shouted, "What's that in the water?" I looked to where the Coastie pointed. "It's her," I shouted. Why it didn't seem strange that she was traveling across the water in her motorized wheelchair I don't know. It didn't make sense, but most of the time, dreams don't make sense. The copter hovered over her and she waved up at me. Next, I found myself climbing down a rope ladder, toward her. I had just about reached her and had my hand out for her to grab onto; however, the closer I got, the further into the water the wheelchair sank. Then, I made one heroic lunge to grasp her from a watery grave when, suddenly, she and the chair disappeared. I stared into the water, trying to see her face, but all I saw staring back at me was a giant red drum with its mouth, like a large sink hole, wide open, with a hand desperately reaching up from deep inside the fish's maw. I tried to force myself to wake up, to make the dream go away, but I couldn't. All I could do was watch as the hand slowly disappeared from view.

Chapter 8

THE *LADY BRYN* finally came to a stop. Where they were, Blythe Parsons didn't know, but she guessed somewhere remote. The air was hot and heavy and thick with mosquitoes that bit at her face, neck and arms, and even through her thin blouse. On her side, with her mouth taped shut and her hands secured behind her back, probably with the same kind of tape, there was nothing she could do except to endure the torture of their never-ending thirst for her blood.

Once she recovered from the chloroform, or whatever he had used to render her unconscious, she'd found herself on her boat in her wheelchair in the middle of the Pamlico Sound, heading where, she did not know. Her abductor had his back to her, piloting the boat. Her immediate instinct was to attack. Silently, she had unlocked the wheels of her chair. The noise of the 225 horsepower Mercury outboard disguised the sound of her turning on the wheelchair's motor and, in the fifteen feet of open space between them, moving forward as fast and hard as she could make it go.

He must have sensed something and turned just as she plowed into him. He yelped in pain, his voice high-pitched and loud. His retribution was swift and harsh. He reached down and, with strength she didn't expect, grabbed the front wheels and flipped the chair backwards, spilling Blythe onto the deck.

What happened next shocked her. He shrieked like a banshee, then, struggling with the weight of the wheelchair, he got enough leverage against the side of the boat to lift it using the right side front and back wheels. The wheelchair, metal and hard plastic, screeched as it was shoved up the gunwale.

How is that even possible, Blythe thought. *It's too heavy.*

Shouting obscenities, when her abductor finally got Blythe's wheelchair to the top of the gunwale, it teetered there for a moment, then, with one final shove, it disappeared over the edge.

While all this was happening, the boat forged ahead, cutting through the water as if it was on a mission all on its own.

He came at her. Blythe struggled, using her hands to push herself backwards, away from him. When she ran out of steam, he stood over her, looked down and said, "You shouldn't have done that." Then he drew his right foot back and the side of her head exploded in pain.

Now all she could do was lie there, immobile, totally helpless, and wait for what would happen next.

Why is he doing this? was the thought that played over and over in Blythe Parsons' mind.

Chapter 9

A SOUND FROM the front of the house startled me awake. For a moment I was disoriented, not sure where I was. I sat up and placed my feet on the floor. I sat there for a short while mentally shaking the cobwebs from my mind.

"Caswell," I mumbled to myself.

Footsteps down the hall. "You awake?"

"I guess," I said. "Knocked back a couple of neats on top of the beer I had at McShane's. Guess I'm not as much of a heavyweight as I used to be."

"The stress from the day," the sheriff said. "Sorry I woke you up."

I stood up and asked, "Bathroom?"

"To the right," stepping out of the door.

After I finished peeing and throwing some water on my face, I wandered out to the front of the house where Caswell was fixing himself an open-faced peanut butter sandwich, which he folded in half.

"Want something?"

"Nah. I'm good." Then, "Maybe some water."

"Got some OJ if you'd like."

"Yeah, that'll work," I said. He got a bottle of OJ out of the fridge and, from a cabinet over the counter, two small empty Starbucks Frappuccino bottles he'd apparently saved, and poured OJs for each of us, handing one to me. "Thanks."

He nodded, then took his OJ and sandwich into the living room area of the great room and sat in the one easy chair. I stayed in the kitchen. "You always patrol until three in the morning?" I asked, noticing the time on the stove's clock. It was actually 3:24 am.

Shifting himself in the chair until he was comfortable, he said, "After you left, I went to relieve Campers on *The Pink Lady* stakeout. He got some zees, then came back and relieved me at three," yawning.

"You really want this guy, don't you."

"It's our job," he said. "Besides, I don't want some jack-wad coming in here and polluting our town with his drugs. I'm not saying there aren't any here now, 'cause there are, but we have to stay on top of it to keep it from getting out of control."

I knew what he meant. Illegal drugs were everywhere, even in quiet little fishing villages and tourist draws like Ocracoke. And there was no good answer on how to stay on top of it. Getting rid of the problem was an impossible task. Getting tough on crime and harsher sentences didn't work, and "Just say no" was pretty much ignored. A joke, really. Now they wanted to legalize it. Maybe that was the answer, I didn't know. If there was a demand, there would always be a supplier, so why not have the government control it. Collect taxes on it. Personally, I'd rather have my roads paved by taxes on alcohol, drugs and tobacco than directly out of the struggling working man's hard-earned paycheck.

"Ever get someone to come down from Hatteras or Dare?" I asked.

"Nope. Say they can't spare anyone, In addition to the usual, they're gearing up for the storm."

"Anything back from the Coast Guard?"

Caswell shook his head. "I'm sure if they found something we'd know about it."

That was disappointing news—or, in this case, no news. "How's that storm looking?"

"We're right in the middle of the projected cone."

"Damn. I guess it's not looking good for getting over to Blythe Parsons' home today?" I asked.

"I'm not giving up on that quite yet. Meet me at the Jolly Roger's Restaurant at . . . say 11:00 am. You know where that is, right?" I nodded. "We'll see how things are looking then." When I didn't reply, he asked, "You come up with any leads from the neighbors?"

I told him about the bike rider.

"Maybe you should use the time in the morning —" he gave a weary smile. "Later this morning," I mean. "Check out bike rental places. Start with the ones at the Harbor and work your way out. Pick up a brochure on the village that lists and locates all the rental places. You have any trouble with them, tell them you're working on it for me. They can call Ms. Terwilliger if you have any problem."

"Sounds like a plan."

Since I was out of options, it was the only plan.

It was about a quarter to eight when I woke up. The sheriff was already gone. I took a quick shower, changed clothes and was out of the house by quarter after.

I wasn't quite sure where to find the brochure that Caswell had mentioned. I went to the three-story brick hotel across the street from McShane's and found one in the lobby. Actually, it was a tri-fold pamphlet with a street map of the town, locating the various points of interest listed by number, the names referenced below. There were five different rental places. I started with the one in the small parking lot where I'd talked to the girl at the boat rental place. In the brochure it was called Silver Lake Bikes and Golf Cart Rentals. They had no sign, but their purpose was obvious.

A kid in his early twenties by the name of Ray (it was on his name tag) was in charge. In fact, he was the whole show. I waited while he finished up with a family where everyone from granny to a precocious four-year-old boy who wanted to handle the whole deal, discussed, argued and, in the case of the young brat, whined about which two carts they would rent and who would ride in which one and where each person would sit. He wasn't nice about it either. There were nine of them. They all thought the annoying kid was cute. He wasn't. When it came time to pay, the kid held his hand out toward his father and rubbed his thumb against his fingers. They all thought it was hilarious. I felt like taking the little brat by the scruff of his neck and the back of his pants, carrying him over to the nearby docks and tossing him in.

When they were gone, I cornered Ray and, using the same tact as with Tammy Wahab, told him I was working for Sheriff Caswell on a case and gave him the description of the bike-riding guy Jenine had given me, including a general time frame when he might have rented a bike.

"Doesn't ding any dongs," Ray said. "I'm here from eight in the morning to nine at night, except for when I'm not here for lunch and dinner," he shrugged, "or a hit-the-head break, you know?"

Why in hell do people add "you know" to the end of their sentences? If I fucking knew, I wouldn't be asking. I gritted my teeth. "Does someone take your place when you're away?"

"No, man. I'm it. Just me, myself and I. I just put a sign out, back in an hour or back in five. Those are the only two signs I have, except for closed, you know."

"So you have three signs, not two." I couldn't help myself.

Ray gave me a dumb look, squinted his eyes, then said, "Yeah. you're right. Three signs."

"I'm always right." Dumb ass. "So, when you're gone, can anyone just take one?"

"One of my signs?"

Groan. "No, one of your bikes. Or one of your golf carts, for that matter." I didn't really care about the carts, but I just wanted to see what he'd say.

"Oh, no, man," shaking his head. "No way that could happen. See." He pointed out the chain that ran through the bike spokes, one end secured to a large eye-bolt in a metal pole, the other end by a key lock in a second pole.

"Thanks, man," mimicking him, and turned to leave.

"Don't you want to know about the golf carts?" he asked.

"Not really," I said. "You know?"

The next place was a sandwich shop on Highway 12 opposite Lighthouse Road. They were so busy doing twelve things at once—food orders, tacky gift sales, golf cart and bike rentals, coming in and going out—that I decided to tack them on at the end and moved on to the third place.

The third place, oddly enough, was associated with the coffee house. The rentals were apparently a side business for them, with a limited number of bikes and no golf carts. One of the guys behind the coffee bar directed me to the back of the shop where the owner also ran a small gift shop. Before I went back, I asked, "You don't know how to make snickerdoodle, do you?"

"Actually, I do," he said. When I looked surprised, he said, "Kinda has become my favorite, too."

"Last time I was here nobody knew what I was talking about," I said.

The guy laughed. "Yeah, that writer lady in the wheelchair came by, gave us the instructions for the blend, waited while we made it, tasted it to be sure it was right, then asked us . . . actually, it was more like an order," chuckling, "to keep it on the menu."

"Yeah, I heard she has a cranky friend who won't drink anything but."

"You the cranky friend?" the guy asked.

I smiled. "Make me the largest one you have, to go," I said, "And give me one of those blueberry scones with it." Until the odors of coffee and baked goods assailed my nostrils, I hadn't realized that I was hungry—I'd forgotten about breakfast. He said he'd get right on it. I told him I'd be right back.

The lady in back—I say lady, because she was fiftyish, attractive in a sophisticated way, hair nicely coiffured and stylishly dressed as if she was going out for a fancy lunch, not like someone running a gift shop in the back of a coffee shop at an island beach village.

She said her name was Milly Post and that she was the only one who leased the bikes during shop hours, which matched those of the coffee shop. If she wasn't here, the person or persons just had to come back. I guessed she was someone who had money in the bank, so to speak, and played at being a business owner.

I told her why I was there. She didn't remember anyone like the person I described, then checked her records. She showed me her computer spread sheet for bike rentals, which included a scanned in copy of the person's driver's license or ID. Maybe she was a business woman, after all. In any event, nothing turned up there, either.

She asked me if I'd checked the other bike rental places and I told her she was only number two. "You know, he could have had someone else rent a bike for him. Or bought one," she added.

Hmm. Damn! I hadn't thought of that. "Something to consider," I said. Then, "You know who sells bicycles here in the village?"

"Ocracoke Village Outfitters. They do rentals, too."

"Thanks. They're on my list," I said and thanked her for her time.

"Give my best to Randy," she said on my way out. It sounded more than the usual canned something-to-say-in-parting message.

"I'll surely do that," I lied.

On the way to the next place, I inhaled the scone as if it was a mere tidbit, but took my time savoring the very large cup of snickerdoodle.

Thank you Bly!

And thank you Barista guy!

As it turned out, the fourth place, a hole-in-the wall down an alley off a side road had only lasted about three years before going out of business. This was according to an elderly couple, probably in their eighties, who told me they had been renting the same house nearby four times a year, and watched the poor guy "drown in his mismanagement and bad decisions." I guess the pamphlet people hadn't gotten the message. "Nobody could find the guy, even if they were looking," the husband said. "I'm surprised he lasted that long," the wife said. "He was a weird dude anyway."

Dude?

The fifth location was back out on Highway 12, not too far down from the sheriff's office, but on the opposite side of the road. Ocracoke Village Outfitters, the one Milly Post had mentioned, was already on my list. It was actually a fishing, camping and sporting goods store. Apparently, it was "the happening place" for everything outdoors. There were at least half a dozen people waiting on customers. All of them appeared to be in their twenties. All wore tan shorts and a yellow shirts with green kayak logo and sandals. All were blonde or had sun-bleached hair with short cuts, and all good-looking, healthy types with that I-can't-wait-for-my-next-adventure look in their eyes. I wondered if they'd been cloned.

After a long wait, I finally collared a young blonde (what else) thing. She was bubbly and bouncy in nature and happy as a lark. If she wasn't, it was a convincing show. I gave her my spiel and she couldn't do enough to try and help. She didn't remember anyone of that description who rented, but did remember a family who had just bought a vacation home in the village and bought five bikes for all of them. "The kids were all twelve and under," she said. Those were the only bike sales over the past two weeks.

Just in case, she asked the other associates, as they were called, and double-checked the rental files on the computer. Like Milly Post at the gift shop, they had scanned-in photos of ID's, but nothing matched the description of the person I was looking for. I was losing all hope for finding out anything more on this guy, but I kept telling myself, if he was on the island for several days before Bly went missing, someone must know something about him, if for no other reason than he must have been sleeping and eating somewhere. I don't know why I hadn't thought of that before. Running tired and angst-ridden, I guessed. I'd ask the sheriff.

My last hope for something on the bicycle was the sandwich shop, rental place, etal near Lighthouse Road. This time around they weren't as busy as earlier. Once I looked at their menu, I realized why a sandwich shop would be busy early in the morning. They did breakfast sandwiches, too. I caught a guy just finishing up processing a bike rental and gave him my story. It was a good thing I had the sheriff's blessing on this round of inquiries. This guy, who said his name was Darin, wasn't as gullible as the rest of the bike rental places.

When he asked for my ID, I couldn't use the from-another-county line of bullshit. I told him I was a private citizen assisting the sheriff's department, who was currently understaffed for the number of cases they were working. The guy gave me one of those "Yeah, right" looks. I asked him to call the sheriff's office. At first he told me to call them myself, then changed his mind, figuring I could be calling anybody that might be working with me to gather information.

"Don't you need a warrant or something?" he snorted and started to walk away. He'd been watching too many TV police dramas and had the suspect's line down pat.

"So, you don't care that someone in the village who is not only an important person but is handicapped and helpless has gone missing and her life may be in danger?" I hated to use the word "helpless" but I wanted to get his attention.

He turned and looked back at me. "And who would that be?" a smirk of disbelief on his face.

"The fantasy writer, Blythe Parsons," I said. That seemed to get his attention.

"The one who lives on Bay Street?" he asked. I nodded. He thought for a minute. "Look, I'd like to believe that's so, but—"

"I'm not asking to look at your records. I just want to know if someone of the description I gave you rented a bike here in the past week, especially the last four days."

"Tell me the description again." This time he thought about it and said the description I gave him did sound familiar. "But he didn't actually rent a bike. When I told him I needed some form of ID, he claimed he didn't have any on him and would have to go all the way back to Hatteras Village on the ferry to get it."

"He said he was living in Hatteras?"

Shaking his head the guy said, "Not really. I just assumed he was. He gave me this sad and pouty look and I felt bad for him."

I wanted to be a smart ass and say, "Maybe I should have looked sad and pouty when you gave me a hard time," but I didn't. "You still didn't rent him a bike though."

"No, but I sold him my old one, which I had in the storage shed," giving a vague gesture to an area behind the shop.

"How much did he pay for it?"

"I asked thirty bucks, trying to be fair but not screw myself, you know?"

"Let me guess. He looked all sad and pouty and you gave it to him for twenty," kind of laughing as I said it so I wouldn't piss the guy off.

He grinned and said, "Actually, he said he only had ten and I sold it to him for that."

Then Darin became distracted, losing interest in me when several people came on to the property, looking around. "I see you're busy," I said, "but give me a quick description of the bike and some details about this person." He told me about the bike and ran through what he remembered about the buyer. "I may need to have Sheriff Caswell or Deputy Campers come by and interview you again," I told him. "What's your full name?"

"Uh . . . Darin. Darin Flinthoffer," his attention back on me since one of his staff had latched on to the potential customers.

"Any chance you can tell me what time it is?"

"Uh . . ." he pulled out his cell phone and looked at it. "Five after eleven."

"Okay, thanks, Darin. Gotta run. Someone may be in touch later today."

Darin looked at me funny and asked, "You think this kid actually abducted her?"

"Could be. Why? He seem too . . . sad and pouty to do something like that?" I just couldn't help myself.

"No, it's just that . . . well . . . I thought maybe he was . . . gay."

"Gay?"

"He had some . . . I guess you could call them swishy gestures. And the pouty face and all. Maybe I'm wrong. I mean, why would a gay boy want to kidnap a . . . well . . . you know. A girl?"

Chapter 10

WHEN I ARRIVED at the Silver Lake Bar and Grill, Sheriff Caswell sat at a table on the deck, right in the middle of everything, a half-eaten cheeseburger in his mouth, chips and a pickle on the plate, with a tall glass of ice tea next to it. I came up the steps, crossed the deck, and so I wouldn't have the sun directly in my eyes, sat down to his left.

"Find anything?" he mumbled while chewing on the chunk of burger he'd torn off.

"Maybe," I said. Then, "Damn that looks good. I caught the eye of a waitress and signaled her over. She signaled back that she'd be with me momentarily. Looking back at Caswell, I asked, "You?"

"You mean on the boat?" I nodded. "Nothing yet. Campers is on it again. I'll have to relieve him as soon as I'm done here." He saw my look and said, "Sorry."

"Hear from the Coast Guard yet?"

"Talked to them about two hours ago. Nothing last evening. They're up again this morning."

More disappointment. The waitress came over. "I'll have what he's having," then asked Caswell, "That sweet tea?" He nodded. Back to the waitress, "Unsweetened for me, thanks."

"Got it," she said and swished away. If she'd come right back for any reason, I probably wouldn't have recognized her . . . couldn't've told you what she looked like. I'm usually very observant, but I was tired, hungry and disgusted with how things were progressing—or, not progressing—and, at the moment my mind was busy with more important things.

"So what'd you come up with?" Caswell tried again.

I gave him a quick rundown on my queries with the bicycle rental places. When I got to the sandwich shop, the name of which I didn't remember, I told him about the conversation with Darin Flinthoffer.

"Yeah, I know Darin. He's an okay guy. Owns the place. It's called Darin's Food and Rentals, by the way. Not very original."

"Guess I'm slipping," I said.

"You got the important stuff," Caswell replied, a deadpan look on his face. Then, Campers or I will follow up when the time is right. You say he gave you specifics on both the guy and the bike?"

I nodded just as a glass of ice tea was placed on the table next to me. I said thank you to whoever it was, then told Caswell, "Darin said the bike was a well-used five year old Walmart special he'd bought up in Kitty Hawk. Model was called a Street Cruiser. Says the blue and white paint was pretty well scratched up but it was still rideable. He'd upgraded about six months ago. Kept the old one as a just-in-case spare.

"And the guy who bought it from him?"

"Said he seemed young. Had slender features, which is what the girl, Jenine, told me. But he saw this guy's face. Had dark brown eyes. Had a baseball cap on. Thought it was dark but couldn't exactly remember. No hair hanging out, so had short hair cut."

"Or bald," Caswell interjected.

"Could be. Can't rule that out," I said. "Guy had on a wrinkled, white short sleeve shirt with a collar, and tan shorts. Was wearing tennis shoes with no socks. Ah . . . said he had a slender nose, close set eyes, thin lips, thin, almost non-existent eyebrows. That's about it. Oh, Darin said he had an odd speech pattern. Talked in soft tones, but in fits and starts."

"Fits and starts? What does that mean?"

"That's why we need a follow-up. He was busy with customers and that's all I could get out of him under the circumstances."

Bobbing his head back and forth, Caswell said, "Well, that gives us a better idea what this bike rider looks like."

"Oh, and one other curious statement from Darin. He said—"

"Oh, thank you," to the waitress who put down a plate with my cheeseburger, pickle and chips.

"Anything else, sir?"

"Not at the moment," I answered, glancing up at her. She looked like every other non-descript server I'd seen over the years. She had a sweet smile. Some witness I'd make if I had to ID her later.

"Darin said . . . ," the sheriff prompting.

"Yeah, he said something odd."

"Curious."

Brows wrinkled, I looked at Caswell.

"You used the word 'curious.' He made a curious statement."

I picked up my cheeseburger, took a large bite, put it back down, held up an index finger, chewed, swallowed, said, "Mmm, that's good." The sheriff waited patiently. Finally, I said, "What he said was, he thought maybe the guy was gay, and wondered why a gay male, actually, I think he said, 'boy,' would kidnap a girl, meaning Miss Parsons."

"Hmm," was all Caswell muttered.

"One other thought I had." The sheriff raised his eyebrows in anticipation. "If he was back and forth on Bay Road like Jenine Wahab said, this bike rider had to be sleeping and eating somewhere around here. I can do the follow-ups, but I don't think hotels, motels and B&Bs are going to give anything up to me. Also, I need some kind of picture or sketch to show around, particularly eating places, to be of any help. I mean, I can give a description but—"

"A picture is worth a thousand words," the sheriff interrupted. "Let me think on all of that for a bit."

I nodded.

Silently, we both worked on our lunch. He was ordering another tea when I said, "I have an idea."

"About the bike rider?"

"No. About your boat watching problem."

"What's that?"

"Let me sit on it while you and Campers go over to Miss Parsons' house and do your thing."

"Hmm," head-bobbing again. "Well," wiping his mouth and mustache with his napkin, "I was hoping you could be there with us in case we have more questions only you could answer. Then again, you could go with Campers while I sit on the boat. I've already been there once and Campers hasn't, so he'll have a fresh perspective. Besides, he's the forensics guy." He pondered for a while. "But it's a consideration. Let me think on it while I work on this ice tea. Didn't get all that much sleep last night."

"You mean this morning," I said.

Caswell barked out a half laugh, then said, "This whole thing is like a cluster fuck. Possible drug runners, a hurricane, a probable kidnapping . . . . Yep, definitely a cluster fuck. And I thought that was reserved for big city police forces."

I saw the sheriff look over toward the street and I followed his gaze. Caswell put two fingers in his mouth and let out a shrill whistle, then called out, "Summer! Hey, Summer!" A young girl wearing a white T, tan shorts and sneakers with ankle socks passing by on a bike, stopped and looked toward our table. She waved back. Before she moved on, the sheriff waved her to come up on the deck.

I watched her get off the bike and walk it up the handicap ramp onto the deck. She moved with purpose, walking the bike right up to us. She was a pretty girl with shoulder-length brown hair under a pink baseball cap. She had a happy smile that made me smile back.

"What's up?" the girl asked him. Her voice was girlish, yet direct and confident. I always wondered what it might have been like to have a daughter. At first glance, this one seemed like she would have been a great candidate. Although, like the crappy job I'd done raising my son, things probably would have ended up the same way with my military career getting in the way and my ex-wife running off to California and marrying a medical doctor.

Before the sheriff responded, the girl gave me a quick glance, as if assessing me, probably wondering if I was a fellow cop. I just gave her a casual gaze.

Caswell made the introduction short and direct. "Summer, this is Webb Sawyer. Mr. Sawyer, this is Summer McPhee." We nodded at each other. Then the sheriff asked her, "You know the writer lady, Blythe Parsons, right?" Summer nodded. "Seen her around lately?"

"Not really," Summer answered. "Last time was at a book signing at the book store." Then Summer scrunched her eyebrows. "Is something wrong?"

This girl is quick, I thought.

Ignoring her question, the sheriff asked, "Where you headed?"

"Just down to feed the ducks."

"Want to earn some money?"

Again, Summer scrunched her eyebrows. "Doing what?"

I was surprised when Sheriff Caswell asked her if she'd like to sit at one of the tables on the dock at McShane's outdoor bar and grill and keep an eye on a certain boat that he'd heard had docked there within the past hour. I didn't know why he lied about when the boat had arrived but my guess was, for whatever reason, he didn't want her to know that he and Campers had already been watching it. Probably didn't want her unconsciously looking for another watcher and making herself too conspicuous.

"Keep an eye on a boat?" she asked. The sheriff nodded. "For what?"

"Wouldn't mind a description of those on board. How many. If anything is being carried on or off the boat. Anybody goes aboard. Whatever. Anything that's going on, that's all."

"Just sit there and watch?"

He reached for his wallet and pulled out a twenty and a one. "Twenty-one bucks in it for you," holding up the money. "Three hours. That's seven bucks an hour. I'll give your mother a call and let her know."

"And you just want me to sit there and watch this boat?" she asked again. Caswell nodded. "How do I know what boat it is?"

Caswell looked at me and said, "She's a budding detective." I gave the slightest of nods. Looking back at Summer, Caswell said, "It's a single-master called *The Pink Lady*. Trimmed out in pink. Like your cap."

He held up the money and Summer shrugged, then, as if deciding why the heck not, snatched the twenty-one dollars out of his hand before he changed his mind. "Three hours?" she repeated. He nodded. "You gonna still be here when I'm done?"

"Nope. I'll catch up with you later." Then, he added, "And if you hear anyone talking about the writer lady, let me know about that, too."

I could see her mind working, but she didn't say anything. "Don't forget to call my mother," she reminded him.

The sheriff pulled out his cell phone as she turned to leave. Once she was back on the side of the road, I watched her stuff the money in her back pocket before she jumped on her bike, waved and took off down the road toward McShane's.

"Caswell," I heard him say into the phone. "Give it another fifteen minutes, then meet me over at Parsons' house." A brief pause to listen, then, "No, I have someone to watch for the next three hours." Pause. "Right, the end of Bay Street." Pause. "See you in a few."

"Where you parked?" Caswell asked me.

I was about to answer when I heard someone call my name. "Hey, Mr. Sawyer! Mr. Sawyer! Hey, Webb Sawyer!" I looked over toward the kitchen area and saw a man standing outside, smoking a cigarette where he shouldn't have been doing so. He looked vaguely familiar, but I couldn't dredge up a name.

"You know that guy?" Caswell asked.

I shrugged. "He seems to know me," The man threw his smoke on the deck and ground it out with a ratty tennis shoe, then headed in our direction. He ambled like a drunken sailor. He was short, balding, wiry looking with a face that looked as if it had gone through a few barroom brawls and had come out the worst for it.

"Hey Duffy," the sheriff said, but the man ignored him, looking at me.

"You're Webb Sawyer, right?" the man asked.

"Yours truly," I said. "And you are Duffy . . . ?"

"Duffy Duffner," the man said, holding out his hand.

When I reached up to shake his rough-looking offering, it hit me. "Duffy Duffner from Norfolk? The charter boat assistant?"

"Yours truly," he said, repeating my phrase."

Caswell waved over the waitress and asked for our checks. "Actually, make it one check," he corrected himself. "He's paying for mine, too," pointing at me.

I ignored Caswell. Hell, I at least owed him lunch. "You living down here now?" I asked Duffy.

"Yeah, for about—"

Caswell cut him off, saying, "Mr. Sawyer, we have to go now. If you want, you can catch up with Mr. Duffner later," suggesting that either I might not, or maybe I shouldn't.

"I'm here until after they close," Duffy said. "I'm the dishwasher. Ain't nothin' fancy but it pays . . . whoever. You know. The people who are always trying to stick their sticky wicket in my pocket and punch my ticket."

It was coming back to me. He was Duffy Duffner all right. I remember that he had an odd way off expressing himself. Duffnerisms, the charter boat captain had called them. Duffy Duffner was one of those guys who made people laugh at him, not with him. He wasn't stupid by any means. Just . . . different.

The waitress brought the bill. It was $16.95 for both of us. It was a good burger, but not that good. I gave her a twenty and told her to keep the change.

"You always was a generous man," Duffy observed. "Gave me a $50.00 tip the time we went out on charter," he said to the sheriff.

"That's good to know, Duffy. I'll try to take advantage of that," Caswell said with a deadpan look on his face.

We stood up. I said to Duffy, "Catch you later." I wasn't sure if that was true or just a platitude. Duffy Duffner stood there and watched us as we departed the restaurant deck.

"Don't forget to call the girl's mother," I reminded Caswell.

"I'll call her on the way over," he said. Then, "You park nearby?"

"Got lucky and found a place in the grocery store parking lot."

"Yeah, well be careful or they'll have you towed if they suspect you're not patronizing one of the businesses there."

"Progress is a bitch," I said.

Chapter 11

WHEN I ARRIVED, Sheriff Caswell was already parked at the end of Bay Street. He'd pulled into the empty half-lot across the street from Bly's house. He leaned against his cruiser. I pulled in next to him and got out of the truck.

"I meant to say something to you earlier," looking at Trusty Rusty. "Now I feel guilty about making you pay for lunch."

"She runs and there are no payments. What more could a man ask," I said, trying to keep it light, but uneasy about going back inside Bly's house.

"Well, Duffy did say you were a generous man. You met him on a charter boat? A fishing charter?"

"Yeah. Been some time since I've seen him. That's why it didn't register with me when I saw him there, particularly because it was a restaurant in Ocracoke Village. I haven't thought of that guy for years. A character, as I remember."

"Yeah, he's a character all right. Been down here a couple of years now. Had him on a few overnighters for D&D."

"Drunk and disorderly?"

"Exactly. There's been some suspicions of petty theft, but no proof, so . . . ," shrugging. "He's basically harmless, but not someone I'd want to hitch my wagon to," warning me off him in a soft and cuddly way. Then, "Okay, here's Campers."

I watched the deputy's cruiser come down the street. There was more room next to Trusty Rusty than on the other side of the sheriff. The deputy pulled in there and exited the vehicle. Caswell introduced us.

Looking me up and down, Campers snickered. "So, this is your new roommate?" When the sheriff didn't answer, he asked, "Does Mrs. McPhee know about him?"

"Don't be a smart-ass, Campers." Then, to me, "The girl you met earlier." I nodded. "I'm seeing her mother."

I gave a semi-eyebrow raise. "If the daughter takes after the mother, this Kim must be a looker."

"Oh, she's hot," Campers chimed in.

"Just get your goddamn kit out of the cruiser and let's get to work." The sheriff didn't sound amused at his deputy outing his love life. Then, looking over my shoulder, "We've got a gawker."

I turned around and looked. It was Tammy Wahab. I waved. She waved back.

"Maybe you should go see if the daughter is home. See if you can get anything else out of her, particularly about the bike. Kids hone in on crap like that," Caswell said.

"I thought you wanted me with you in the house," I said.

"I do. Come over when you're finished there. We'll process under the garage and the elevator first." Then, to Campers, "Get him some footies and gloves."

Before Campers got them and gave them to me, he looked at the Wahab house and said, "What's with the pink siding?"

"It's the new fashion statement," I said.

Ignoring our repartee, the sheriff said, "Put them in your truck. Put them on before you join us."

"We'll leave the lights on for ya," Campers quipped.

Shaking his head, Caswell said, "You sure you're up for this, Campers? Maybe a little slap-happy from lack of sleep?"

Deciding he'd best tone it down on the smart remarks, Campers said, "I'm good, Sheriff."

"Let's go then."

While they crossed the cul-de-sac, such as it was, I headed over to the Wahab house. Before I reached it, I checked the house across the way. The Suburban was gone and I saw no sign of life. Probably went to the beach. Tammy was on the deck waiting for me when I arrived.

"Come back to see me," she said.

I gave an internal groan. "While it's a pleasure to see you again, Ms. Wahab, actually, I'd like to speak with Jenine."

"Jenine? What for? She don't know nothin'."

"She here?"

"She's off to a friend's," now put off by what I'm sure she considered to be my "attitude."

"Catch her later then," I said, trying to stay upbeat.

"Hey! What's going on over there with the sheriff and all? Is there a dead body or somethin'?"

It was all I could do not to wince. "Nope," I said, heading back down the stairs. I could see Caswell and Campers working the area under the house near the elevator. Then, I stopped, turned around and said, "If Jenine comes back before I leave, tell her I need to talk with her. You do that and I might be able to share with you what's going on." *Not likely*, I thought. Then continued my way down the steps. I began to understand why her daughter was searching for another personal identity for herself.

Behind me I heard Tammy whine, "That would be nice." Then, "It's my street, you know!" louder.

"Fuck you," I said under my breath.

I went to Trusty Rusty and got out the plastic booties and gloves, waited until I got closer to Bly's house, then put them on. When Sheriff Caswell saw me, he said, "Point out where you walked." When I did, he told Campers, "Concentrate over there, in case he came in from that direction," meaning from the side of the house the garage was located.

I watched Campers walk the grid on the area I hadn't foot-printed up. He stopped several times, bending down to look at the ground. When he was done, he looked over at us and shook his head, saying, "Nothing."

“All right. Now the elevator,“ from the sheriff. The deputy came over and Caswell asked me to hang loose while they worked it. While Campers looked for and processed foot prints and finger prints, Caswell told me I’d have to come up to the office and give samples of mine. When they finished he motioned me into the elevator and we all rode up to the main level.

“Just stand over by the window until I say otherwise,” the sheriff said.

I complied.

The sheriff took another wander around the house while Campers finished up the elevator door. When Campers was done there he went into the kitchen. I saw him staring down at the counter top on the island. “I guess it’s low like this so she can work on it from her wheelchair.”

Counsel of the obvious, I thought.

With a gloved finger, Campers reached down and touched something.

“What?” I asked.

“Looks like bread crumbs.” When I wandered over to the counter, Campers said, “I thought the sheriff told you to stay over there.”

I ignored him and leaned over the counter top. “Hmm. I missed that before.”

"What?" came the sheriff's voice. He'd just come back out of the guest bedroom.

"Crumbs on the counter," I answered before Campers had a chance. "Your deputy spotted them."

"So?"

"She would never leave crumbs on the counter, not unless she was trying to tell us something."

"Yeah? Leave it to Campers to spot it. He's got an eye for minutia and a nose like a beagle. In fact, he can smell a fart that was left yesterday."

"Very funny, sheriff." Then to me he asked, "What kind of message?" He looked closer at the crumbs, as if something might have been written in them.

"As I've told the sheriff. She's very meticulous. Check the dishwasher. She cleans up after herself anytime she makes something in the kitchen."

Campers turned, found the dishwasher, a top-of-the-line Bosch, and looked inside. "A few things in there."

"Are they clean?"

He picked up a butter knife and looked at it. "She rinse stuff off before she puts it in here?" I told him she did. "Not this time," he said.

"That may have been her only way of telling us she wasn't here alone. And if she left a mess behind that she didn't leave of her own free will."

"Damn, if my house looked this clean, I'd win an award in *House and Garden*."

The sheriff came over and looked at the crumbs, then came around the island and looked in the dishwasher, then at the butter knife Campers still had in his hand. "Peanut butter," he said.

"And some regular butter, too," Campers said. "Seems like she made a sandwich."

"Or sandwiches," I said. When I opened the refrigerator, Campers shot me a glance. I held up a hand and wiggled my fingers, reminding him I had gloves on.

He came over and looked inside. "Anything out of order here?"

"Yeah," I said. "She didn't tie the bread wrapper shut."

"Huh." Then, "Why don't you check the cabinets. You might spot something I'd miss." I took him up on it, but found nothing else amiss. I had to squat down to check them out. When I stood back up Campers asked, "She have any male callers you know of?"

While I contemplated the question, the sheriff cut in with, "I used to see her at the Silver Lake Bar and Grill with Roy Smith when he was playing for the evening tourist crowd."

I knew that Roy had returned to the Louisiana Delta. His son had died in Afghanistan and had left behind a baby boy with an elderly great-grandmother. When she become ill, Roy went back to his boyhood home to take care of both the grandson and the great-grandmother.

"Roy was a good guy," Caswell said. "They were an item, I guess."

They were, but I didn't bother to say so.

"Anyone else?" Campers asked, looking back and forth between the sheriff and me.

"She was good friends with John Tucker, the wood collage artist. Just friends," I added. "She bought that piece from him," pointing to one of Tucker's works on her wall behind the short end of the couch.

"Yeah, John's a good guy, too," Caswell said. Then, "Why don't you go talk to him after we're finished here," looking at me. "See if he has any thoughts."

"Shouldn't one of us be doing that?" Campers asked.

"We have other things to do. Besides, I trust Sawyer. We wouldn't even be here unless I did," the sheriff said, in a matter of fact tone. Deputy

Campers merely shrugged and let his eyes drift away, not really buying his boss' assessment.

They cleared the front room and moved to the back. Nothing seemed amiss. Campers did ask something about a couple of *Bait and Tackle* magazines on Bly's night stand. I told him she was not only a subscriber but an avid fisher.

We spent more time in Bly's office. I told Campers my fingerprints were all over everything. He wasn't pleased, but took some samples several places anyway. He also wasn't pleased about the broken window pane. "And you know about this?" he asked the sheriff.

"I've already dealt with Sawyer on that matter," was his reply. Campers snorted. "If we're done here, let's check the dock."

Campers also snorted when I suggested the only logical route from the house to the dock and the best places to pull prints. Even so, he took my advice. But once he saw there was a combination lock, he asked if there were any windows. When I said there weren't, he lost interest and asked about the van entrance door.

"Same problem," I said.

"Back burner," Campers said, unconcerned.

"We'll check it later," the sheriff said.

We went out to the dock, Campers dusting for prints and looking for footprints on the way over the gates and out the boardwalk. Along the way, he took some samples of both.

Standing there on the pier, Campers said. "So what we know is, she may have left little messes to let us know something, who knows what. That she apparently doesn't have any jealous current or ex boyfriends and that she missed her appointment with Sawyer, and her boat's gone." He shrugged, his arms out. "Don't really know what we have here," looking at the sheriff.

"Just process what you have and write up a report," the sheriff said, eyebrows furled.

Realizing he probably pissed off his boss, Campers looked around and said, "Anyway to get that arm back to the dock?" He was talking about Bly's mechanical boarding system.

"Not unless you have the remote," I said. "Then again, if you want to climb out on it, I'll consider pulling you out if you fall in." On one hand, I couldn't afford to aggravate the deputy, but he was annoying the hell out of me, so I just had to give him my little zinger.

"Funny as a boil on baby's ass." Campers wasn't amused.

"We done here?" the sheriff asked, looking at his watch. "We gotta get back on the survail. You using Smiley's launch?" he asked Campers.

"Yeah, but that's only good until about six or so. He's going out for a couple hours of fishing after he gets off with Nickdot." I knew he meant NCDOT. Smiley apparently worked for the ferry system.

"I'll use it until he needs it. You relieve me for dinner at six. Wear civvies. In the meantime, meet Sawyer at the office and pull foot casts and finger prints for comparisons." Campers didn't look all that happy and just nodded. "Sawyer, when you're finished with Campers, get that damned door pane fixed, then, if you have time, talk to Tucker if he's in his shop or whatever he calls it."

They all stood there looking at each other. Then, clapping his hands like a football coach, Sheriff Caswell busted out with, "Okay. Chop-chop! Let's hit it. Places to go, things to do, people to watch," then headed down the boardwalk.

"I fucking hate it when he does that," Campers said under his breath.

Chapter 12

ON THE WAY out of Bay Road I looked for Jenine at the Wahab house. The Civic was in the driveway, but I didn't see her or her obnoxious mother. I'd lay money that the whole time we'd been in Bly's home, Tammy Wahab had been in one of the west side windows, binoculars glued to her eyes.

I followed Campers' cruiser out onto Highway 12, all the way to the sheriff's office. Once there, it only took about a half hour for Campers to get what he required. There wasn't any conversation between us except for what was needed to accomplish what the sheriff had asked of him.

I was about to go out the door when Eloise Terwilliger got off the phone and said, "That was the sheriff. He said to tell you I'd be calling the hotels, motels, B&Bs and house rental places to see if anyone of the description he gave me registered with any of them." I smiled and told her it was good of her to do that. "Just part of my job," she said. "The sheriff said you were on your own with the eateries."

I nodded, then asked, "Anybody here a sketch artist?"

Terwilliger laughed. It was one of those deep, throaty, unstable ones that conjured up images of her hawking up something I didn't want to contemplate. "Campers there is the best drawer we got, and he only does stick figures." She looked back toward him and said, "Where's that drawing you did of that crime scene a while back with all the stick people in it?" When he glared back at her, not saying a word, she turned to me and said, "I guess he's too busy to find it."

Feigning disappointment, glancing back at him, I said, "Maybe I'll get him to show me some other time." He was still glaring. I gave him the thumbs up and turned to leave, saying to Terwilliger, "Appreciate your checking on the hotels."

"And motels and B&Bx and house rentals," she reminded me.

"Those, too."

Outside, I sat for a minute inside the truck's cab, trying to come up with a plan of action that didn't waste time. The clock was ticking and I was no closer to finding Bly than when I began.

And Angela was coming.

There was a hardware store just down 12, a few minutes from the sheriff's office. I expected one of those old-timey places that had a little bit of everything here, there and everywhere. There aren't many of them around, but over in Hertford, a little town just southwest of Elizabeth City with a picturesque waterfront and not much more, had one—a place you could spend hours just browsing around, looking, touching, blowing the dust off and, in general, being amazed at the craftsmanship of early to mid twentieth century vintage hardware. But, hey, that's just my take on it.

Dad used to say, "Don't expect nothin' and you won't be disappointed." He was correct. What I got was a small, independent version of Ace-is-the-place.

"Have to order it from a place in Nags Head. Be faster to drive up there, have it cut, and drive back."

Great!

"I can sell you the putty and grout though."

I settled for a piece of heavy duty tin. It was three feet long and sold by the foot. At least the guy cut it to size for me. No charge. *Hooray for my side*!

The next stop was John Tucker's studio. It was actually on the brochure, along with the bicycle rentals and other places of interest. However, I hadn't noticed that his place was on Back Road, just down from the coffee shop. So I stopped there first. When the Barista saw me come in, he smiled and said, "snickerdoodle, large?" I nodded. A few minutes later I was back inside Trusty Rusty and pulling out of their lot.

I didn't have far to go. One block, in fact. I had already gone by his place several times. If you weren't looking you wouldn't notice it. There was a variety of shrubs and trees behind a three foot brick wall with another twelve inches or so of wrought iron on top of that. Once I turned into a gravel driveway, arched by trimmed, overhanging tree branches, a white two-story stucco house revealed itself from behind more shrubs and trees.

I went to the door, ready to knock or ring a bell when I saw a hand-written sign that said: I'M OPEN. COME ON IN. It also had a smaller sign that said "No Food or Drink, Please." Coffee cup still in hand, I took several long gulps, then returned to the truck and stowed it in the holder. Back at the door I obeyed the bigger sign. As the door opened inward, I heard a *ding-dong* from somewhere at the back of the house. Then a voice calling out, "Come on back." To my right, stairs led upstairs. A baby gate, closed, blocked the way. Residential quarters? Probably. A house/studio combo. My power of observation was unparalleled.

The front room housed a display of John Tucker's work The work on exhibit was all wood collages and wood sculptures. Each piece hanging on the wall, and the two sculptures on display stands had small plaques covered with plexiglass giving the titles of the works, the dates and the author's name.

I followed the voice down a short hall that opened through an archway into a substantial studio. Most of the space was taken up with stacks and piles of timber and pieces of wood of miscellaneous shapes and sizes. The man at the other end of the long, rectangular space sat on a backless stool, leaning over the only other piece of furniture in the room, a worktable. He had a gauging tool in his right hand. He turned his head and looked at me over his left shoulder. Oddly, he had on a natural-colored Fedora styled Panama straw hat with a narrow brim. Other than that, his attire seemed normal: a plain black t-shirt, a pair of light tan cargo shorts and dark brown fishermen's sandals. He didn't wear glasses, but a pair of Ray Bans hung on his chest from a white twisted cloth necklace. He didn't appear to be a big man, but it was difficult to tell since he was sitting down.

"John Tucker, I presume," I said.

"That you, Stanley? I hope it was it a pleasant trip down the Nile," he quipped. When he saw the confused look on my face, he laughed, then turned back to his work. "John Tucker here," he said as he studied the piece of wood he had before him. He meticulously gauged out a small piece, then studied it again. When I didn't reply, he asked, "How may I help you?"

I guess I was a little dense. Maybe a lot dense. Or maybe, just a lot tired. It finally dawned on me that he was mimicking the famous meeting in Africa between Dr. David Livingstone and Sir Henry Stanley. "Sorry to bother you, sir, but I wonder if I could have a moment of your time."

He stopped what he was doing and, still seated, turned around to face me. "You don't sound like an admirer or a buyer," a hint of a smile at the corners of his mouth. "You selling something?"

I gave him a forced smile. "I'm a friend of Blythe Parsons."

"Miss Parsons. The writer."

I liked him right away. Particularly since he didn't say, "Miss Parsons, the writer in the wheelchair."

I gave him the whole story, up to the moment I walked in his front door. When I finished, he said, "Well, that's quite a tale, and all news to me." He paused, frowning. "But I'm certainly willing to help in any way I can, although for the life of me, I can't see how. She bought one of my pieces," he tacked on to the end of his matter-of-fact statement.

"I take it you have no idea who the person on the bike is?"

Tucker gave a slow, deliberate head shake. "No. Not at all."

"Do you know anyone who Miss Parsons may have had trouble with?"

Again the head shake. "You realize that I've only seen Miss Parsons twice, strictly for business. Once when she visited the studio to look at my work and the second time when she returned to buy a piece she liked." Then his eyebrows furled. "Well, that's not exactly true. I remember that I delivered the piece to her house and actually hung it for her. The short end of her couch in the great room, if I recollect. So it's the first thing someone coming off her elevator can see. At least, I'd like to think that," giving a closed-mouth, air-from-the-nostrils snorting laugh.

"That was not too long after she'd moved in," I said.

Pursing his lips and nodding. "Seemed so. It's been a few years."

"And you haven't seen her since then?"

"Just around the village. To wave and say hello. But I read about her from time to time. She's done very well for herself."

"And you have no idea about her acquaintances?"

"Not at all."

"One more question, then I'll let you get back to work."

"Shoot."

"What was the procedure for her letting you inside?"

"Procedure?"

"You rang the buzzer on the elevator and . . . ?" waiting.

Tucker thought for a moment. "Been a while. Hmm. I think there was an intercom." A slight pause. "Yes, an intercom. I think she said something like, 'Is that you Mr. Tucker?' I said it was. Shortly, the door opened and there she was, greeting me. I unloaded the wood collage, brought it upstairs and installed it. She might have offered me something to drink, but I don't really remember. That's about it." He thought for a minute. "From what I remember, she had an interesting place. Designed to meet her needs."

Pretty much the same routine she used with me. She expected me. She expected him. Surely, she hadn't expected the bike rider. I'd have to mull over that one. I waited for a moment. When he offered nothing more, I thanked him for his time, turned to leave, turned back—he was still watching me—and said, "Your work is very interesting. I wish I could afford it."

He smiled. "I wish you could, too." Then, "I hope you find her unharmed and soon. Guess you've heard. Hurricane's coming our way."

It surprised me how blasé everybody was. They lived on nothing but a big friggin' sandbar, for Christ's sake.

When I pulled out onto Back Road, I thought about starting in on the eateries. Maybe get lucky and find someone who remembered the bike rider. There were a lot of places to visit, all the way from small burger bars to informal eat-on-the-deck places to full sit-down-inside establishments. A lot of time would be spent and I wasn't sure I'd come away with anything worthwhile. I decided to go to Bly's house and secure the open window pane. Then think about the eateries.

It only took me a little over twenty minutes to put in the temporary fix for the broken pane. The time spent was a guess as I didn't wear a watch. To me, it was either day time or night time. Now it was day time. The new glass would have to wait. I needed to put my time and attention into finding my friend.

Back on the street, I looked up at the front of Bly's house. Windows. She could see if there was a vehicle outside. One she was expecting or recognized. Unless they pulled up under the house. But would commercial vehicles do that? I didn't think so. I did because she was expecting me and I intended to stay there, not just come and go. Was she expecting someone or simply tricked into letting someone in? That didn't seem likely. Bly was careful. It couldn't have been just anyone who had talked their way into her house. Could it? I tried to come up with a scenario where that might happen, but nothing came charging forward.

I looked toward the sky. Odd cloud formations were already beginning to drift in from the southeast—far-reaching outer bands from Angela, like probing fingers, testing the air above and the waters below. I walked over to the edge of the Pamlico

Sound where it lapped against the rocks that had been piled there at the end of the street, sort of a half-assed breakwater. I searched the sky for Coast Guard search planes or helicopters but, except for contrails off to the west, the sky was free of flying objects. The horn from a ferry coming in from either Cedar Island or Swan Quarter broke the silence. I looked, but couldn't see it. Apparently, it had already turned into the channel between Ocracoke and Portsmouth Island.

People heading home? More tourists? Didn't they know death and destruction was coming? Would Bly be caught out on the open waters and swept overboard? Or had the bike rider taken her to ground and, if so, where?

Back in Trusty Rusty, I was almost to the end of Bay Road when I glanced to my left. Something that had been niggling in the far recesses of my mind finally exploded into a coherent thought. I stopped, then backed up and into the driveway of the unoccupied house.

What I was looking for was still there.

I exited the pickup and my eyes trailed back toward Bly's house.

Why would she let someone she didn't know into her house?

Chapter 13

HOW COULD I have been so stupid?

As Blythe Parsons lay on the deck of the *Lady Bryn*, bound and gagged, that was the question that haunted her. She'd lost sense of time, but she knew she must have been there for hours. The continual torture from the swarms of mosquitoes drove her mad. She'd tried the trick of taking her mind to other times and places. Even into her fantasy world of Nnyw. What would Bryn Carter, her fictional heroine, do? But this wasn't fiction. *I can't write my way out of this one*, Blythe Parsons lamented.

The mind games only worked for a short time. Her skin crawled with the hungry insects, sucking out her blood like vampires, one drop at a time.

* * *

At first she ignored the buzzer from the elevator. Her fingers froze, hovering over the keyboard of her Dell Optiplex 3010 desktop with its twenty-one inch LED screen. It annoyed her to no end to be interrupted in the middle of writing, not to mention right in the middle of a thought. She'd decided to ignore it when there was another long, mind-jarring buzz.

"Dagnabbit!" as her dad used to say. He wasn't a cusser and neither was she. She rolled her chair back from the computer desk and swung it around. As she headed down the short hallway between her writing room and her bedroom area there was a third buzz. Was Webb here early? She went through the only door allowing entrance and exit from the back of her house to the front. Another buzz. "Jumpin' Josephine! Hold yer horses!" she spit out.

She rolled up to the window nearest the elevator and looked out onto the street. Nothing. It could be Webb. He usually parked under the house. But he wasn't due until mid afternoon, and it was mid morning. She rolled over to the elevator and pressed the intercom. "Who is it?"

Shortly a voice came back, "I have a special delivery for a," there was a short pause, "a Blythe Parsons."

Special delivery? "From who?"

"Ah . . . it's from a . . . ah, Imagine Books. From ah, New York." The voice was soft and feminine.

She could almost see the person studying the envelope. Something from her editor? Sounded like it. "I'll be right down."

When she reached the ground, she opened the elevator door and—

How could I have been so stupid? Blythe repeated in her mind.

Chapter 14

THE BIKE STILL rested where I'd first seen it. Thrown on the ground behind the empty house next to the vacation house the Suburban guy temporarily occupied. The bike was pretty much as the sandwich shop guy had said. It was a rusted and flaked faded blue and white trimmed 10-speed. Beat up. Scratched up pretty good. Front fender bent. Back fender with a six-inch gouge in it. The seat, however, looked new. Replaced.

I stood about ten feet from it, concerned about walking over footprints next to or near the bike. Should I take a chance? Save time and put the bike in the back of Trusty Rusty and take it on out to the sheriff's office? I'd have to pick it up without getting my prints on it. I looked back toward the truck. It was the wrong season for gloves; however, I did have a couple of towels folded and stored in a plastic bag in the lock box in the truck bed behind the cab.

What to do?

I decided to go back to the sheriff's office and get Campers.

Unfortunately, when I arrived, Campers wasn't in. He'd been called out on a dispute between two neighbors having a heated argument about a branch of one person's tree that might be blown down during the expected storm and damage a carport belonging to the other person. This from Ms. Terwilliger. For some reason she liked me and, while the interest was not reciprocal, I didn't discourage it. She was a good conduit for information and I needed her on my side.

At my suggestion, she called Campers on his cell and told him I had found the bike-rider's 10-speed, had left it on site, and needed him to pick it up and pull prints. She said he'd be back as soon as he was done with the cranky neighbors. I preferred to deal with the sheriff, but Campers was the fingerprints man, so all roads led back to the deputy, anyway.

I was getting antsy waiting and was about to go check the snack bar I'd seen not too far down the road, both for something to eat and to run the bike rider's description by them, when Campers called in. Terwilliger handed me the phone.

"So where'd you find the bike?" he asked, getting right to it. I told him. "I'll meet you down there," he said, " but gonna get something to eat on the way." When I told him my plans, he said, "Yeah, that's Sarah's. Was heading there myself. Meet you there." Before I could reply, he hung up.

On my way out of the office, Terwilliger said, "Sure is a terrible thing about that writer woman in the wheelchair, isn't it?" When I gave her a frown, she said, "I mean someone kidnapping her and all."

I started to say that we didn't know what happened to her, but in my mind, that wasn't so. For whatever reason, someone had taken both her and her boat to parts unknown . . . and that I'd bet my pension on.

As I was heading up the steps to the deck of Sarah's Snack Bar, Campers pulled into the parking lot. I waited for him, figuring it would carry more weight if he was asking the questions. He didn't have a happy look on his face, which is why I was surprised when he said, "While we're getting some grub, we'll see if our guy made a stop in here during the past week or so. Seems like he might have been staking Parsons out for a while."

So he was finally buying into the fact that our bike rider was, in fact, a perp. That he had done something with Bly. Progress.

"You ask the questions. I'll buy the food. What's your pleasure."

"My pleasure would be to kick the sorry asses of those two idiots fighting over a tree branch that may or may not fall down when Angela hits. Told 'em if they were smart they'd get in their cars and haul their asses up the road and out of the way."

"You think it will be that bad?" asking as we went inside.

"Even nor'easters here are bad, particularly if they push water in from the sound like Irene did."

"That one did cause a lot of flooding problems out here."

"Damn thing tried to cut a new inlet on Pea Island. Guess you came over the temporary-turned-permanent bridge they put up." I nodded. "I got a bad—"

Campers was interrupted by a thirtyish blonde thing behind the counter. "Hey Camp. What can we get yah?"

"Gimme two cheeseburgers, a large order of fries and a large root beer. He's paying," gesturing toward me.

"Trading off for a speeding ticket," the woman joked. At least I assumed she was joking. Maybe he'd let her off once for a free lunch or two.

The woman, who I soon learned was Sarah herself, passed on the order to a young girl with mousey brown hair, dishwater eyes and a nose as long and thin as her mouth was wide. I pictured a girl living in a beat-up single-wide with two snot-nosed kids and some loser who was always between jobs.

That thought aside, she was quick and efficient. While Campers and Snack Bar Sarah jawed at the other end of the service counter, the girl with the mousey hair, whose name tag said her name was Lindy, got together both Campers' order and my whitefish sandwich with tarter sauce, hush puppies and a side of slaw. As soon as she rang me up, Campers and Sarah wandered down towards us and he went through his ID questioning.

To my surprise, Lindy said, "Yeah, I remember a young guy like that. Came in like four days in a row, early on before the lunch crowd came in. Always ordered the same thing: one hot dog and a small Coke. You don't remember him, Sarah?" Sarah shook her head. "Huh. Maybe Diana was on then." She thought for a moment. "Yeah, I guess she was here too, but was in back with you unboxing supplies and stuff."

"Anything you can tell us about him?" Campers asked. While they talked, I laid the trays back on the counter. Sarah waited on another customer while Lindy thought it over.

"Hmm. I remember he had a few bills but mostly change he pulled out of a fanny pack. Must have been heavy, cause there was a lot of coin in there."

"Anything else?"

Lindy shrugged. She had one of those looks that people get when they think of something, but think it's too stupid to mention. I saw it all the time when I ran investigations. "What?" I asked her.

Again she shrugged. "It's just that, you know, I don't want to be all inappropriate and all, but . . . ." I waited, raising my eyebrows as a prompt. "The guy seemed kinda . . . well . . . you know . . . gay."

"Gay?" from Campers.

"How so?" I asked.

"Just talked a little funny. You know, soft and all. Kinda girly."

"You talked to him?" again from Campers.

Shrugging. "Not really. Just him ordering. Was very careful about counting out his money and all, as if he didn't really have all that much." Again, the shrug.

"Interesting," Campers said. "That it?"

Another shrug. "Yep."

"That my tray?" Campers asked to some invisible person between me, the counter and Lindy.

"That's it," I said. Then, to Lindy, "Thanks," doing Campers job of reminding her to call him or the sheriff if she thought of something else . . . or saw the kid again which, if he was the guy, was highly unlikely.

While ordering was done inside, there was no place to sit in there, so we went outside on the deck and took one of the picnic benches. Campers lit into his first cheeseburger as if it was on fire and it was his job to put it out. After the third bite, which just about polished the thing off, he jabbed his right index finger toward me and said, "About three days ago there was a break in over on Scrub Tree Lane and the only things taken was a piggy bank and some food." Then, correcting himself, he said, "Actually, only the money from the piggy bank was taken. The bank was broken open and left on the floor."

I pursed my lips. "Could account for all the change the guy here had in his fanny pack."

"There was three one-dollar bills in there, too."

I just nodded. "You get prints."

Campers polished off his first burger before answering. "I did. And I'd lay the points on it they're the same as on the bike."

His phrasing was a gambling term. I wondered if he had done some betting at the track or played the sports pools.

Quickly changing the subject, Campers said, "Don't take the banter between the sheriff and me to be anything more than light-hearted jest."

If his statement was meant to take my mind away from his gambling colloquialism and take me off guard, it did, I gave him a Lindy-like shrug and said, "I really don't care one way or the other. Sometimes I get into enough trouble with the police when I'm just minding my own business, so I certainly don't want to get into the personalities and politics of local authorities." I gave a half-assed smile when I said it, just to throw *him* off.

"I heard Caswell talking about you on the phone. Only heard his side of the conversation, but got the impression that you're trouble." He waited for an answer. I ignored him and dug into my own food. I was hungrier than I realized. "So are you?" he asked.

I took another bite of my sandwich. It wasn't great but it wasn't all that bad either. The hush puppies were a little too heavy and the slaw a little too sweet but, as I said, I was hungry. Campers was still looking at me, waiting for an answer. Finally, I said, "Only if someone harms one of my friends."

He stared at me a while longer, then finally said, "I guess that would piss a man off." Then, "That what that Serb did?"

My fork stopped halfway to mouth with a load of cole slaw on it. I looked Campers right in the eyes and said, "I'd tell you to ask him, but I blew an extra hole in the asshole's face and he stopped giving interviews," then downed the cole slaw.

I followed the police cruiser over to Bay Street. Campers pulled into the driveway, but not far enough for me to pull in behind, so I drove onto the grass beside him. We both exited our vehicles, but I hung back and let him do his thing.

When I looked to my left, the guy with the Suburban stood on the front deck, bottle in hand, watching. When he saw me looking at him, he tried to act nonchalant and eventually wandered back inside. I checked across the street at the Wahab's. No watchers there. At least none who could be seen.

I turned my attention back to Campers. He was precise. Methodical. I appreciated that aspect of the man. I didn't particularly like him, but he was good at what he did. I had a feeling he thought he was better than good, knew more than he thought he did, but I didn't give a damn about that. If he could help me get back my friend, I could deal with his snotty attitude.

He asked if he could put the bike in my truck for transport back to the office. It was easier than trying to cram it into his trunk, which was still full of crime-scene processing kits and equipment. I was happy to accommodate him. Anything that would bring me closer to finding Bly was on the top of my to-do list.

Traffic was light and we were back at the sheriff's office in less than six minutes.

The moment we walked in, Terwilliger held up the phone for Campers, saying it was Sheriff Caswell. Campers and the sheriff talked for several minutes. I could tell they were working out schedules for watching the pink boat in the harbor. Campers went through what we'd found and how he was about to take prints and make a comparison with those from the food-and-change break-in.

There was also back and forth about what to do next with the prints. When they were done, Campers handed me the phone, then rolled the bike to the back of the office, where he immediately went to work pulling prints.

"You staying over again?" Caswell asked me.

Actually, I'd considered staying the night at Bly's, but at that moment I'd decided against it. Somehow, it just didn't seem like the right thing to do. "Yeah, that would be great. And I appreciate the hospitality."

Caswell chuckled. "Yeah, well. Not much of that, but it's a place to lay your head, fill your belly and whet your whistle."

It *was* that.

"I may ask a favor of you regarding the boat-watching business, but it will be up to you." My guess was he wanted me to take some stake-out time. With only him and Campers trading off, I figured they were both starting to run short on sleep and needed some help. "I know your mind's on other things but—"

"You're sure that kid wouldn't do a better job?" I interrupted.

He laughed. "You're a real smart-ass, aren't you, Sawyer?" When I didn't reply, he said, "You're a hard guy to figure out, you know that?"

"I'm sure my lady friend and you would love to compare notes."

It didn't take long for Campers to pull prints from the bike and make a match. I'd walked to the back to watch him work. "Only two sets," he said. "The other one must belong to the sandwich shop guy. I'll get a control set if I need 'em for a court case, but . . . ." He looked back and forth between the bike sets and the break-in set through a hand-held magnifying glass. He pushed one of the bike sets to the side, then waved a finger back and forth between the two that were left. "Looks like a match to me. Wanta look?"

That surprised me. I said, "Sure," and did. "Yep an obvious match," then surprised him when I talked about matching ridge-end and bifurcation points. I was by no stretch of the imagination an expert but, compliments of a friend who was a detective with the Kill Devil Hills police department who had studied fingerprint identification techniques, I knew just enough to sound knowledgeable.

"Huh," Campers grunted, but didn't comment further.

"Can you send these off somewhere to get an ID? The FBI maybe?"

"Well, if you want to get an answer in a week to ten days, we can send 'em to the feebees, or if you want something within twenty-four hours, we can send them to NCSBI," which I knew was the North Carolina State Bureau of Investigation. "That's where I'll start, but if the guy hasn't been arrested here in state, they'll have to send it to Washington. That's the best we can do for now unless the Coast Guard comes up with something."

"That's more than I'd hoped for," I replied.

"In the meantime, between this damned boat at Silver Lake and trying to get ready for the storm coming up the coast, you're on your own."

"I understand." I could only hope that finding the bike, getting good prints and sending them out for an ID was not too little too late. At least things were turning in my favor . . . and I hoped Bly's.

"Get me a report from NOAA," Campers said to Terwilliger.

"Call them?" she asked.

"No, don't call them," Campers growled. "Go online and see what the current tracking is."

The poor woman looked at me, her face all red. Her "Okay" drizzled out like a little girl who'd been told no for dessert.

I wandered over and stood over her shoulder while she brought up the NOAA web site and clicked on the National Hurricane Center Link. The map for the Atlantic came up and she clicked on the only storm being tracked, Angela.

The cone wasn't all that wide. If it stayed on the projected track, it would come right through the middle of Bly's house.

Angela was two to three days out.

Chapter 15

I WAS LIKE a rat in a maze, not sure which path to take next. With no plan or idea about what to do, I went back to Sarah's hoping to squeeze another tidbit of information out of Lindy. She was already gone and Sarah was there by herself. Since she hadn't seen the guy, I left, got into Trusty Rusty and the next thing I knew I was at the coffee shop. The guy who'd helped me twice before wasn't there and I had to walk another young fellow through the recipe, hoping he'd get it right. Somehow he prepared it as a cappuccino. Reluctantly, I took a sip and surprised myself when I declared it fit to drink. Old dogs can learn new tricks. Nan told me that once, but she wasn't talking about coffee.

Thinking of her, I realized she was probably wondering why I hadn't called, particularly with the storm heading our way. I decided to find a pay phone and call her cell, then decided to wait until later. While I was gone, she was working days at her restaurant, the Shallowbag Pub in Manteo, and was letting Nehi cover the evening shift. Nehi was Nell Etheridge, called Nehi because she had a penchant for the old fashioned Nehi grape soda. Nehi had been with Nan since she opened, and while the girl was something of a mess in her personal life, she was a totally dedicated and reliable employee at the business.

I took my coffee outside. I've never been good at waiting. I've also never been one who was lost or confused about coming up with a plan of action. Plan A, plan B, Plan C. If nothing came back on those fingerprints, what would I do then? A wave of apprehension came over me. What if I didn't find Bly in time? Suddenly, the coffee left a bad taste in my mouth. I threw the half-finished cup in a nearby trash bin and got into my friendly pickup. I couldn't wait until later. I needed to talk to Nan now.

A few minutes later I sat in Sheriff Caswell's living room, calling Nan from his land line. I'd just leave a five on his counter to cover the cost, as it was a long distance call from there. Even though

Bly'd never actually said anything, I could still hear her now, giving me a hard time about not keeping the cell phone she'd given me. "It's times like this when you need it the most . . . ."

Nan's cell started to kick over to messaging when she picked up. "Yes?" Tentative. She didn't recognize the number or the caller ID name.

"Sorry to bother you at work," I said.

"What's wrong?" She heard it in my voice. I gave her the whole story, from the time I arrived at Bly's house until now. "Holy crap! Is someone looking for a big payday?"

"No one has surfaced asking for money or anything else."

"What else would they want?" she asked. Then, "Oh crap! I hope she's all right. She's so . . . vulnerable."

"The thing is, if those prints don't hit, I'm not sure what else to do. And the one who usually steers me in the right direction is Bly. And she's not here. And— "

"Can Randy help you in any way?" meaning Randy Fearing.

"Not really. Even though he had no concrete proof, Deputy Campers went out on a limb and told SBI this was a kidnapping and the finger print match needed the highest priority."

"I thought you said he was kind of an ass."

"Well, maybe he is, but he's also a professional, and he knows there's been a crime here."

There was a long pause on the line. Finally, she said, "And a storm is coming right at you. I was going to call Bly's cell later today and tell you to get the hell out of there and bring Blythe with you, but—" Interrupting herself, she asked, "You try Bly's cell?"

I hesitated, then said, "The day I got here and she wasn't around. But not since then."

"Want me to try?" Nan asked.

'Sure," feeling stupid I hadn't thought of it before. We hung up.

A few minutes later, Nan called back."Out of service. No signal available."

"How could that be?"

A long pause. "If it was in the water."

"Crap. Not good." The thought of her phone, and maybe her and her boat, at the bottom of the sound . . . or, the ocean, was unsettling. On the other hand, the guy who kidnapped her wouldn't want her phone being tracked, so he might have done just what Nan suggested. Thrown it in the water.

"But, what about the storm?"

I knew she was trying to deflect my worries, the storm being the least of them.

"You know," trying to sound casual, "that reminds me. She has storm shutters that need to be closed. Her house might be the safest place to be in the middle of a storm."

"You're not coming back until you find her, are you?"

I packed up my things, left a five and a note for Caswell, then headed over to Bly's house. Even though I felt uncomfortable about staying there, the place needed to be secure, and that included the fact that the elevator was left in operation mode and no one but Bly knew the code to lock it down.

What a friggin' mess.

The house the Suburban guy was renting appeared empty. I guessed he'd decided to pack up and head out before the roads got too clogged with people trying to get off the Outer Banks. I knew someone who had been stuck inside their car on Highway 12 in Avon during a tropical storm. They said it was the scariest thing that had ever happened to them. I couldn't imagine being in that situation during a full-blown hurricane. If you were caught up at Mirlo Beach or Waves, you could literally be washed away when the ocean surge came across the road. Hell, whole houses had been swept away during Isabel.

I pulled in under Bly's place, called the elevator down, and took it upstairs. I'd been thinking about her computer. It remained on but would have to be shut off once the weather started getting ginchy. The problem was, once it was shut off, unless I knew the password, I couldn't get back into it. Once, with the help of my son's girlfriend, I'd broken into a computer, but that was just pure luck.

Also, both the sheriff and Deputy Campers said neither one of them were computer guys and if it came down to it, and the computer needed to be gone through, it would have to be taken and sent to someone in Dare County who knew what they were doing.

My thought was, maybe there was something on it that might offer a hint, although I doubted it, because we spoke briefly before I came down she didn't even hint at anything odd in her life—and she would have if there was a situation brewing. Unless, maybe it was something innocuous that she didn't pick up on. What that might be, I didn't have clue.

I hated living out of a suitcase or backpack. I unpacked my things and put them in the dresser in the guest room. Once that was done, I got myself a bottle of water from their fridge and headed into her writing room. I grabbed the folding chair she used for guests—a seldom occurrence in that room—and sat down at her computer. I hit the space bar and shortly the screen came alive. It was still in the middle of the page where she'd stopped writing. I clicked on "Save," closed the file and clicked on her Internet Explorer icon. Her home page was Yahoo. In the upper right hand corner of the page was the "Envelope" icon labeled "Mail." I clicked on it.

It opened.

I knew she had two emails addresses. One was for her personal stuff, the other, her professional matters. As I scrolled down the emails, this one was appeared to the one for her writing business, as most were many emails from Elaine Norton, the woman I knew to be her editor at Imagine Publishing. There were only eight in her queue. All had been opened and, I presumed, read. I noticed folders listed on the left of the screen, one for Imagine and four others with various labels. I decided to go back to the top of the email list and just open and read each one. Maybe I'd find something helpful. I'd look at the folders next. I felt extremely awkward about doing this. Like I was snooping into her personal business. Even so, the investigator in me took over my thought process and I opened the first email in the queue. I had no idea what I was looking for, just anything that jumped out as odd or unusual.

Nothing did. Six of the emails were from her editor. Most of the discussions were about her current book project, talking about characters and which ones might be best used for future books in the series and ideas on how to do that. I could tell from the back and forth that Bly was leading the conversation with Norton just throwing out thoughts and ideas, most of which Bly deflected or, sometimes, just flat shot down. You could tell that Bly was in charge of that business relationship, and rightly so. Her books were on the best-seller list and her editor's job at this point was to keep her happy.

Of the other two emails, one was from Imagine's marketing department, trying to talk Bly into attending several conventions and to do more book signing events. I knew she did some, but they were far and few between. Traveling was enough of an ordeal without having to get around in a wheel-chair. She'd gone to the very first science fiction and fantasy awards ceremony to accept her Best First Novel award, but the next time she was nominated, she'd arranged for someone to accept on her behalf. The only other one I knew she went to was the Sci/Fi and Fantasy convention, which met once a year in the fall in Virginia Beach. She attended because she could drive to and stay two or three nights without too much trouble.

The other email was from an on-line writer friend asking for advice about plot structure in her soon-to-be-started fantasy novel. It was all cordial and friendly, so there was nothing that raised any hairs.

Next, I went over to the folders. There was one for IMAGINE, one for FWM (I wasn't sure what that was), one for WRITERS and one that read MISC-PUB, which I presumed meant miscellaneous publishers. I went to the Imagine folder, where I spent the next hour or so opening-reading-closing, opening-reading-closing . . . . I came up with nothing.

I needed caffeine.

I returned to her refrigerator, as I knew she kept her coffee containers in there. "It keeps them fresh longer," she claimed. She was probably right. She usually is about most things. She liked Starbucks Espresso and bought it in bulk when she did a periodic drive up to Nags Head in her converted van. When she knew I was coming, she also stocked snickerdoodle. When I saw it, it hit me that she'd probably had it blended at the coffee shop on Back Road.

She also had a six pack of Red Drum Beer, a local micro-brew she favored, and a six pack of Grolsch she stocked up on when I was coming down. She was a thoughtful person. A flash of rage surged through me. If this person who took her did her any harm, when I found him—and I would find him, that was for sure—he might not make it to trial.

I took out the sealed jar of snickerdoodle and spent the next ten minutes preparing and waiting for the four-cup brewer she had on her counter next to the fridge to do its thing, then fixed myself a mug. The one labeled Webb's Doodle. Funny girl.

I didn't want to take the chance of spilling it on her computer desk, so I decided to drink it at the couch. I found a stack of four coasters on the end table with the lamp, took one, put it on the coffee table, and looked around for the TV remote. I wanted to see what the Weather Channel had to say about Tropical Storm or Hurricane Angela, whichever category it currently was.

I couldn't find the damn thing, so I just got up and turned the TV on manually, waiting to see what level the volume was set. I didn't have to adjust that but had no clue about the number of the Weather Channel. I started at two and worked my way up. Finally, I found it and returned to the couch. I sipped coffee for about eight minutes before they got to the storm.

It didn't look good. As the NOAA tracking had shown on Terwilliger's computer, the center of the projected track of Hurricane Angela was still the same. Angela was still a tropical storm but, unless the track changed it would certainly intensify and would hit the islands in about three days. I wondered how long the Coast Guard would keep up their search. Not much longer, I suspected. Then, the most they would do was what they probably already had done, and that was put out a watch for her boat up and down the East Coast. By now, they probably figured it had left the area. Or sunk.

Back at the computer, the next folder was FWM, which I soon found out stood for Fantasy Writers Magazine. The most recent email stored in the queue was over two months earlier. It was a thank you for being one of the judges in a short fiction contest and asking Blythe if she would consider writing a work of short fiction based on her fictional world of Nnyw. Bly had replied that she would consider it when her schedule permitted.

The several dozen emails prior to that were either from the magazine editor or from the two other judges, all discussing the merits, or in most cases, the non-merits, of the hundreds of stories that had been submitted. One from the editor to all three judges about a specific submission that wasn't on the log-in and might have gone missing. All pretty much routine business. It was pretty much the same with the WRITERS and the MISC-PUB. Routine business. Nothing antagonistic or even the least bit disagreeable.

Even though I thought it was useless, I logged out of her business email and typed in the address for her personal email, which I retrieved from the miniature address book I carried around in my wallet which, every time I took it out in Nan's presence, she laughed, asking if it was in the Guinness Book of Records for the smallest address book in the world. The problem was, while I had the email address, I didn't have the password.

I tried several different tactics. First I tried a combination of her family names, at least the ones I knew. Nothing. Then I tried character names and places from her books. Nothing. Then I tried local names and places in the village and on the island. Nothing. It was hopeless. Now I couldn't get into her personal email and couldn't get back into her business email even if I wanted to.

I sat back in the not-so-comfortable folding chair and stared at the computer screen, trying to strain my non-techie brain, searching for other things I might search for on her machine.

The honking of a car horn broke my concentration.

Chapter 16

I GOT UP, went into the front room and looked out the window. Standing next to his cruiser, looking up at me, was Sheriff Caswell. As soon as he saw me he walked under the house. I sent the elevator down for him. Shortly, he was in the room, hands on hips, looking around.

"You know, you could have pushed the buzzer on the elevator."

"I could have." Then, "Technically, this is still a crime scene, you know."

"I'm investigating," I said.

"Investigating what?"

"I just finished going through all her emails." I didn't tell him how I was now locked out of both email sites.

"Anything?"

"Business as usual."

"I guess you'd know."

"Since I'm not much of a computer person, I was trying to think of something else we could look at that might lead us somewhere."

"Oh, so now that I'm here, it's us and we, is it?"

I glared at him. "You think I'm going to sit around twiddling my thumbs while you spend hour after hour staring at a pink boat?"

Ignoring me, he said, "You look at her bookmarks? Some systems call them favorites."

"Hadn't thought of that yet."

"Check her browser for the places she's been visiting recently?" He asked. I shook my head. "Her document files? Besides the files on her books, we could see what else she's writing about."

"Did you say we?" giving him a wry smile.

Ignoring that, he said, "Seems like a lot more to do. Glad you thought of it. My mind has been on this damn boat thing. I just can't figure out what in the hell the guy is doing here with his wife and kid. The only place he goes is up to the grocery and they have taken some meals at McShane's. He's up to something, but I don't know what. But he's got to make a move soon. You know, with the storm coming and all."

"Maybe he's waiting for somebody to show up. A meet here in the village."

Caswell nodded. "Yeah. Makes sense. You're probably right about that." Then, "She got anything to eat here, or am I gonna have to go out and bring something back?"

My jaw twitched, wondering if the bastard who took her was giving her food and something to drink. With Bly's physical situation, if she didn't have regular fluids, her kidneys could shut down. "Well, she eats like a bird, but I'll look. She usually has a stock of fish on hand, particularly when I'm coming." I'd have to look out on the hot tub porch, where she kept a freezer.

"Here's the deal," Caswell said. "If you're going to continue on with the computer search, I'll go get something. If I'm going to search, you can cook something."

I liked to cook but, to be honest, I didn't trust him not to miss something. To gloss over something I knew would be out of character. "I'll go back on the machine. But if you're gonna fly, you're also gonna buy."

"I'm not taking special orders. You eat what I bring back."

I nodded. "Just the food. There's plenty to drink here," meaning plenty of what I liked to drink.

"Leave the elevator at the bottom," he said.

I nodded.

I followed his suggestion and clicked on the "Favorites" link which, after a few misdirections I found was the star icon, located between the house and something that looked like a cog, which was for something called "Tools." As with the emails, she had everything sorted into folders labeled: MISC, PERSONAL, PUBLISHING, MARKETING, RESEARCH and WEBSITE.

The miscellaneous folder was empty. I presumed that links to sites went in there when she needed them and deleted when she was finished, like a temporary file. Her Personal folder had three individual links, one for J. C. Penneys (I knew she liked to buy clothes from them), one called Allure that looked like a hair products site (it was), and the third one for Dell Computers. The folder that surprised me was a sub-folder labeled WS. *Huh*? I opened it. I wished I hadn't. Inside were several links to articles and news reports on yours truly.

WS. Webb Sawyer.

I didn't open any of them. I knew they were out there, but never wanted to read any of them, and when someone tried to discuss them with me, I cut them off. I'd once talked to Bly about them. She'd just shrugged and said, "Sort of like reviews. If you get a bad one and you don't read it, it doesn't count." Yet, she'd looked up and book-marked mine. "She's going to chronicle my deeds and misdeeds for herself, like some proud reclusive aunt," I said aloud. I decided that, no matter what, I'd keep this discovery to myself. I moved on to the Publishing folder.

It had the Imagine link, the Fantasy Magazine link, both of which were on her business email folder list. It also had links to an agent, who she had recently been in contact with about selling both foreign rights and film rights and options. I didn't see any reason to look at their websites. As for other agents, I saw none. Bly didn't use an agent with Imagine. When she once told me that she felt she was taken advantage of on the first book deal, I asked why she didn't get an agent, and she told me, "Now that I know better, and since my books are on the best seller list, I have them by the short and curlies." I'd asked her where she'd learned that kind of talk. She'd said, "I've been around, too, you know." When I smirked, she'd said, "You don't know the half of it," then laughed. I guess I didn't know, and I didn't want to.

The Marketing folder was much of the same as the one for publishing. All the usual online bookseller links, several groups related to writers, readers, reviewers and sites where reviews were published and the like. I decided it might be productive to go through the user groups just to see if there was anything there, maybe a nasty comment or the like, when I heard the elevator.

Good time for a break.

The sheriff had bought and brought Spanish mackerel po-boys along with fries and cole slaw from McShane's. Actually, he'd brought three sandwiches, saying, "One and a half for each of us. I'd have gotten two each, but the jury is still out on whether you're worth it or not."

I gave him a half smile. "Just for that, I'm not going to offer you a Grolsch."

While searching through her cabinets for plates, he shot back over his shoulder, "Thank God for that. Too damned bitter for my taste. I'll stick with one of those Red Drums I saw in there," meaning in the fridge.

"In the island. Cabinet door on the far left."

"What?"

"The dishes," I said, getting the beers out of the refrigerator.

Caswell shuffled around inside the cabinet and came up with some inexpensive green plastic dishes. "Might as well eat in style." He then set out the food on the plates.

I uncapped the beers and handed him the Red Drum, then took my plate and the Grolsch to the dining table. I sat at one end. He pulled a chair around from the side and sat at the other end.

"Find anything yet?" he asked.

"Nothing."

"What do you think this guy wants with her? A disgruntled fan who didn't like her killing off his favorite character? Or just some weirdo who wants to have sex with a crippled girl?"

I winced at the last thought. The thing is, I'd wondered the same thing. What was this guy's motive? As much as I hated to admit it, I thought Caswell might be right about the sexual angle. If that was so, I hoped if he tried something she'd rip his nuts off. She had the capacity to do it, too. She worked out her upper body every day, including hand strengthening exercises with rubber balls.

"You've known her a long time, I guess?"

I told him about our days at the Weeksville School. How she'd first arrived there at the start of the fifth grade in a beat up old wheelchair that squealed and squeaked as she went down the halls, about the bully who said unkind things about her to others, right in front of her face. How I'd beat the crap out of the guy and got suspended.

"So, you've been her guardian angel ever since."

"Not really. Just good friends. If you knew Bly, you'd know she didn't need a guardian angel. Despite the fact that her parents were overly protective, she's always been very independent. The thing is, they lived poor but had money stuffed in the mattress and wouldn't spend it. They were old time country folk that 'saved their money for a rainy day.' They could have given her anything she needed to better her life, but they didn't. The only reason they finally let her go to public school was because she 'fussed, cried and threw a tantrum,' as she said. After her parents died she inherited a bundle, and moved down here to write."

"She tell you that? The tantrum part, I mean."

I gave a half smile. "Yes, she did."

"Sounds resourceful."

"She is."

"Why'd she move here?"

"Randy Fearing and I used to go fishing all the time and she'd beg us to take her, but her parents were reluctant to let her go. Finally, one day, we just showed up at her place at six in the morning. She told her parents she was going fishing and that was that. As we got her and her wheelchair into Randy's junker, they just stood there on the front porch in their robes, with their mouths hanging open.

Finally, one Saturday we were coming down here for the day and, once again, she wanted to come along. By then, her parents had given up on saying no, except they told us we couldn't stay overnight and had to come back that day. Well, as you know, it's about a three and a half hour trip down here. It was even longer then. My dad had a friend who lived here then and the guy let us use one of his boats to fish in the sound. We didn't stay the night, but we didn't get her home until after 11:00 pm. Her parents weren't happy but they didn't say anything to us After that, Bly was hooked on Ocracoke Village. Said that one day she was going to move here . . . and that's exactly what she did. She's come a long way from that rickety old wheelchair to the red and white spaceship she rides around in now."

"Yeah, I can see that she's spared no expense in making the place here handicapped friendly."

We finished our meal in silence.

Before I got back to the computer, Caswell asked the obvious. "I suppose you're going to stay here for the time being."

"Look, I know you don't—" I started before he held up a hand.

"No, I get it. Unless it's from the computer, I don't think we're going to get anything else from here. Plus, she's your friend. You feel like you're doing something. Accomplishing something, if nothing else than holding down the fort for her." Then, "Campers know you're here?"

"I didn't decide until I'd returned to your place."

"Just as well. Campers would have thrown a fit."

I chuckled. "I get the impression he'd like to have your job."

"Yeah, well," nodding, "he thinks having a two-year degree in law enforcement from the community college up in Dare gives him the edge. What he doesn't really understand is that people down here like to have one of their own in this position. Someone who understands how people here think. I'm fourth generation here and I just barely qualify as a local," chuckling to himself.

"Camper's an outsider?"

"Originally from Raleigh. Moved to Nags Head out of high school. Did the life guard bit, sharing a house with a bunch of guys, working odd jobs and going to school during the off-season." I nodded. "Don't get me wrong. Campers is a smart guy and does a good job, but he could use a few more 'bullshit and brogue' skills if he ever wants to be elected sheriff in Ocracoke."

"Kinda sensed that right off," I said.

"Anyway, I have a favor to ask." I waited. "I'd like you to take a six hour shift watching the boat."

"Six hours."

"From midnight until six in the morning. There are a number of things I just have to get done in the morning, and I can't do them on no sleep. You can relieve me and then Campers will relieve you."

"Campers okay with this?"

"I'm the goddamn sheriff, remember. Campers takes orders from me."

The mood between us had suddenly turned sour. I guess Campers got under his skin more than he wanted to admit. Throwing my hands in front of me, I said, "Hey! Just don't want to get any crap from him. I need him on my side, too. I don't give a rat's ass about any office in-fighting between you two. I just want to find Blythe Parsons and return her home unharmed. If we get the asshole who took her, that's a bonus."

This time, it was Caswell who threw up his hands. "You're right, I'm wrong. I apologize."

"I accept."

"So, will you take my stake out?"

I laughed.

"What?"

"Nothing. Where do I meet you?" He proceeded to tell me which pier to go down and which boat to board. When he finished, I said, "I'm going to get back on the computer." Caswell stood up, started to grab his empty plate when I interrupted with, "I'll take care of cleaning up."

He nodded. "Midnight," he reminded me.

"I'll be there."

"Let me know if you find anything," meaning on the computer.

"I will."

I watched him get in the cruiser and leave before I headed back to Bly's writing room.

I guess I should have thanked him for the meal.

Chapter 17

I SAT BACK down in front of the computer when I realized I really didn't know how to search Bly's browser history. Or any browser history. I was tired and frustrated and my brain wasn't functioning at a hundred percent. Maybe not even fifty percent. Even so, I made several attempts at figuring it out. Finally, I gave up, thought about a large cup of coffee, decided if I was going to spend all night peering out a window looking at a boat bathed in the diffused illumination of dock lighting I'd better get some sleep. I'd get some guidance from Caswell when I relieved him on his stake-out.

I didn't even take my shoes off. I was asleep moments after my head hit the pillow. Actually, it was the spread pulled up over the pillow.

I woke up with a start. I hadn't had even the hint of a dream. Had I overslept? Missed my time to meet Caswell? I jumped off the bed and scanned the room for a clock, in my haze not remembering whether or not there was one in the room. As I said before, I don't wear a watch. Hadn't since I'd left the Army. I shuffled into the great room. I could turn on the TV. No. Go into the kitchen. There was a clock on the stove and the microwave. I relaxed. It was only 10:45 pm. I needed coffee. There was still some in the pot. I decided on a shower and change of clothes first.

When I finally returned to the kitchen it was twenty after eleven. I poured out what was left and made a fresh pot of coffee—snickerdoodle, of course. While that brewed, I dug around and found something with which to make a sandwich. I had to settle for an old-fashioned PB&J, in this case the "J" standing for jam. Bly liked cherry jam. She also liked whole wheat bread and the natural chunky kind of peanut butter. I made two sandwiches, wrapped them in some tin foil, then went down to the truck and retrieved my thermos. As soon as the coffee was ready, I poured myself a mug, then filled the thermos with what was left.

I showed up at the docks with ten minutes to spare. I'd parked all the way down at the public parking lot near the museum, then walked up the long block. When I stepped on the boat, Caswell whispered from inside the galley, "In here."

I ducked inside the galley door.

"Right on time," Caswell said, glancing at his watch.

"Early, actually. So what's the marching orders?"

Caswell then told me that there were three of them on the boat, one being a kid around eleven or so named Ellie Antonelli, Ellie's mother Gloria, and a man named Jed McManus, who was the primary target. "If he leaves the boat, follow him."

"Suppose the woman leaves and he doesn't?"

"Tough call. She could be a decoy to pull us off him, so—"

"You think he knows he's being watched?" I interrupted.

"Don't think so, but you never know. Whether he does or not, from the report I got, he seems to be the cagey type, which is why he's still roaming around and nobody has nailed him yet."

"Arrogant, too," I added, thinking again, *who in the hell would ride around peddling drugs in a pink boat*?

"A guy I'm gonna catch," Caswell said. "At any rate, if the woman goes out alone, call me and I'll come over and sit on him while you go after her. So, if you see her leaving, do not give her any lead time. Call me right away."

I laughed. "On what?"

Caswell handed me his cell. "Keep it on. I've set it so all you have to do is hit call and it will dial my land line."

"Hope you're not a heavy sleeper."

"I'm not. In any event, you call if *anyone* leaves that boat. In the middle of the night, it won't be for just a walk in the midnight air."

"What if the kid leaves?"

"I doubt that. She's been vetted by Summer."

"Vetted?" I laughed. "You mean by that kid I met at the restaurant?"

"Yep," terse.

"You mean to tell me you trust the word of a . . . what is she, eleven? Twelve?"

"The kid on the boat isn't a problem, trust me on this."

I shrugged. "If you say so."

"I do. End of conversation."

The sheriff left the boat, thermos in hand, saying, "Hope you brought your own. Mine's empty."

* * *

By three o'clock—I checked the time on the cell too often, making the minutes and hours pass too slowly—my thermos was half empty. I was hungry and wolfed down one of the PB&Js.

Standing inside the cabin peering out a porthole was incredibly tiring, not to mention boring as hell. Since Caswell's instructions didn't include restrictions as to my watching post, I decided to go out on deck and sit on the bench seats along the leeward side of the boat, facing my objective.

I'd done many stakeouts in the military and knew what worked and what didn't, and standing up, looking through a window for six hours didn't work for me. I'd already done three hours and that was enough, thank you very much. Besides, the pier I was on was totally dark. The light on the post at the entrance was either burned out or turned off on purpose by the sheriff—I suspected the latter. So I could sit there in the darkness without being seen while, at the same time, see anyone leaving *The Pink Lady*, the target boat. The pier light was on over there.

While I sat there staring into the gloom, I thought about Bly. I should have been sitting in the back of her boat, trailing a line, waiting for that red drum catch that would outweigh her best catch and win myself a free meal at a local restaurant of choice. Of course, that had yet to happen. She always seemed to pull out the winning catch for whatever fish we were after. Thinking about food made me hungry again. I downed the other PB&J.

I thought of the story I'd told Caswell about Randy Fearing, Bly and I racing down to Ocracoke for the day, trying to get as much sound-fishing in as possible before having to race back to Weeksville. What I hadn't told the sheriff was how she out-fished us, in variety, number and length and weight of catches. Randy and I had been flabbergasted. "Next time we go I'll give you guys a few tips," she'd chided.

The thing is, after we got her home, her parents had time to recover from her early-morning rebellion and clamped down on her social activities. The following week at school—we were in the eleventh grade then—Bly told us her parents were really upset with her and she was going to cool it for a while. She realized they meant well and only wanted to protect her and she didn't want to upset them any more than she already had.

I knew she was a voracious reader and a big fan of fantasy. She'd started working on a fantasy novel and, once again, by the end of the next school year she was feeling restless to "do something fun."

There was a senior field trip planned to the Chrysler Museum of Art in Norfolk. A week before the trip, Bly cornered me at lunch in the cafeteria and said, "There's a fantasy convention in Virginia Beach and I want to go. You know, meet and mingle with real writers. Get some tips. Learn stuff."

Then she asked me how to let air out of a car tire. "Why?" I'd asked. Then she laid out her plan. Actually, it was more like a plot, bordering on a caper. I'd laughed, thinking, she is just talking. Playing along, I told her you only had to uncap the air valve, then poke something into the opening and press down on the metal stem. Then she wanted to know how she could get the cap off, since she was in a wheelchair. That one I didn't have an answer for, but she said she'd figure it out.

I soon found out she wasn't kidding. She was determined to go to the convention. By then, Randy Fearing was concentrating on getting into college and making good grades and wasn't up for anything that might screw up his chances, so I was on my own for this one.

The day of the field trip, we were supposed to be at the school by 6:30 am, which meant we had to be leaving home by six or so. Bly had already gone through the motions of bringing home the approval form for the trip and getting it signed. Somehow, it never reached the school's front office. She wasn't on the list of those going. I didn't bother with the approval form. My parents didn't even know there was a field trip.

That morning I borrowed my mother's Buick LeSabre because "I had to stay late after school to help plan the upcoming prom." My mother was pleasantly surprised to find out I was involved in that and was more than happy to lend me her car. I wouldn't be home until after 6:00 pm.

By design, I just happened to be driving by Bly's house on the way to school when I saw Mr. Parsons standing in his driveway, hands on hips, looking at two flat tires. I pulled in and got out. "What happened?" I asked, looking past him at Bly, who was in her wheelchair, an amused look on her face. After some brief chatter about how he only had one spare and how Blythe had to catch the bus for her field trip, I offered to take her with me. "I'm going too," I said, "So I'll bring her back home as soon as we get back on the bus from Norfolk." Mr. Parsons was too disgusted with his tire situation to contest or complain.

Bly loved the convention. She went to readings and Q&A sessions and cornered every writer she could, asking questions, talked about writing. It was literally a fantasy come true for her. Many years later, she told me that was just the boost she needed to make a real commitment to her writing.

On the way back from Norfolk, I'd asked Bly, "How'd you get the caps off?"

"Used dad's pine-cone picker," she'd said. "Squeezed the ends around the cap and kept turning it until they came off." She'd also used my idea of using the point of a long stick to push on the metal stem and release the air.

"Where were your parents while you were doing all of this?" she asked..

"Dad was taking a nap. Mom was making dinner."

"You're a tricky girl."

"Yes I am," she'd said.

Thinking about it now gave me hope that she still was that tricky girl I knew in high school. That she'd find a way to turn the tables on the little bastard who took her.

Six in the morning was a long time coming. Actually, it was 6:10 am when Campers finally showed up. By then I was back at my original post inside the cabin.

Campers did the classic double-take, then growled, "What in the hell . . . ." he let his surprise and apparent indignation drift off, then just shook his head. "First he uses a kid to gather information, now an out of town wanna-be who's the friend of the alleged local celebrity kidnap victim."

"If I were you, Campers, I'd watch your mouth."

"Oh, I forgot. Anyone pisses you off, you just shoot 'em," he scoffed.

I wanted to smack him in his smart mouth, but I let it go. I still needed his help. I gave him a quick look in the eyes, picked up my thermos, and moved past him, saying, "By the way, in case you're interested, there's nothing to report from *The Pink Lady*. Enjoy your watch," then stepped from the boat onto the pier, wondering if the coffee shop was open this early.

It was. I ordered a large snickerdoodle and a blueberry scone, "Fresh from the bakery," the girl said. That made three Baristas who could make my brew.

I sat outside on the front deck, sucking down the coffee and filling my belly with the scone. Well, not really. I went back in and bought a second one. After I pounded down that one, I sat there, sipping the final third of my cup, trying to come up with a plan of action; what I could accomplish for the rest of the day, but I was just too damned tired to put together a coherent thought.

I finished the coffee and drove back to Bly's.

* * *

Once inside, I went through the house, opened the door to the back deck, went outside and wound my way down and around to the dock where Bly's boat should have been.

I stood there for an indeterminable amount of time staring across the cove, mesmerized by the rays of the early morning sun glimmering off the rippling blue-green of the Pamlico Sound.

Where are you, my friend?

Chapter 18

BLYTHE PARSONS TRIED to get a handle on where he had taken her and where she was. She'd asked him to take the blindfold off and untie her. "I can't go anywhere," she'd pleaded.

He'd only chuckled. "Soon enough," he'd said. "And that won't be all I'll be taking off."

The audacity and the casualness of his statement pissed her off. Was his whole plan to kidnap her, take her to a secret location and rape her?

"If it's money you want, I'll pay you. But you'll have to take me back home first."

Laughter. "Oh, I'll be getting your money, alright," he'd said.

What did that mean?

He wasn't a big kid. She thought of him as a kid. She'd studied him before he'd tied her up and blindfolded her. He was only about five-five, maybe five-six, slight built, with delicate facial features; a slender nose and narrow lips. His eyebrows, set over closely set eyes, were so light colored they appeared to be almost non-existent. The dark blue baseball cap with no logos or writing on it, covered either short hair or hair that might have been pushed up under it. He even could be bald. He hadn't taken the cap off. He also wore an old, white, short sleeve shirt with tan shorts. His tennis shoes were black, off the discount shoe store rack. He didn't wear socks.

He'd struggled to carry her off the boat, then she'd felt him staggering as he'd splashed through shallow water, carrying her in his arms. As soon as he'd left the water he'd set her down on something that felt like a hard bench. Shortly a small engine started up. Whatever he'd placed her on, or in, began to move over solid ground. She'd gotten the impression it was a golf cart, or at least something akin to one.

It had been a short trip before they came to a stop. She'd tried to use her senses for clues to their location. Mosquitos still fed on her. She was almost numb to it. She'd felt the transport shift as he got out, or off of it. She hadn't heard him move away and sensed that he was still there. Finally, she'd asked him, "Where are we?"

At first he didn't answer, then laughed and said, "Making sure company has gone."

Just to nettle him, she'd said, "You know, if you hadn't thrown the wheelchair overboard, it would be easier to get me from one place to another."

Again the thin, reedy laugh. "No problem. With all the money I'll have, I'll just buy myself a new one." He spoke in choppy bursts, as if writing the words on paper.

Another odd answer, she'd thought. She'd have to consider what it meant.

Chapter 19

THE FIRST THING I decided to do was get back on Bly's computer and see if I could figure out how to access her browser history, but when I hit the enter key, the screen didn't light up. Then I realized that the computer was off.

What the hell?

I hadn't noticed when I'd come through the house earlier. Had someone been here and turned it off? I went back to the front of the house and checked the kitchen stove and the microwave. The clock was off on the zapper and blinking on the stove. Apparently, there'd been enough of a power fluctuation to knock out the clocks. I didn't remember seeing the dock lights blink or go off. Then again, maybe they were on a different circuit.

I went back to the computer and turned it on. Maybe she hadn't set up a password to get online. I soon found out she had. Of course. That's how Bly ran her life. Being cautious. Which is why it still bothered me that someone got into the house and took her away. Then something hit me. The garage. We'd been so intent on the theory that she'd been taken away in her boat that when Campers saw there was a coded lock, he didn't want to bother breaking in. Caswell had said we'd deal with it later, but that hadn't happened.

I jumped up from the computer and went outside. Hands on hips, I stared at the code pad, as if by magic the access code would come to me. Then I remembered. She'd once told me what it was. Well, not exactly what the numbers were, but that she'd used her mother's birth date, so she wouldn't forget it.

Huh!

My guess was she kept all her addresses, contact info and probably even birth dates and anniversaries on the computer. If so, that wouldn't help me. But maybe she had an address book somewhere in the house. I decided to look around, hoping she'd understand my reason for further invading her privacy.

First, I looked around her writing room. I found nothing helpful. Next I checked her bedroom area. Nothing in the night stand. I hesitated, but finally went into her dresser drawers. Nothing of use there. Next, I tried the great room. Still nothing.

I went back to the writing room and looked out the window toward the garage. Should I kick open the door? I wasn't ready to do that. At least not yet. I was convinced she'd been taken away on her own boat. I had two options. Find a phone. Call Nan and have her go online and look for Bly's mother's obituary. That would probably give the date of birth. Or . . . .

I decided to drive up to the sheriff's office. I'd get Terwilliger to do it, and also see if she had any updates from either the Coast Guard or the SBI.

I needed gas and figured I'd better get some before the storm hit and knocked everything out. I stopped at the grocery store/gas station and filled up. I was paying twenty cents a gallon more than further up the island, but I had no choice. When I walked into the sheriff's office, Terwilliger was the only one there.

"You playing sheriff this morning?"

"Oh no, I could never do Sheriff Caswell's job," taking my comment seriously.

I started to make the obligatory "just kidding" comment, then changed my mind and asked, "Have you heard anything from the Coast Guard?"

"Oh, didn't someone tell you?"

I waited.

"They called off the search and put out a bolo, or whatever they call it, for the boat and Miss Parsons." When she saw the look on my face, she said, "Sorry."

"No, that's okay. I was expecting it. Still, it's disappointing."

"Yes. Yes it is," nodding.

"What about the SBI on the fingerprints?"

"Nothing yet," shaking her head. "Sorry. I'll ask the sheriff when he comes in. I was expecting him by now, but—"

"There's something else you could do for me," I interrupted. She looked at me, waiting. "I need a birth date on someone who's passed away."

"Really?"

"It's Bly's . . . Blythe Parsons' mother."

"Why in heavens would you need that?" scrunching up her face like I'd just let out a loud belch. She was a simple woman for which anything out of the ordinary or the least bit unusual created a brain fart inside her oversized head and undersized intellectual capacity. Were my thoughts mean? Yes, and probably unfounded. It's just that the longer Bly was missing and the closer Hurricane Angela got to Ocracoke, the shorter my patience.

I tried to make up for my unspoken ill temper with, "It will help me with something in my search for Miss Parsons." Keep it simple.

"Oh, okay," smiling, as if that was a revelation she could understand. Her fingers hovered over the computer keyboard. "What's her name?"

"Harriet Parsons," I said. Her mother had died almost ten years earlier, so I wasn't sure there would be an online record. I stood behind her and watched her type in the key words I'd given her: Harriet Parsons Obit. She scanned down the list of possible sites. I scanned down the list of possible sites.

"I don't see anything for her. How long ago was it that—"

"I need you to call someone who might know." When she hesitated, I said, "This is really important," stressing the word "really."

"Well, if you say it is. I trust you, Mr. Sawyer, and I know—"

"The number is 252-555-6878."

"Uh, but that's a long distance call and I need either the sheriff's or a deputy's approval to—"

"I'll pay for the damn call," I said in a near shout, reaching for my wallet.

"What's the problem?"

It was Sheriff Caswell.

"I was explaining—" Terwilliger started to say.

"My bad, Sheriff. I wanted her to make a long distance call from your phones here and she was just explaining that she needed your approval."

Caswell looked at his secretary, who blushed and said, "I think it has something to do with the Parsons thing,"

He looked back at me. I explained my thoughts about the garage, then added, "It might also work on the computer." Then I told him about the power flux and how I couldn't get back on her machine without a password.

He furled his brows. "If she was taken away on her boat, why do we need to look in her garage?"

I didn't want to tell him it was just in case I was wrong about what happened, so I said, "I was looking for an address book that might have some information in it."

"Such as . . . ?"

"Her mother's birth date, passwords . . . whatever."

"You think she keeps passwords in an address book in the garage?"

"In her car, maybe. I checked the rest of the house and couldn't find anything."

"Who's he want to call?" asking Terwilliger. She told him the number.

"Who's that?" he asked.

"My aunt. She keeps all that kind of information."

"Why don't you call Miss Parsons' mother?"

"She's dead."

"Oh my," Terwilliger uttered, as if it was the first she'd heard about it. I wanted to roll my eyes, but I restrained myself—just barely.

"It happens," Caswell said, then to me, "Seems case-related to me. Make the call. Use the one on Campers' desk." Then, "By the way, I didn't tell him," meaning Campers, "that you were babysitting last night," looking, waiting for my reply.

"He seemed annoyed," was all I said. Caswell laughed, then said for both my and Terwilliger's benefit, "I have to go talk to the mayor about the upcoming storm event," as he called it. "Anything from SBI yet?" to Terwilliger. She shook her head. "Call me if they do, or if anything else comes up." Then to me, "I'll catch up with you later."

I nodded.

Fortunately, Aunt Tabby was home. She was my mother's sister. Since both my parents and her husband had long since passed, and she was alone with her newly acquired German shepherd in a big old farm house, she was so happy to hear from me that when I told her what I needed, she ignored it and went right into the local gossip about who was at church the past Sunday (she belonged to the local United Methodist Church there in Weeksville) and who wasn't, who was sick, and with what, who died, and from what, and all the rest of the news that may or may not have been fit to print. I let her ramble. When she finally ran out of steam, she asked, "What was it you asked?"

Of course she wanted to know why. I hadn't had much time to come up with a good bullshit story. So I gave her the first thing that came to mind, that I was putting together a family history surprise for my friend Blythe Parsons, whom Aunt Tabby knew, and was missing her mother's birthday. The story seemed to fly. Just for the hell of it (actually, just in case I needed to try it) I had her come up with both Bly's parents' birth and death dates. Aunt Tabby kept a scrapbook of everyone who belonged to the church who had been in the local paper, no matter what for. I once asked her what she was going to do with it. She said, "I've willed it to the church when I die."

Okay then!

When I finally got her off the phone, Mrs. Terwilliger was staring at me with an amused look on her face. "That was quite a story you told your aunt."

"Guess I'm going to rot in hell."

Back at Bly's, I tried the mother's birth date on the garage code pad. I wasn't sure how may ways there were to punch in January 13, 1943. I tried 11343. To my surprise, it worked. Every now and again something turns out the way I'd hoped.

I eased open the door and stepped inside. There was a sensor located on the door jamb, and the lights came on automatically when the connection was broken. I looked around. Nothing seemed out of place. Her van was there. It was a specially converted silver Chrysler Town & Country van with the license number NNYWLAND. Nnyw, of course, the name of the fantasy land Bly had created. I tried the handle. Locked. I walked around it and looked in the windows—the rest of the doors were also locked. At least I knew she wasn't in the van or the garage.

I reset the code box and went back into the house. I sat down in front of her computer and turned it on. When the request for the password came up, I tried the mother's birth date. It kicked me back, telling me it was an incorrect password. I played with variations that included her mother's name. Then I tried the father's. Then I tried Bly's. I knew hers. It was a total bust. So much for getting back onto her machine.

I sat there for a while, trying to come up with something productive while I awaited word from the sheriff's office about the SBI. The only thing I decided was that I was getting hungry again. I went into the great room to the kitchen and opened the refrigerator. After a while I found myself standing there, door open, staring into it without really seeing anything.

"Forget this," I told myself. I decided to go over to the Silver Lake Bar and Grill and let them do the cooking.

When I pulled out from under Bly's house and turned up Bay Road I saw Jenine sitting at the top of the steps to her mother's house. I waved. She waved back.

I was coming up British Cemetery Road, about to pass the cemetery when, up ahead, I saw a man strolling toward me on the opposite side of the road. Darned if it didn't fit the description of the guy from the pink boat. I went up to the intersection, turned onto Back Road, came to a stop and backed up, heading back toward the cemetery. By that time, the man was turning up the lane that ran between the cemetery and a small trailer park.

I eased back down the road when I suddenly realized there was someone I recognized sitting on a bench in the small park that housed the British Cemetery. It was the young girl I'd met at the restaurant—the one Sheriff Caswell had paid to watch the pink boat from McShane's. She had her eyes glued on the man.

"Well I'll be darned."

I drove past, went all the way to the end of the road, turned around and drove back again. This time I noticed a bike in the park's bike rack. The man was nowhere in sight. So the sheriff had her on the job again. I wondered what happened to Campers. Maybe the sheriff needed him for some emergency and he'd missed out on catching the guy leaving the boat for a meet.

As morose as I was over the business with Bly, I had to chuckle about it.

At the Silver Lake Bar and Grill I took a table at the back of the deck overlooking the water. It was too early for lunch and only a few people were there. Shortly, a waitress came up and introduced herself as "I'm Sandy. I'll be your server." She was tall and thin with dusty blonde hair and a thin mouth. She wasn't exactly pretty, but there was a certain sexual tension that hovered over her. Or, maybe it was the perfume that smelled like lilacs. I like the smell of lilacs.

"How fast do you serve," I said, being a smart ass.

I thought I was catching her off guard, and was surprised when she smiled and said, "A hundred and thirty miles and hour, one mile an hour faster than the world record set by Venus Williams at the 2007 U. S. Open."

"I'm impressed," was all I could come up with in response.

"You should be. What can I getcha?"

"Still serving breakfast?"

"Yep."

I ordered three eggs, scrambled, sausage links, English muffins with butter and jelly and orange juice. I just couldn't bring myself to order coffee.

Chapter 20

I WAS LOOKING out across Silver Lake Harbor when I heard my breakfast plate and glass of OJ being set down on the table. I turned my head, expecting to see Sandy. I was surprised when I saw Duffy Duffner standing there.

"Hey, Duffy."

"My friends just call me Duff," he said.

I guessed he hadn't heard of my stingy qualifications for friendship and had decided, since he knew me, we must be friends. To humor him, I just nodded and said, "Okay, Duff it is."

"No coffee?" he asked. "No man can start the day without a cuppa jo."

"I'm particular about my coffee, Duffy," I said. "Remember?"

"Duff," he reminded me.

"Right."

"It's not too bad here," he said.

"Sorry, Duff, but not too bad is not good enough."

He shrugged, pulled out the other chair and sat down, then jumped right back up, saying, "Hey, I'm supposed to be on a coffee break and I ain't got no coffee. What's with that?" He started to leave, then stopped and said, "If you change your mind on the coffee, let me know."

"Okay."

"Okay, you want some?" I shook my head. He shrugged again, then headed off to the kitchen.

He was back before I had two thoughts put together, a large mug of coffee in his hand. He sat down, once again without asking.

I wasn't in the mood for chit-chat. "Whatcha need Duff?" I asked in as polite a tone as I could muster while I dug into my breakfast.

Oblivious to the hint that I preferred to eat breakfast alone, he said, "I heard you was friends with that writer woman." When I didn't answer, he followed up with, "You know. The one in the wheelchair."

Huh! I suddenly decided to be more accommodating. Maybe he knew something that would be helpful. "You know Miss Parsons?"

"Just seen her around. Used to come around more when her boyfriend—I guess he was her boyfriend, you never can tell."

"What do you mean, Duff?"

"You know. A woman is with a man, you don't know what their business is."

I wasn't sure if Duffy Duffner was, as dad used to say, "just dense, clueless or, worse, a Republican." The first time I met Duffy was on a charter fishing trip I took with my friend Dave "The Wave" Meekins and a few others who'd joined up to fill in the party of six. Had he been this annoying back then? I couldn't remember.

"Anyway, I heard he left town to take care of a sick aunt . . . uncle . . . whatever," Duffy said. "You been seeing her now?"

Apparently, he hadn't heard about what had happened. I decided not to tell him. I didn't feel like being on the receiving end of a hundred troubling questions. "I hate to burst your fantasy, Duff, but we're just friends way back from our school days." Figuring I wasn't going to get rid of him without being terse, It didn't seem to phase him. I decided to change the course of the conversation, hoping while he yapped, I'd eat. "So, how'd you end up down here, Duff?"

"From where? You mean from Knott's Island or from Norfolk?"

"You were at Knott's Island?"

Duffy tilted his head and slurped his oversized cup of coffee. It was a manly mug, as my dad used to say. "Yeah, but, you know, it didn't work out so well there . . . ." then he went on to tell me his sad tale of misadventure.

Duffy had a penchant for finding himself involved in petty crimes and misdemeanors. He wasn't a bad guy. He just had the bad luck of being cast as an educationally challenged Ratso Rizzo in the movie of life.

His story was that his supposedly vast supply of friends dried up after he'd been arrested several times on drunk in public, drunk and disorderly, and disturbing the peace.

"Cops love to cause trouble for people who drink. One time I was nabbed for drunk and disordinary when I wasn't. I was totally ordinary. When he told me I was too drunk to have the ability to know, I told him my ability was just fine. That I could walk and talk and everything." When I asked Duffy what happened, he said, "I don't remember. I think I passed out."

This was pretty much how his life went. And while Duffy's misadventures at living were much more colorfully told by him, I will give you my more understandable version.

He'd lived with his mother and she bailed him out when she could. Sometimes, however, he just had to ride it out in the can. Then his mother died suddenly from an ongoing heart condition. Since he couldn't afford the rent, he found himself out on the street, looking up old and new friends and acquaintances, begging couches to sleep on.

The final straw for him in Norfolk was when he was arrested for assault and battery. The A&B, he claimed, was because he was defending a woman in a bar from the unwanted advances of a person he described as a lecher. Actually, he called him a "leecher," but I suppose that could also apply.

When, between bites of my breakfast, I asked him what happened with that one, he said, "I don't remember. I think I passed out." That seemed to be his standard *modus operandi*. In any event, when he woke up, he found himself in a jail cell with a guy whose mouth was as big as an elephant's asshole (his words, not mine). "The guy called me names and shouted out terrible things about me to the guards and the other prisoners. I should have sued him for defecation of character," Duffy complained. "To make it worser, he was a damn Yankee. From Massatooshits, no less."

Duffy was so serious about his observation, t was all I could do not to laugh. I kept the rim of the glass of OJ I was about to ingest pressed hard against my bottom lip so I wouldn't.

I was interrupted by the waitress named Sandy, who asked if I needed anything else. I was dying for a cup of coffee and dared to chance it by asking, "Do you have some half-and-half and some cinnamon I can doctor it up with?" She said she'd check and breezed back toward the kitchen.

"You like cimminum in your coffee?"Duffy asked, scrunching up his face as if it was the most ridiculous thing he'd ever heard.

"Yep. Love that cimminum," mimicking his butchery of the word. It soared past him like a fart in the wind.

"Huh! I think I'll try some." Then, "Did I tell you why I left Norfolk?"

"Nope. Sure didn't."

Then he went on to tell me how after he'd gotten put on probation, he'd decided to leave the Hampton Roads area and went just across the border on Route 168 to the North Carolina state line town of Moyock, telling me, "I lived there for a few weeks but didn't have an address." I took that to mean he was homeless and hunkering down wherever he could, probably until the local police rousted him and he left town. I didn't want to ask.

"Got me a ride down to the town of Currituck, where the guy was taking the ferry to Knotts Island. So I says to myself, 'self, I guess the good Lord wants me to go to Knotts Island.' So I took the ferry there. I stayed in this guy's pickup so I didn't have to pay extra. Smart move, huh?"

"Yep."

Sandy brought me a steaming cup of coffee, several packets of half-and-half and a shaker of cinnamon.

"Fastest serve in the world," I said. She just smiled.

"She's a looker," Duffy said after she'd gone.

"If you like 'em tall and bony."

"I like 'em every which way."

My guess was he might have liked them every which way, but wasn't getting any no way. "What'd you do on Knotts?" I asked. Actually, his story was so odd, that I really was curious about how he found his way down to Ocracoke Village; it just might be worth becoming a victim while he relived his life.

While I doctored the cup of what they called coffee, Duffy continued with, "Actually got me a little job helping a guy with his fish selling business; you know, helping customers and cleaning up and all. He even had a little shed out behind the store where he let me put up." I was contemplating asking him how he fucked up that little gig when he saved me the trouble, saying, "Then I turned up in the right place at the wrong time."

"If it was the right place, it wouldn't have been the wrong time." I couldn't resist at least one little zinger, but he didn't get it, anyway.

"Yes it wasn't." Then he said, "I got arrested for doin' nothin'. Got a hundred and eighty days in the lock-up. If I'da actually done something, I'da probably got six months."

Duffy Duffner certainly had an entertaining way of expressing himself. I waited for the rest, but when he didn't say anything else, I prompted, "And . . . ?"

"You was drifting' off. I thought you weren't interested in what I was saying."

So he was aware. At least when he thought he'd lost his audience. "Just trying to decide whether I hated this cup of coffee, or if I just loathed it," I said. I'll give him this. He was an amusing diversion.

Duffy laughed. "Loathed. Now that there's a funny word, ain't it?"

"It's hilarious."

"You're a funny guy, Webb, you know that?"

"I'm hilarious," I said, smiling.

Duffy laughed again and asked, "You wanna hear what happened?"

"I'm all ears." It was what I came to know as another typical Duffy Duffner story.

"Game warden snuck up behind me while I was fishing—"

I interrupted asking, "You had all that fish in front of you every day in the shop and you had to go out and catch your own?"

"Ain't no fun if'n you don't catch 'em yourself," he replied. Then proceeded to tell me how the game warden said he was going to give him a ticket for catching over the limit. Then, Duffy told the warden that he was only planning on keeping the amount he was supposed to, that he was going to sell the rest, and that he didn't have a license anyway, so it shouldn't matter.

The rest of the story was convoluted and confusing, but what I got out of it was that Duffy got belligerent with the warden and the man called in the sheriff's department. When they took him in and ran an arrests-and-warrants on him, they found that he was wanted in Norfolk for breaking the terms of his parole. He'd left the jurisdiction without permission.

"So that's how you got the six months?" I asked.

"A hundred-eighty days," he reminded me.

"Oh, right. Sorry." Then, "You live nearby, Duff?" keeping the conversation going, just for shits-and-grins, as we used to say back in Somalia. Let's lob a mortar round over that way, just for shits and grins.

"Oh, yeah. Right up the end of Lighthouse Road," waving a hand in the general direction. "Share me a little salt box house with an old guy who ain't there much cause he works for the state on the ferry systems and pulls long shifts. It's the yellow one with the paint peeling."

I presumed he meant the house, not the ferry or the old guy.

A shout from the kitchen area came wafting across the deck riding on the clanking sounds of a bussed table and silverware, telling Duffy that his break was up five minutes ago and that if he wanted to keep his job he'd best shake a tail-feather (that's actually what the girl said) back to the kitchen before the manager got back.

Oh, the joys of having to pay the rent.

"Well, guess I gotta run, Webb. Sure's been nice talking with yah."

I nodded.

"Glad we're friends again," he said, then gave me a half wave and hustled back to his post.

Friends again? Funny guy.

I've been wrong about a lot of things in my life and as it turned out dismissing his well-intentioned gesture was one of them.

Chapter 21

I LEFT THE restaurant wondering not only what I would do next, but if there was anything else I could do but wait. Resigned to that fact, I headed for Trusty Rusty. I'd parked her on the side of the road half-way between the restaurant and the marina. I'd almost reached my pickup when I noticed the girl I'd seen earlier—the one who followed the man from the pink boat. Now she stood there with her bike, peeking around the corner of the three-story brick hotel across the street from the marina.

I stood by the driver's side door, watching. What was she up to now? Was she still tailing the guy from the boat? It wasn't long before the boat guy came out the front door of the hotel. When he did, the girl pulled back out of sight. The man strolled across the parking lot as if he didn't have a care in the world. It was obvious that he didn't have a clue that the girl had followed him.

The boat guy wasn't halfway across the lot when another man came out of the front of the hotel. It was Campers. Curious. Were Campers and the girl working together? Interesting thought, but it didn't make sense. The boat man continued out of the parking lot and across the street to the marina, with Campers after him, making no effort to hide his presence. By the time Campers was across the street, the boat man was walking down the pier to his gaudy craft. When Campers kicked a nearby signpost, it was all I could do to keep from laughing.

Just when I thought the amusement was over, the girl rode her bike across the street and stopped on the walk behind the deputy and said something to him. In response, he turned around and glared at her, then started giving her grief—at least that's what it looked like from where I stood. The girl, however, seemed unperturbed by whatever he was saying. Shortly, she got on her bike and headed up the road toward me. Campers watched her for a few seconds, kicked the post again, then headed off in a huff toward the museum parking lot at the end of the road. By the time the girl rode by, I was in my truck. She didn't look my way.

Again, I laughed. The whole scenario unfolded in my mind. The boat guy aware that Campers was on him, went into the front door of the hotel. Campers had probably looked around, couldn't find him, figured he was meeting someone in one of the rooms at the hotel. While Campers was busy investigating that non-event, the boat guy, who had already slipped out the back entrance, was on his way to the actual pre-arranged meeting place.

The only thing I wasn't sure of was how the girl got on to the boat guy. Presumably by chance, because it didn't look as if Campers knew anything about what she'd been doing. In any event, this girl who's mother the sheriff was seeing was one smart and resourceful kid. Campers being bested by a twelve-year-old, and a girl, no less, had to be humiliating as hell for a man with his ego. The whole business gave me a temporary mood boost.

I sat there in Trusty Rusty long enough to see Campers come past in his cruiser. His jaws were clenched tighter than a face lift. He didn't notice me, either.

I watched a young fit looking couple jog by, both with blonde hair, hers long and flowing, his short and curly. They wore matching black jogging shorts with matching lime green shirts with yellow dragon logos on the right shoulder. Might have been ones on the left, too, but I couldn't tell. They both had black New York Yankee ball caps and blue- and lime- soled black shoes that I'd bet cost well over a hundred bucks a pop. Maybe more. I'd also lay money there was a rag-top Beamer somewhere in the picture.

My mind wandered back to the man in the pink boat. If what the sheriff said was true, it sounded like the guy was a small time drug runner. I hated people like him. Back in Dare County, it was a constant game of cat and mouse between law enforcement and assholes like him who were trying to bring their poison into the northern Outer Banks.

With nothing else to do but wait, I got back out of Trusty Rusty, locked her up, and headed down to McShane's. There was only one table occupied by a family, and a half-dozen people at the bar. Since they didn't have any coffee or beer that was palatable, I ordered an unsweetened ice tea and found a two-person table close next to the docks where I could watch the pink boat. The electric blue mast was a nice touch. If it wasn't so serious, a drug runner around in a pink and blue boat would be laughable. Maybe he was an arrogant man who enjoyed thumbing his nose at the authorities. If so, sooner or later it would be his downfall.

Now, thanks to the girl, the local contact person had been identified, I guessed Caswell would pull off the 24/7 watch on the boat and shift it over to the guy in the trailer park. I sipped on my tea, my thoughts fluttering between the pink boat, what was happening to Bly and why it was taking so long to get a hit on the fingerprints from the bike.

My friend, Randy Fearing, always laughed about how the various cop shows on TV tracked down leads, got fingerprint and DNA hits within minutes and solved the case in an hour—less if you took into consideration all the advertisements for pharmaceuticals with names that had to have at least one of, or some combination of J's, Q's, X's , Y's and Z's. Pills with clever names to cure your smoking habit, or migraine headaches, or spastic colon, or whatever; as long as you didn't mind the side effects such as, uncontrollable vomiting or diarrhea (or both) loss of eyesight, toes dropping off, and a zillion other terrible things that were worse than the cure. All this read to you at the speed of an auctioneer; a guy copping a little side money im-personating an announcer.

My mental self-amusement was interrupted by a fishing boat pulling into the dock. A couple of men on a boat the next pier over shouted at them, inquiring as to their success. One of the guys who'd just arrived reached down into the hold and pulled up a nice-sized Spanish mackerel, after which, a lot of "alrights," "Way to goes," and "Good eatin' tonights," were exchanged across the bows.

Still trying to keep my mind off things I couldn't control, I thought about the reason I came down here in the first place—besides the good company and interesting conversation always provided by Blythe Parsons.

Fishing!

"What'd you use to hook him?" I shouted across the deck to the man proudly displaying his catch. I knew that while Spanish mackerel were aggressive, vicious predators, they were rarely caught with natural bait. That said, anglers had differing views on the best artificial lure to go after this run-and-gun fish.

The man, dressed in a once-white t-shirt, khaki shorts and flip-flops gave me a big snaggle-toothed grin and said, "A seven-foot spinner with a 12-pound test line and a four-buck Got-Cha jig, dude. Cool, huh?"

"Not too shabby," I said. Keeping in the spirit of his jargon, I gave him the thumbs up. The man took a can of what I call cold-piss beer from one of his boat mates, popped the top, tipped it up, downed it, did a one hand can-crumple, dropped it on the deck, then held out his hand, fingers giving the bring-on-another-one sign.

Our conversation over, I turned my attention back to the pink boat. While I'd been talking to fisher-dude, a young girl had come out of the cabin on to the deck. She was sprawled across one of the benches, reading a paperback novel. I'd have to ask Caswell about her. What was a drug dealer doing with a young girl on board? Cover? He'd've been better off painting the boat white.

Thinking about fishing as a means to draw away my profound feeling of dread, I decided to give up on the girl reading a romance novel, or whatever young girls read these days, and head back to Bly's. I knew she stored her fishing equipment in the garage and, since I now had the code, I decided to distract my angst with some fishing off her dock.

As I drove by, the teenager, Jenine, was still on the steps of her house, playing with her cell phone —texting, tweeting, who knows what. She waved. I waved back. By the time I'd pulled Trusty Rusty under the house and got out, she was heading across the street toward me. I stood by the truck door, waiting to see what she wanted.

"You find Miss Parsons yet?"

The question annoyed me but, since she'd been helpful, I humored her, "The investigation is still ongoing," I said. Noncommital and true.

"You need to get those NCIS guys to help you out," she said.

My eyebrows furled. "That's TV bullshit, Jenine. This is real life stuff."

The look on her face said I'd hurt her feelings. "Sorry." Then she tried to make amends with, "Let me know if I can help in any way."

"Sure, Jenine," trying not to sound too dismissive.

She looked down at the ground, said, "Okay," then turned and walked back towards her house.

People who mean well can be annoying. I called down the elevator, rode it up, grabbed a bottle of Grolsch out of the fridge, then went through the house and out the back to the garage. I keyed in the code and went inside. Once the lights were on I found a small cooler (she usually had two each of small, medium and large coolers, all in red and white—red being her favorite color). One of her large coolers was missing. Had she put it in her boat in anticipation of our fishing trip? I half filled one of the small coolers with ice from an ice box/fridge combo she kept out there, then went to the unlocked floor-to-ceiling cabinet she had at the back of the garage, selected one of her eight rods, a seven-foot spinner, then fed the line and tied it off. After going through her draws of lures, sinkers and the like, I set up one of the empty tackle boxes from a selection of five, and headed out to the dock.

On earlier visits, I'd caught some speckled trout, flounder and puppy drum. Puppy drum was my best bet. I went out to the end of the pier, set the cooler down, rigged the line with three soft plastic, bright green and pink tails, about ten inches apart, cast my line and set the rod handle into one of the three plastic pipe holders, then sat on the edge of the dock, legs dangling, and sipped on my Grolsch.

As it turned out, I didn't need the cooler. I caught two small puppy drums, and one ugly fish whose identity was undetermined, and threw them all back. I wanted to drop kick the cooler into what Bly called the bay and I called a cove. I might have if it hadn't belonged to her. At least she had some fish she'd caught stored in the freezer, although not as many as I'd expected. I'd have to settle for that.

The rest of the day I tried to work off my frustration with sit-ups and push-ups, interspersed with bottles of Grolsch. A ridiculous combination of conflicting purposes, but what can I tell you? I took two frozen flounder I found in Bly's freezer, carefully defrosted them in the microwave and fried them in butter, garlic and parsley, with a nuked potato on the side. I also finished off three stalks of celery I found that had been pushed to the back of the fridge.

After I cleaned up the dishes, silverware and cookware, I spent the rest of the evening channel-surfing. I watched a few innings of the Atlanta Braves playing the Mets. When it got to 8-1 Mets, I switched over to a heads-up Texas Hold-'em poker tournament. Annie Duke was playing. She was a woman with four kids, learned how to play from her brother, Howard Lederer, and was one of the few world-class women players in the game. When she lost in the semi-final game to Phil Hellmuth, I lost interest.

I flipped to the Weather Channel. It looked like within forty-eight hours, it would be on us. I made a mental note to reintroduce myself to Bly's storm windows. She'd showed me once how to secure them, but it had been a while. I'd do that tomorrow. Try one of them and be sure I knew the procedure so I could shut them all when the time came.

Disgusted, and with no way to ease my worries, I knocked back a Black-Jack over ice and hit the sack. I lay there for well over an hour, running possible post-abduction scenarios through my mind. All were troubling.

I woke up with a start. The clock on the night stand said it was 4:13 in the morning. I sat on the edge of the bed for what I thought was a short while, but when I looked at the clock again, it said 4:24. Eleven minutes had passed and I hadn't even realized it. Had I been sleeping sitting up? I stood up and wandered into the great room. I slept naked and didn't think about it until I found myself standing on the back deck, staring out at the dock, the place I where knew Bly had been taken away in her own boat.

After all my mulling, I still didn't have an answer as to where the young man had taken her?

Or why?

Chapter 22

THEY WERE ON the move again. After he'd "made sure company was gone" as he called it, he'd started up the golf cart, which is what Blythe decided it was. She knew there were golf cart rentals in the village of Ocracoke, used for the most part by tourists. Were they somewhere in a hidden cove on the outskirts of town? Blythe didn't think so. They'd traveled longer than just around the southern tip of the island, so they had to be somewhere else. But where? On the mainland? Somewhere desolate, but with golf carts. Were they at a golf course? That seemed odd. Too public. She tried to think of various places along the coast where he could hide both her and her boat where they wouldn't be seen.

They rode for about ten minutes, maybe more, before they came to a stop. She was pretty sure they'd gone over two more short, arched bridges.

She felt the cart shift as he got off. There was a long period of silence. Then, suddenly, a scream that seemed to go on forever. Since her abduction, Bly had put on a brave front, but now she was frightened. From the few nonsensical responses he'd given her, and now this, she was more than frightened. She was terrified. Whoever he was he was unpredictable. Someone she couldn't reason with.

Minutes of silence followed his outburst before she felt the cart shift when he got back in. As he drove, he muttered incomprehensibly. They returned over what she presumed was the same two arched bridges they'd gone over earlier, then continued on. Finally, they came to a halt. The mosquitoes were enough to drive her insane. Still talking to himself, she heard him take items off their transport and move away.

"It would be nice if you'd spray me with some mosquito repellant, you know!" she shouted, assuming he was still within hearing distance.

Nothing.

When he returned, she tried again. This time, he answered with, "Shut up or I'll kill you now and take my chances." Then she heard him rummaging around. Shortly, she heard the release of spray from an aerosol can and felt the wetness on her neck and arms. He must have moved around in front of her, because he said, "Close your eyes and mouth and don't breathe. You don't want to ingest this stuff. It'll make you sick" All of a sudden his anger had changed to caring accommodation. She obeyed and he sprayed her face.

After that, she heard him moving back and forth between the cart and wherever they were now. Eventually he got around to her. He struggled, but finally picked her up. With arms under the back of her knees and armpits, he staggered, stumbling twice. She braced for the falls, but they never came. She felt him take three steps up and on to what sounded like a wooden-planked porch.

She heard door hinges protest, then felt them moving inside. Were they in a house? Without warning, he plopped her down onto a hard wooden chair or bench, she wasn't sure which. Then he walked away and she heard him clattering around. Then it sounded as if he went up a wooden stairway. Soon she heard him moving around upstairs.

When he returned she decided to see if she could get him talking. "You said you had plenty of money. If that's so, what do you want from me?"

"Plenty of money!" He giggled. "Oh, I'll have that when I have your identity. I want to know everything you know. I want to be Blythe Parsons. I will be Blythe Parsons."

"And then what?" Blythe Parson asked. "You'll kill me?" When he didn't answer, she followed up with, "Are you crazy? You can't be me. You can walk. I can't. You don't think anyone will notice?"

She heard his footsteps as he stormed over to her and suddenly her face was knocked to her right as he slapped her so hard she lost her breath.

"Don't you ever call me crazy, bitch!" he shouted, his voice high-pitched, bordering on hysterical. "I'm not fucking crazy!"

At that moment she knew that, in fact, he was as crazy as a shithouse rat.

Chapter 23

WHEN I FINALLY went back to bed, I slept until after eleven, something I never do unless I'm physically or mentally exhausted. Worry and emotional stress will do it every time. Cup of snickerdoodle in hand, I stood looking out the street-side windows. Outer bands of the hurricane had already begun to roll in from the south and southeast, bringing with them intermittent rain.

By the time I took a long hot shower and got dressed, I'd already frittered away half the day. I was hungry but wasn't sure I wanted to suffer the chit-chat of Duffy Duffner at the Silver Lake Bar and Grill, so I secured the last five eggs from Bly's fridge and made myself a mess of scrambled eggs, flavoring them with garlic salt, pepper and cumin —she kept a well-stocked spice cabinet (not just a rack, but the whole cabinet) with things even I hadn't heard of. On Ocracoke, when you ran out of anything considered unusual or exotic, you waited for a shipment, took a drive all the way up to Nags Head, or stocked up.

I figured Caswell and Campers were too busy with the drug runners to think about Bly and me. As soon as I'd cleaned up behind myself, I jumped in the truck and headed to the sheriff's office. About seven minutes later I parked and walked through their door. The only one there was Terwilliger. She looked up, gave me a smile and said, "They're both out."

"On the pink boat business?" I asked. She nodded. "Anything in from the SBI yet?" A frown settled on her face and she shook her head. "I'll check again later." Annoyed and disappointed, I turned and left. What else could I say or do?

I was almost back to Bly's when I had a thought. I remembered that Randy Fearing had an old college buddy who worked with the SBI Crime Lab in Raleigh. Maybe he could make a call, see if he could move things along. I thought about driving back to the sheriff's office, wondering if it was a good idea to use their phone to make a call that was pretty much back-dooring their efforts, when I saw Jenine on her bike, coming down her driveway. I stopped, rolled down the window and waved her over.

She rolled over, stopped, and said, "Hi, Mr. Sawyer. I'm sorry I bugged you yesterday. I know you're worried and all that about Miss Parsons, but—"

Yesterday I hadn't considered that, if it hadn't been for Jenine I wouldn't have a description to shop around. Now I needed her help again. Holding up the palm of my hand, I said. "Jenine. I'm the one who needs to apologize. I was abrupt and rude and I'm sorry."

"Oh, no, Mr. Sawyer—"

Again, I interrupted. "I need your help with something." Was I being two-faced? Nicing up to her just because I wanted a favor? Maybe that was part of it but, despite her kooky get-up, for a teenager, she was pretty cool.

"You do?" Innocent. Anxious to be of assistance.

"I do. I—" Crap! Suddenly, her mother was on the front deck, waving and heading for the stairs. "You have a cell with you?"

"Uh. Yep." She started to reach for her back pocket.

"No-no. You like to fish?"

"Sure, but—"

"Ditch your mother and meet me behind Miss Parsons' house in about half an hour. I'll be out on the dock." She started to say something, but I gave her a quick wave and drove over to Bly's, hopped out of the truck, called down the elevator, and rode it up. When I looked out the front window, Jenine was heading back up the stairs to the deck. Her mother stood there, hands on her hips. Despite everything, I had to laugh.

I had recreated my setup on the dock from yesterday when she showed up. I'd gotten out a second rod and additional tackle, but she'd brought her own stuff.

"Get anything yet?" she asked as she walked up behind me.

"Nope." I'd set my hook and cast out, but had secured my rod in the holder. I sat with my feet hanging over the end of the dock. I'd been running through my mind the upcoming conversation with Randy Fearing. "Just waiting for you. Got the phone?"

"You don't have your own?" she asked.

"Phone, you mean?" She nodded. "Nope. They're more trouble than they're worth."

"Apparently not," she said, pulling the cell out of her back pocket and waving it in the air.

"For Christ's sake, it's pink," I said.

"I like pink."

Girls and drug runners!

After a session of twenty questions as to why I needed her cell, who I needed to call and why, she went about the business of getting ready to drop her line. Her only question about fishing was, "Not the best time of day for this, but what do you think?" running through four or five species.

"Flounder is out. I'd go for puppy drum." Then, "If my friend isn't in, we might be here a while." She shrugged. I punched in Randy's office number from memory. Francie, Randy's secretary, answered the phone.

"Hi Francie. I need to speak to Randy, ASAP."

"Is this Mr. Sawyer?"

"Oh, sorry, Francie. Yes, it's me, Webb Sawyer. I need to speak with him right away. It's extremely important."

"You in trouble again, Mr. Sawyer?" There was an uneasy chuckle accompanying the question.

"No, Francie. Nothing like that. It's a friend of mine. She's—" I wasn't exactly sure how much to tell her. "There has been a crime committed against my friend. Actually, Randy knows her, too. We all went to school together. It's important that I talk to him about it right away."

"Is this in our jurisdiction?" she asked.

"No. I'm in Hyde County. But this girl's life is in danger. Tell him it's Blythe Parsons I'm talking about."

"The author?"

"Yes."

I could almost hear her thinking. "He's over at the Java Hutt with a couple of his attorney friends," she whispered. "I'll get in touch with him and have him give you a call. What's your number?"

"Hold on a sec," I said, then asked Jenine what the number of her cell was. When I started to repeat it to Francie, she told me she'd heard it.

"Sit tight," she said, and hung up.

While I waited, Jenine and I fished. I was surprised when she started talking baits, lures, lines and best times to fish and for what.

"You really know your stuff," I said.

"You seem surprised?" When I laughed, she asked, "Is it because I'm a girl?"

I laughed again. "Not at all. Bly is one of the best anglers I know, and she's wheelchair bound."

"Bly? You mean Miss Parsons?" I nodded. "I heard you say you went to school with her. You her boyfriend?" she asked.

"Just good friends and fishing buddies." Bly was a private person and I didn't want to divulge too much to a teenager who lived across the street. I changed the subject asking, "Who taught you how to fish?"

A look came over Jenine's face. "My dad used to take me out all the time. Before he hit the road." Then she seemed to drift off in thought, then turned her attention back to fishing.

"Sorry," not knowing what else to say.

Jenine shrugged. "He just couldn't deal with mother any longer." She was jigging her line when she said it. I wasn't sure this was a conversation I wanted to have, but when I didn't answer, she continued with, "You saw how mother is. I mean, I love her, but she can really get on your nerves."

I wanted to agree. Her mother annoyed me to distraction, and I'd only just met her. Instead, I gave her the tried and true bullshit answer, which was, "Family dynamics are difficult."

"Do you have any kids?" she asked, still looking out into the bay, working her line.

I drew air through my nostrils. "A son."

"You have a good relationship with him?"

"It could be better," I admitted. "He was raised by his mother and a step-father. I was in the Army and was away a lot," as if that was a real reason.

Then, she threw me a curve ball with, "Do you think I'm weird?" When I didn't answer, she shifted her body around and looked at me. How in the hell was I going to answer that? She gave me a little head nod, accompanied by an eyebrow raise.

I gave her an unsure half smile. "Well, you dress weird, and you hair is weird and I'm not real crazy about the nose ring and the stud in the tongue things, but . . . ." I once made the mistake of asking a woman if it didn't hurt to have that stuck in her tongue and she'd said, "The last guy I used it on didn't complain." I shoved that image out of my mind as, given the current circumstance, totally inappropriate.

"But what?"

"But no. I don't think you're weird at all." What else was I to say. I figured she'd get over all this stupid stuff soon enough, unless she was planning on being a rock star, so why create trouble for myself. After all, she was helping me.

She laughed. "Yes you do, but that's okay. My dad is a normal guy and I think he's okay."

It was an odd conversation, which is why I was happy when her cell took that moment to play a refrain from some tune I wasn't familiar with.

"Nerveline," she said, then picked up the cell, which was on the deck next to her, and looked at it. "For me. I'll get rid of them." She did. It only took four words. "I'll call you back," then clicked off.

"Nerveline?"

"A grunge band from Seattle," she said.

I should have known.

We fished for another hour or so, casting, then jigging the lines and reeling them in. Jenine was correct when she'd said earlier it wasn't the best time for catching anything. Neither one of us got a bite; not even a nibble. Finally a squall came by, dropping rain on us and we gathered up our gear and made it onto the back deck, undercover.

I was about to give up on hearing from Randy when her cell chimed again. Jenine whipped it out of her back pocket, looked at the screen, and said, "I think this one's probably yours." But instead of handing it to me, she answered it, listened for a moment, said, "I'm Jenine. Mr. Sawyer's investigative assistant," then, straight-faced, handed the phone to me.

While he was probably still going, "Huh?" I asked, "Randy?"

Without preamble, he answered, "Investigative assistant? Have you officially gone into the P.I. business now?" He was serious. Ignoring his question, I asked him if they were serving Gigantiques at the Java Hut now. "What in God's name are you talking about, Webb? And what's this about Blythe being in some kind of trouble?"

Since he didn't get my bad joke about taking so long to call me back, I went right into what was going on. I'd wished Jenine wasn't there to hear all the details, as I didn't want it going out on Facebook and Twitter just yet, but . . . . When I was finished, Randy asked, "What can I do to help?"

"Didn't you once tell me you had an old school buddy at State who worked at the SBI Crime Lab?" When Randy said he did, a guy named Jack Gurganus, I explained how time was not only of the essence but, with Hurricane Angela looming on the horizon, that time was running out and I needed a name that went with the fingerprints Sheriff Caswell had sent along to the SBI, and needed it yesterday.

We spoke for a short while longer. When we were finished, Randy said, "You know, if Jack can do anything, he's going to have to report it directly to the sheriff there."

"I know, Randy, but can you have him call me, too. The sheriff and his one available deputy are in the middle of a drug case and I'm not entirely sure this is at the top of their queue right now. And with the storm coming . . . ." There was a long bout of silence. "It's Bly we're talking about here, Randy," I reminded him.

"I'll ask him, Webb. Give him the circumstance. Tell him it's a personal favor request."

"Thanks, buddy. Oh, and if your guy calls and Jenine answers—"

"Jenine?"

"The girl who took your call. I'm using her cell as a point of contact and she will probably have the phone when he calls."

"Oh, right. I forgot. You're the no phone, off-the-grid guy," riding me.

"Yeah, well, when he calls—"

"If he calls, Webb. If he calls. I'll do my best. Keep me in the loop."

"I will. My best to Rebecca," even though she wasn't my biggest fan.

He gave a half-hearted chuckle, said, "Sure," and hung up.

When I handed the cell back to Jenine, she said, "You sure know a lot of cop type people, don't you:?" I gave her a non-committal shrug. "From what I heard you tell your friend, it's a good thing you do."

Chapter 24

JENINE WANTED TO leave her cell with me, but as anxious as I was to hear from the SBI Crime Lab guy, I didn't want to deal with her incoming personal calls. And I trusted her to find me when the call came. If the call came.

That evening I wandered around the television stations, spending a lot of time on the Weather Channel, hoping the storm would take a turn, preferably east and out to sea. While I didn't wish any harm to the people farther south on the east coast, if it went that way, that was fine by me, too. Unfortunately, all the tracking cones brought it straight through Ocracoke Village; and it was closing in fast.

Already the intermittent rain and breezes had ramped up to bands of rain lasting several hours, with irregular intervals. Winds were already steady at fifteen to twenty miles an hour, with gusts up to thirty-five.

I stayed up until 1:00 pm watching, of all things, a movie called *The Perfect Storm*. Afterwards, I dreamed I was on the *Andrea Gail*, riding up the crest of an impossibly large wave. George Clooney and I, facing doom together. When the fishing boat toppled over backwards and pushed under the water. I struggled to find my way to the surface, but every time I was close, I was dragged under again. I woke myself up so I wouldn't drown.

I checked the bedside table clock. It was only 2:35 am. As if on remote control, I fixed myself two fingers of Jack Daniels, neat, then turned on the television and watched the Weather Channel for a while. Nothing had changed. It was going to be a rough ride for the islands. My only hope was that wherever Bly was, she was out of harm's way.

I woke up shortly after 10:00 am. I hated sleeping late. I was not a person who liked to lay around doing nothing—at least not for long. This whole waiting business was getting on my nerves to the point I wanted to break something, maybe even an annoying person's nose. I fixed a fresh pot of snickerdoodle, poured it into the largest mug I could find, and went out onto the back deck. I was standing there sipping java when I heard an inboard approaching from the south. From the sound of it, it was near shore, and coming fast.

I walked to the west end of the deck to get a better view, and there it was. Three men. I recognized two of them: Sheriff Caswell and Deputy Campers. The boat looked like the one docked at the wharf where they sold day excursions to Portsmouth Island, some sort of flat-bottomed Fischer or Alweld with a custom built open cabin over an inboard engine at the back. When I say it was coming fast, I mean as fast as a boat like that will go. All I know is that it sounded as if whoever was piloting it had the engine wide open.

I watched them go past the bay and continue north. *Has to have something to do with the drug suspects*, I thought. My next thought was, if information about Bly's kidnapper came into the office, they wouldn't be there to do anything about it. And who knew how long they'd be wherever they were off to. I was assuming, of course, that if Randy's friend had, in fact, responded to his request to get an answer chop-chop, he might just call the Sheriff's office and leave me out of the loop. After all, why would the SBI guy want to risk his job letting a private citizen in on state secrets. I was being facetious, but maybe not. That's how bureau-weenies thought.

I downed my coffee, took a three-minute shower, didn't bother shaving, and was down the elevator and in Trusty Rusty as if I were a volunteer firefighter off on a call. I thought about stopping at the Wahab house and letting Jenine know where I was going, but changed my mind when I noticed her mother puttering around on the front deck. She waved but I pretended I didn't see her.

When I reached the sheriff's office and went inside, Ms. Terwilliger was giving some older man a hard time, telling him that he was wasting his time waiting for the sheriff, that he was out on a case and wouldn't be back for quite a while. The man turned and, with a disgruntled look on his face said to me under his breath, "Whatever you want, don't waste your time," then left. Terwilliger gave me a quick smile, then went back to whoever she had on hold, saying with an annoyed look on her face, "As I said, ma'am, I'll have the sheriff call you when he returns." Then, "No, I don't know when that will be." She hung up and pasted on a happy face. My guess was, unless someone was a reasonably good-looking, mid forties, available male somewhere in the range of five-eleven and a hundred eighty-five pounds, he'd be lucky to get a "what do you need?"

"Sheriff's not in," she said.

"I know. I saw him and Campers go by in a boat heading north up the sound."

"In a boat?" When I nodded, she said, "I didn't know they had a boat."

"Borrowed one, I guess." I didn't bother telling her whose it was.

"I wondered why Deputy Campers ran out of here so quick when the sheriff called in. Must be after someone."

"Must be." Then, "Nothing yet from the SBI?"

"Uh, no. Not really. Sorry," shaking her head just a little too vigorously, giving me a pouty lower lip as if the fact she couldn't please me saddened her.

Not really? "Could I have one of your sticky notes?" pointing to the yellow pad on her desk.

"Sure," tearing off the top piece of paper and handing it to me.

I took a ball-point pen out of my pocket, wrote down Jenine's cell phone number, and handed the sticky note back to her. "Could you call me right away when they call?"

"You got a phone?"

"It belongs to a friend."

"Oh." She studied the number. "It's a cell number."

"Right," I said. "I appreciate all your office is doing for me," trying to give her something positive to hold onto as I turned and exited. I wondered why Caswell kept her around. Maybe she'd been there when he was elected. Maybe she was the mayor's sister. Who knows?

Mrs. Wahab was nowhere in sight when I returned to Bly's. The rain had started up again and it was very breezy. The sky had gone gray and ominous. After I parked, I called down the elevator and rode it up. When the door opened I froze. I hadn't left the TV on, had I? No. In fact, I hadn't turned it on. At that moment I wished I had my mother's Autauga MK II .32. It was a small sub-compact semi-automatic pocket pistol with an eight-pound trigger pull and a snag-free fixed front with rear sights. It wasn't particularly powerful, but it held seven Winchester silvertip cartridges and could do damage.

I did a quick look around the great room, then slid behind the kitchen island and was moving toward the one door that led to the back of the house when Jenine came out of the guest bedroom door. When she saw me, she jumped back, throwing a hand across her mouth. "Oh! You scared me." When I didn't say anything, she said, "I saw how you got the elevator to come down, so I tried it and here I am. Miss Parsons has a pretty cool place."

"And you didn't think it would be a good idea to wait until you were invited inside?" I was annoyed, but didn't want to be too confrontational. She was the one with the phone. My lifeline to information.

"Oh. Sorry. But I didn't want Mother to know what we had going—Oh, not like that—Oh, you know what I mean." I couldn't help but smile. "Anyway," she reached into her back pocket and pulled out her cell, waving it at me. "The guy called!"

"The guy from SBI?"

"Yeah. Jack Gurganus. But I was over at Laney's house—she's a friend—So. I jumped on my bike and came right here. I didn't want Mother to get involved, 'cause you know how she is and—"

"Okay, okay, I get it. Did you write down what he told you?"

Jenine pointed at her head. "Got it right up here."

I hoped whatever he told her she remembered it all. "He said . . . ?"

"Get this," she said, her eyes wide, excitement written all over her face. "The fingerprints belong to a girl, not a guy. Her name is Elizabeth Traynor and she escaped from the Harrow-Martin Psychiatric Hospital about nine weeks ago."

I waited. When she didn't provide anything else, I asked, "That's it?"

Jenine shrugged. "I asked him if that was all and he said he hoped to have more by tomorrow, but he couldn't guarantee it."

"A girl." I could feel my face wrinkling up. Actually, it made sense. Everyone who described him . . . her, talked about the slight features and some commented on her effeminate affectation.

"Oh, and something else," Jenine said, interrupting my thoughts. "Gurganus said he would have called you sooner. That he'd gotten tied up with something else, then had to slip outside the facility so no one could overhear him. I got the sense they monitor calls there, too, but I don't know," shrugging.

"Hmm." Since Terwilliger said they hadn't called there yet, he must have called me first. While that thought ran through my mind, Jenine said, "He did say that he'd already called the sheriff's office."

"Huh." What time did you get the call?"

"Just before ten," she said.

"Before ten?" She nodded. *Damn*! I thought. That meant Terwilliger lied to me. They had already called them when I got there. She'd said that Campers had gotten a call from the sheriff and left in a hurry. That son-of-a-bitch must have told her not to tell me if I came in inquiring. "Asshole!" I said out loud.

"What? Who?"

"Never mind. Now I have to get in touch with this Harrow . . . what was it again?"

"Harrow-Martin Psychiatric Hospital."

Damn, she's good. "Right. We need to get in touch with them . . ."

Jenine was already working her smart phone while I was talking.

". . . and get a name—"

She held up the phone. "Got it right here." When she saw the expression on my face, she said, "Im-pressed, aren't you?"

I wasn't sure if my expression was so much that I was impressed as relieved; relieved that I was finally making some progress again. Jenine punched in a number and handed me the cell. "Ask for Dr. Avery Janowitz. He's the chief of staff."

"You're a princess," I said to Jenine. The voice on the other end of the phone said, "Well thank you sir. I've been waiting all my life to hear someone call me that." When my reply became stuck in my mouth, the voice gave a muffled giggle and said, "This is Emily Cobellisi. How may I help you?"

Finally, I unstuck my words and said, "Hello, Miss Cobellisi," then gave her my name and where I was calling from. "I'm hoping to speak with Dr. Avery Janowitz, and it's extremely important that I do so right away."

"I'm very sorry, Mr. Sawyer, but Dr. Janowitz is out of town and not expected back until tomorrow morning. However, Dr. Courtland is in her office. Possibly she could help you. Can you tell me the nature of your inquiry?"

I hesitated. One thought said to keep the information for someone who would be authorized to tell me what I wanted. The other thought said to tell anyone who would listen and see what happened. You never knew where a tidbit of information might come from. I told her what happened to Bly and how I was working with the sheriff's office but they were in the middle of a drug bust and with the hurricane bearing down on us how time was of the essence.

"Hmm. I understand," Emily Cobellisi replied. "Has the sheriff deputized you?" I told her they hadn't but that I had been assisting them with the investigation. "Hold on," she said. "I'll ring her office."

I waited for a good five minutes. Finally, Emily Cobellisi came back on the line and said, "I'm sorry, Mr. Sawyer, but Dr. Courtland is busy with a patient. She did say that she would speak to Dr. Janowitz in the morning, when he comes in and have him give you a call."

"You did tell her that time was running out, didn't you?" frustration permeating the tone of my voice.

"I did tell her that, as you put it, 'time was of the essence.'"

"Can anyone reach Dr. Janowitz by telephone?"

"Actually, he's on vacation in his mountain cabin and there is no cell phone service there. Even if there was, I doubt he'd answer anyway."

Then I lost it. "Jesus fucking Christ. Are you telling me it doesn't matter to anyone there that my friend's life is in danger and one of your *escaped patients* is responsible?" My voice headed from baritone to tenor as I spoke. "What kind of perverted rules do you people operate under, anyway?"

Jenine looked at me with silver dollar eyes, her face as red as a baboon's ass.

Her voice calm but concerned, Emily Cobellisi said, "I totally understand, Mr. Sawyer. Tell you what. As soon as Doctor Courtland is free, I will speak with her in person and let her know the severity of the situation." I was still trying to calm myself down when she followed up with, "Just hang in there, Mr. Sawyer. I understand why you're upset. I would feel the same way. I will follow up on this. I promise."

I took a deep breath. "Okay . . . Emily. I'm sorry I took it out on you. I apologize."

"Don't worry about it."

"Did I give you my number?" I was so agitated, I couldn't remember.

"I got it on my ID when you called in." There was a pause, then I heard another line ringing. "Gotta go," she said. "I'll stay on top of it," then rung off.

"Sorry about the language," I said to Jenine.

"I've heard worse," she said, making an attempt to blow it off. "It did scare me for a sec, though," giving me an uneasy laugh. "I wouldn't want to get you mad."

"It's just that my friend is out there somewhere with who knows what happening to her and nobody seems to give a god damn." I knew that was frustration speaking. Even though Campers was an asshole, I knew Caswell did care. He just couldn't be everywhere doing everything at the same time.

"Maybe I can Google Elizabeth Traynor and see what comes up," Jenine suggested.

"Better than nothing," I replied.

Chapter 25

JENINE GOOGLED THE name Elizabeth Traynor on her cell phone. I expected there would be something about her escape from the Harrow-Martin Psychiatric Hospital, but there was only one hit. Her name was mentioned as the surviving daughter of Miriam Traynor, nee Tolson, a member of the Shiloh Baptist Church. The mother was living in Grayson County, Virginia when she died. It was a short obit with no other information provided. I asked Jenine to check the name Miriam Tolson, but the only thing that came up was the same obituary. I retrieved a piece of blank paper from Bly's printer and copied down the information.

"Do you want me to hang around to see if they call back?" Jenine asked. When I was indecisive with my reply, she said, "I can leave the cell with you. Just don't answer it unless the number for the psych place comes up. Any others can just go to voice mail. I got nothin' all that important going on," which surprised me, because most teenagers are so self-absorbed that a newly discovered pimple was a major event in their lives they had to share immediately with everyone on their call list.

"Maybe that would be best. If you don't mind. I know kids without their cell phones are lost in cyberspace."

"Good one," she replied, pointing at me. She walked past me and laid the cell on the kitchen's island counter. "Guess I better go."

I gave her one of Bly's Dr. Peppers from the fridge as a parting thank you gift. Not much for what she'd helped me with.

Once she'd gone, I looked at the clock. It was closing in on the noon hour and I was both hungry and pissed off. I was pissed off at that friggin' Campers. Why would he hide the fact that the SBI had called him about the Traynor girl? He knew how important this was to me . . . and for Bly. I wondered if he'd told the sheriff about it. What an jackass. I decided to go up to the sheriff's office and, if Campers wasn't there yet, wait for him. But I had to get something to eat, first. Otherwise, I just might tear Caswell's office apart and end up in a jail cell. That wouldn't be fair to him, Bly or myself.

It was still raining with a steady breeze of about fifteen miles an hour. Soon it would graduate from a breeze to wind. I could have put down a plate of eggs, sausage and biscuits, but I didn't want to risk running into Duffy. Instead, I drove up Back Road to the coffee house. I'd get something more substantial later.

I took my large snickerdoodle and blueberry scone and sat out on the covered porch until the breeze became a little too gusty and blew the rain, which was coming in from the east, into my space. I was the last one to give up the porch and, by the time I'd gone back inside, there was no place to sit down. I leaned up against a support post and watched a couple of guys playing chess. It wasn't a game I was adept at. That said, even I could tell the younger guy was being chewed up by his older challenger.

When the clock on the wall said it was 1:00 pm, I moseyed on out to Trusty Rusty and headed for the sheriff's office. When I pulled in, there was a police cruiser in the parking lot. I was pretty sure it was Campers. I was still pissed off, but decided that rather than grabbing him by the front of his shirt, running him up against the wall and giving him a nose-to-nose tongue-lashing, I'd confront him with sarcastic oratory—and try to restrain myself from punching him in the mouth when he got snotty with me, as I knew he would.

When I entered, Terwilliger was busy typing something into her computer. She looked up to see who'd interrupted her and when she saw it was me, got a look on her face. Campers was in back. He didn't bother to look up.

"Uh," Terwilliger groaned. I could see the hamster go from a lope to a full-blown run on the wheel inside her head. Jerking her thumb behind her, she whispered, "He's really busy right now."

"That's good," I whispered back, then walked around her desk and headed toward the back of the room.

"But . . . ." her hand in the air, finger pointing in the general direction of the ceiling.

When I reached Camper's desk, without looking up, Campers said, "Can't you see I'm busy?"

"What I see is a person who doesn't want to talk to me." Campers didn't answer. "Is it because you don't want to tell me why you told your secretary, receptionist, or whatever you call her, not to tell me the SBI called with the ID on the fingerprints?"

Campers stopped working on the report he was filling out and, slowly, his head raised up so he was looking me in the eyes. "I guess she didn't do what I asked," he growled, then looked to the front of the office, where Terwilliger had stopped whatever she was doing and was staring at us.

I wasn't going to deny or confirm how I knew. "You think—" I started to say, when he cut me off.

"I think you should stay out of the way and let someone who knows what they're doing take care of this investigation." Our voices were rising with each exchange. I could hear Terwilliger on the phone trying to reach the sheriff.

At that moment I realized that, from now on, I was on my own; that I could not expect any further assistance from this asshole. I wanted to punch out the smart-ass expression on his face. Instead, I withheld my fist, but not my tongue. If nothing else, I wanted the satisfaction of nettling this jackass. Was I being childish. Probably. Did I give a shit. No. I laughed. "Someone who knows what they're doing? You aren't even qualified to follow a suspect. What makes you think you're qualified to conduct this investigation?"

Campers bolted out of his chair. "What are you talking about, Sawyer?"

"I'm saying, Deputy Campers, that it was a kid who picked up your slack and found out who the contact was for the suspect on the pink boat." I returned the smug look he'd given me only moments before.

"What do you—" He interrupted himself. Looking past me at Terwilliger, he shouted, "I hope that's not a personal call, Terwilliger. Don't you have work to do?" Then, back to me, pointing and shaking a finger, said, "You'd better watch out, Sawyer. I'm very close to arresting you for interfering with a criminal investigation."

"If you remember, sir, I'm the one who brought this case to your attention."

"I'm not talking about this supposed kidnapping case. I'm talking about the drug investigation."

"Don't be ridiculous, Campers. And what do you mean, 'this supposed kidnapping case?'"

A smirk on his face, speaking slowly and deliberately, he said, "What I mean is, I think your little writer friend is a lesbian and has run off with this cross-dressing boy, who's really a girl. And you're just pissed off because she got tired of what you had to offer and traded you in for another player."

Without thinking, I leaned over his desk and, with both hands, grabbed him by the shirt and pulled him toward me. "You little piss-ant. It's people like you who give law enforcement a bad name. If you weren't wearing that uniform, I'd take you outside and kick your ass."

While I was ranting, Campers reached for his weapon. He had it halfway out of his holster when, from the front of the office, Sheriff Caswell shouted, "What the hell is going on here, Campers?"

I released my hold on the deputy and pulled back. Campers returned his weapon to his holster. When neither one of us said anything, To my surprise, Terwilliger spoke up on my behalf and told the sheriff, "Deputy Campers just insulted Mr. Sawyer's writer friend, and—"

Ignoring Terwilliger, Caswell strode past her and up to Campers' desk. "Well?" he asked.

I didn't bother answering or looking at the sheriff. I glared at Campers, and he glared back, his face screwed up into something hate-filled and angry. To Campers, I growled, "Why don't you tell the sheriff that you got a call from the SBI about the bike rider. And that you've done nothing about it. And while you're at it, tell him what you said about Miss Parsons and about the kidnapping investigation?

When he didn't answer, Caswell said, "I think you'd best leave, Mr. Sawyer. I'll deal with you later. Right now we've got one man locked up and another one on the run. I'll deal with the Parsons business as soon as I get this other mess cleaned up."

Without saying anything, I turned and marched out of the sheriff's office. As I left I heard Caswell saying, "I'll deal with this stupidity later. We need to have a little sit down with—" That's all I heard as the door closed behind me.

"Cocksucker," I mumbled to myself. I wasn't normally a curser, but Campers drove me to reach into my lock-box of profanities and use them with more liberty than my parents would have condoned. And it wasn't just Campers. It was this whole frustrating business of dealing with people who didn't share the same sense of urgency about the situation. That said, I asked a silent forgiveness to Mom and Dad, even though under the circumstances I felt my uncouth vocabulary was justified.

There was a break in the rain, so I decided to drive down Highway 12 to Silver Lake Harbor and see if the pink boat was still there. My guess was that is was not. My guess was correct. I was about to turn onto British Cemetery Road when I saw someone pull out of a parking space. The rain had stopped; at least for the time being so, on a whim, I whipped into the opening. Actually, my growling stomach made the call. A yuppy in a black Saab coming the other way gave me the finger as he drove by.

I walked across the street to McShane's and grabbed one of two empty seats at the bar. While ordering a Spanish mackerel sandwich with fries and an unsweetened iced tea, I felt a tap on the shoulder. I looked around. It was the Saab guy. He looked about mid twenties. He had on a black muscle shirt, black jogging shorts and black Reeboks with no socks.

"You took my parking spot," he said, with the phoniest British accent I'd ever heard. Either that, or the Mother country should be ashamed of their output.

I had a brief thought about rearranging his smug gen-x face, but decided on, "Yep. Sure did." At that moment, the bartender/waiter put down my iced tea, so I turned away from Saabus Interruptus and took a long swig of the unsweetened liquid. I felt him behind me for a while, then he turned around and walked away. I wondered what he hoped to accomplish with that mini-confrontation. As crappy a mood as I was in, I had to laugh.

The Spanish mackerel with a little malt vinegar was delish. I ate about half the fries and gave the rest to a hungry looking teenager who'd been eyeing them since after I'd finished my sandwich.

On the way out, I gave the Saab guy, who was giving me the stink-eye, the thumbs up. He'd met up with some skinny blonde thing who I guess he was trying to impress. Actually, she looked as if she really *was* impressed. Go figure.

Just after I turned onto Bay Road, Jenine's cell rang. I had it in my right front pocket and had to pull over to extract it. My mood temporarily improved when I saw it was from the psychiatric hospital. It was Emily Cobellisi.

"Mr. Sawyer?"

"Princess?" I was surprised at the depth and heartiness of her laugh.

"I can only talk for a moment," she said. "I wanted to let you know that a man identifying himself as Deputy Billy Campers of the Ocracoke Island Sheriff's Department called. He wanted to speak to the director. Or, as he put it, the guy in charge."

I had no intention of telling her about my confrontation with Campers. "Who'd he speak with?"

"Actually, nobody. Dr. Courtland was busy with a patient and, as you know, Dr. Janowitz won't be in until tomorrow morning."

"Thanks for letting me know." Now I felt bad, since I'd gone off on her earlier. "Is Dr. Courtland still planning on calling me back, or will she put me off now that the sheriff's office got in touch with you?"

"The deputy just said he'd call in the morning, so I guess she'll be talking to him." It was a nice way of saying I was not on Courtland's radar." Then, "Aren't you guys about to get hit with this weird June hurricane coming up the coast?"

"This whole situation is a nightmare, Miss Cobellisi."

She said she could imagine and wished she could do more. "But I'm not a doctor and I'm not authorized to go into the private files." She seemed apologetic.

"I understand. And, once again, I apologize for acting the fool when we spoke this morning."

"I've already forgotten about it," she was kind enough to say.

"Would you try again with Dr. Courtland," I pushed. "I think it's important we speak."

"I'll remind her," Emily Cobellisi said. I knew she meant it.

As I expected, Courtland didn't call. I waited until 6:00 pm before I tried the hospital. The phone went to an answering machine, advising me that if it was an emergency I should call . . . and they gave another number.

I called that number, which immediately went to voice mail. I left a message that my call was an emergency, but didn't expound on what it was. When I received no call by 9:00 pm I gave up hope. I had a feeling I was suddenly *persona non grata* at the Harrow-Martin Psychiatric Hospital.

Outside the rain had returned, much heavier than before.

Chapter 26

THE NEXT MORNING there was another break in the rain, but the winds were still steady—I guessed around thirty or so miles per hour sustained. I've ridden out a few hurricanes in my life, but never one on Ocracoke. I'd heard stories about flooding so bad that cars just washed out into the sound, and some even out to sea. That's why most people with any brains lived in stilt houses. Bly was smart when she went with a concrete ramp up to her garage that, like the house, stood eight feet above the ground.

I decided that any hope of obtaining additional information about the probable abductor, Elizabeth Traynor, would have to wait until after the storm had passed. In the meantime, I would go ahead and secure Bly's storm shutters and secure the house the best I could.

First, I took all the chairs and tables off the back deck and moved them into her garage, which had more than enough space to hold them. I also took everything else she had that could be blown away, or worse into somebody else's property. She only had a few planters and flower pots—one was actually a Ficus tree. Bly was a minimalist. She had to be. It was too difficult for her to take care of extras. When I visited, she usually put me to work watering, pinching off dead leaves and once in a while, repotting, so I was just as happy she didn't have a full-blown deck garden. Not that I didn't appreciate plants, trees and flowers. I did, as long as they belonged to someone else, or in their natural habitat.

Once that was done, I closed the storm shutters. Bly had a company in Virginia Beach custom make all her "storms," as she called them. Securing them took less than a minute. Once I thought about it, I remembered I only had to click a switch on the wall next to the elevator and they all unrolled and locked themselves into place. Once that was done, I felt as if I was inside a tomb.

After coffee and a fish sandwich—I'd saved a chunk of pan-fried fish—since I hadn't heard from

Jenine, I decided to brave an encounter with her mother and headed across the street to return the girl's cell phone. I knew there wasn't a chance in hell that Dr. Janowitz or anybody else from the psychiatric hospital would call me back. Why would he or any one else there talk to me now that law enforcement was involved? And, who knew how hard Campers would actually push on getting information. My guess was the only reason he'd made the call when he did was that Sheriff Caswell ordered him to. I'd have to make sure Caswell either stayed on his asshole deputy or would follow up, himself.

Goddamned Campers.

I knocked and waited for someone to answer. When no one did, I turned to leave and was at the top of the landing when Jenine opened the door. "Mr. Sawyer." I turned. "Sorry. I'm the only one here and I was in back on the computer."

I got lucky. The mother wasn't there. "Returning the phone," I said, holding it up.

She gave me a big grin that soon turned to a frown when I told her that no one called back and I didn't expect them to. That they were dealing with the sheriff now. I didn't go into details.

“I hope they find out something,” she said. “I’m worried about Miss Parsons.”

“I am, too, Jenine. Thank you for trying to help me.”

On my way back across the street the rain began again. The wind, blowing from the east had picked up another ten knots or so, whipping the rain against my face and body. I ran the last several yards to get under the house. I had just reopened the elevator door when I heard, “Mr. Sawyer! Mr. Sawyer!” Jenine was running toward me through the rain.

When she reached the house, she pulled her cell from her back pocket. “I hope I didn’t disconnect her,” she gasped. She was drenched from the sudden downpour. “The psych lady,” thrusting the phone at me.

I took it, put it to my ear and said, “Webb Sawyer.”

Whispering, Emily Cobellisi said, “I’m not supposed to be talking to you, but screw them.” Then she asked me if Portsmouth Island was anywhere near Ocracoke. When I said it was and asked why, she said. “Because I took a quick peek at Elizabeth Traynor’s file and it says that her grandparents had a home on Portsmouth Island and, you know, I was hoping . . . ."

Portsmouth Island? That must mean Portsmouth Village, right across the channel from Ocracoke Village. "You know something Miss Cobellisi. You really are a princess."

She gave a whispered chuckled and said, "I was hoping you'd say that," then hung up.

"You're smiling," Jenine said. "What she tell you."

"I think I know where Miss Parsons might be."

I dug around in the lock box in the back of the truck, found my rain slicker and threw it on. I was at the sheriff's office in under four minutes. It was fortunate that British Cemetery Road and Highway 12 were devoid of traffic. Everyone was holed up and battening down the hatches. At a glance, as I passed by I noticed the water in the semi-protected harbor was already getting rough. A fisherman struggled to secure his fishing boat, which was being buffeted in the turmoil. I knew it would get worse. Much worse.

When I reached the office, the only one there was Terwilliger. Right away she began a rambling apology for not telling me right off about the SBI call. "But he threatened me that I'd lose my job," she whined. That seemed like a lame excuse, since she spoke up for me with the sheriff during my confrontation with Campers. No matter, I thanked her for that and told her I hoped she didn't get in trouble for doing so. She gave me a jumbled reply that I didn't understand and didn't care one way or the other.

"Is the sheriff anywhere I can reach him?" I asked. She told me that he and Deputy Campers were out on patrol, getting ready for the storm, whatever that meant. I realized that any assistance from them would not be forthcoming until Angela passed through. Even then, depending on the damage, it could be days, even weeks, before they could turn their attention back to Blythe Parsons.

"The guy who runs the charter to Portsmouth Island, where does he live?" I asked.

Terwilliger gave me a questioning look. When she realized I wasn't going to give her a reason for my query, she said, "You mean Austin Meads?" I nodded. "He's over on O'Neil Road," she said, then asked why.

"Need to talk to him about something," was my noncommital answer. "Can you give me an address?" She got out the local phone book, looked it up, and gave me the street number, then showed me a street map.

"Thanks," I said. "Stay safe."

Before she could answer, I was back out the door.

I took Old Beach Road to Middle Road, then left on Trent Drive. O'Neil was the third right. O'Neil was paved and turned right into Elizabeth Lane. I found the name a bit ironic. Apparently, I missed the number and drove back to Trent.

"Huh?"

I turned around and drove back to the end of the street, where I discovered I'd gone by a sandy lane just at the turn into Elizabeth. There was one house a few lots down on the right. It was Meads'.

There was a pickup in the front yard. I would have said the driveway, but the only thing that identified it as such were the tire tracks. The truck was white and rusty, about the same vintage as mine. So far, the driveway and yard had absorbed the rain.

The house was a fairly new two story rectangular shaped box. Nothing unique or special. It sat right on the ground. While it did sit on a two-foot grade, the Pamlico Sound was less than a hundred yards away. No storm shutters, either. *Kinda dumb for a waterman,* I thought.

I parked behind his truck, went up to the door and knocked. A guy about five-foot-ten sporting a gray, close-cropped beard and moustache, wearing jeans and a blue and white plaid short sleeve shirt with a pocket over the left breast—typical chain store fare—answered the door.

"Looking for Austin Meads," I said.

"You're lookin' at him," he answered. Then, "You better come on in out of the rain fore you drown."

Once inside, we stood in the foyer, me dripping all over his tiled floor. "You're the guy who runs the charter over to Portsmouth Island, right?"

The man threw his head back and laughed. "I ain't takin' you over there today, if that's what you want. Probably not tomorrow or the next day, neither."

I spent the next ten minutes telling him about the situation with Blythe Parsons, what we'd found out about the kidnapper (I gave the sheriff credit for everything) and that we suspected he was holding her somewhere in Portsmouth Village.

When I finished, he pursed his lips and asked, "How come the sheriff ain't here tellin' me all of this?"

"Because he and Deputy Campers are out patrolling and getting ready for the storm," repeating what Terwilliger had said. "Randy," evoking Caswell's Christian name as if we were best buddies, "asked me to come talk to you about it." The lie rolled off my tongue like an oil slick from a floundering tanker.

"Well Randy must think I'm crazy if I'd chance goin' across that channel in this weather. And it's only gonna get worse," shaking his head. "No siree, you can just tell the sheriff that it's gonna have to wait until this nasty woman they call Angela passes north."

I tried another approach. "You know Portsmouth Village pretty well, right?"

"Yeah?"

"Does the name Traynor or Tolson mean anything to you as families who once lived over there?" I knew that Portsmouth Village, founded in 1753, had been abandoned in 1971 by the last of the old time families, most of whose ancestors had founded the settlement.

Again Meads pursed his lips. "Hang up yer slicker on that coat tree and follow me," he said.

I did as he requested and followed him down a short hall to a room on the left. On the way, a woman's voice from upstairs called down, asking, "Who was it, Austin?" He answered, "Just a friend." I guess I'd gained instant status, like you would on Facebook. At least that's what I've been told. I wouldn't know Facebook from Assbook—

and I suppose there is something like that online, too.

"My office," he said as we entered a twelve-by-fourteen room with a black Ikea bookcase, a desk with a laptop and printer on it, and not much else except a few papers, and an easy chair facing a 32-inch flat-screen TV on the opposite wall. "I call it my hidey-hole."

I laughed.

On the wall behind the desk hung a large satellite map showing Ocracoke Village, Portsmouth Village, including houses and buildings, and the channel between the two villages. The map sat in an inexpensive wood frame. Except for the TV, it was the only thing on the walls of his hidey hole.

"Tolson," he said, then pointed at the map of Portsmouth Village. "There was a Benjamin and Rebecca Tolson who lived south of the village in the middle community." He pointed to a spot on the map. "Right here, not far from Egret's Cove."

"Tell me about the other buildings there."

Meads was patient. He went through each house, who had once lived there, and each building: the post office/store, the church, the school, the coast guard barracks, and other places of interest.

"You know anything about the Tolson family?" I asked.

Meads shrugged. "Benjamin and Rebecca Tolson were one of the last families to leave the village; hung on until the very end. Had a daughter Miriam who married some loser from the mountains of Virginia. I actually knew Miriam. Not well, but after her parents died, she used to come down to visit the old homestead. I'd carry her across the channel, then bring her back. Nice lady, but always seemed like she was somewhere else when you spoke with her."

"This Miriam have a daughter?" I asked.

Meads was about to answer when his wife came into the room with a tray in her hand. "Brought you some hot tea," she said. She had a soft, pleasant voice and wore a kind smile on her thin face. She'd probably been pretty when she was younger. Her husband didn't introduce me, and she didn't inquire about me. He thanked her and had her place the tray on his desk. She left without another word. A wife who didn't say much. Go figure.

Meads took one of the cups, I took the other. Thank goodness it wasn't coffee. I wasn't as particular about my tea. Actually, I seldom drank tea unless it was iced.

"You were asking about a daughter?" I nodded. "I'd heard she had a girl, but I never met her and don't know anything about her." When I didn't reply, he asked, "Anything else?"

"Just one other question. Can you tell me where Duffy Duffner lives?"

Chapter 27

I ASKED AUSTIN Meads about Duffner because I remembered Duffy saying that when Meads had charters but couldn't make the trips Duffy would make the crossing. Meads said Duffy Duffner lived in a saltbox house on Lighthouse Road. When he said it, I vaguely remembered Duffy telling me that. Meads also told me that Duffy didn't have a boat and, if he did, even he wouldn't be crazy enough to take me across the channel during a hurricane. I told Meads I agreed with him, that I or anyone else would be crazy to try it. I wasn't lying. I just didn't tell him that, in fact, I felt a little bit crazy.

Just a few days ago, Duffy Duffner was the last person I thought I'd ever need help from. It's amazing how life can throw curve balls at you and you don't even see them coming. My only hope was that Austin Meads was wrong and Duffy Duffner was just a little bit crazy, too. Maybe a cash incentive would convince Duffner to overlook the insanity of it all. I'd do what I had to do to convince him. If not, there was Plan-C. I would have to figure out how to do it myself.

I found my way across the village back to Highway 12, then down to the north end of the harbor where I turned left onto Lighthouse Road. The rain now came down steadily and it was hard to see. I had no idea where on Lighthouse Road Duffy lived. I seemed to remember him telling me the color of the house but, for the life of me, I couldn't dredge it up. I drove slow and kept my eyes peeled for a saltbox house. I'd been down the road before and knew that there was at least a dozen or more houses that fit that description.

The first one I came to was on the right, just past the Ocracoke Lighthouse. Even though it was mid-afternoon, the light was in operation, warning unwary sailors that land was there. My thought was, if sailors were out to sea in this storm, they had more to worry about than running aground. Then I laughed at my own thought. What was it I wanted to do?

The rain slicker gave little protection from the wind and rain as I ran up to the front door and knocked on it as hard as I could. There was no overhang and no gutters and, even though the house had a flat roof, water poured off the edge like a waterfall.

Finally, someone opened the door a crack and stared out at me as if I was a mad man. “I’m looking for Duffy Duffner’s house!” I shouted.

“Don’t know ‘em,” the person said, and closed the door in my face. I didn’t even register if it was a woman or a man I’d seen.

I ran back to the truck and jumped in. The driver’s side of the bench seat was already sopping wet. I hoped Trusty Rusty would forgive me for the abuse. I backed out into the street and crept up the road until I saw the next saltbox house. There were two of them in a row. I repeated the process from the first house, including getting drenched. Someone must have been peeking out the window because when I reached the door, it opened and a middle-aged woman with short blue hair frantically waved me in, as if she’d been expecting me. I obliged and stepped in out of the wind and rain.

“My God, man!” she said, her voice was cigarette husky and forceful, eating me with her dark brown eyes. “What are you doing out there in this mess?” Not who are you and why are you at my door, but what am I doing out in this mess. When she saw me looking at her unruly, dark brown hair, she touched it and asked, “You like it?”

Actually, I did, but I wasn’t there for a social visit. “I’m looking for Duffy Duffner’s place. You know him?”

“Hey, wait!” she said, pointing at me. “I know you!” When I frowned, she said, “You were the guy Duffy sat and talked with a couple of days ago at the restaurant.”

“Okay,” I replied. Then, “You know Duffy, then?”

“Yeah,” she said. “I’m a cook there. Duffy plays like he’s a dishwasher.” Then she laughed. That wasn’t encouraging. Had I been eating off the plates he’d played at washing? “Yeah,” again. “You lookin’ for a place to hang out during the ‘cane? You know, Duffy only has his room with an old guy roommate who works on the ferries. And I’m sure he ain’t out on ‘em right now,” laughing.

“I appreciate the offer—“

”Jamesy,” she interrupted.

“I appreciate the offer, Jamesy, but I just need to talk to him, and it’s important.”

“Well, after you talk to him, you’re welcome to come back here and hang out. I already made up some chili and got plenty of beer, so . . . ." I couldn't believe she actually batted her eyelids at me.

Just to get it over with, I said, "Maybe I will, Jamesy."

She smiled. Her teeth were yellowing and not in all that good shape. "Next one up," jerking a thumb over her shoulder.

"Much obliged," I said and bolted for the door before she threw me over her shoulder and carried me to the back room. Nan would get a kick out of this story—then again, maybe I'd just bury this one. As I ran out into the storm I heard, "I'll be waitin' for yah!" She didn't even know my name.

I dared not leave my truck there, so I went through the routine of getting back in, backing out onto Lighthouse Road and driving the thirty feet or so up to the next driveway.

I knocked. I knocked again. I was about to knock the third time when an older man opened the door a crack and peeked out. "Looking for Duffy!" I shouted.

"Sleeping!" the old man shouted back and started to close the door when, like a traveling salesman who wasn't about to lose a sale, I stuck my foot between the door and the jamb. The old man looked down at my foot as if he didn't believe what I'd done.

"Look," I said, loud enough to be heard but not sound threatening. "It's important that I speak with Duffy. He and I are friends," I lied. "Actually, it's literally a matter of life and death," deciding from the unsure look on his face that he needed to hear something dramatic. Unfortunately, my words were actually true. It very well could be a matter of life and death.

Reluctantly, the old man pulled back and beckoned me in. He looked me up and down, shook his head and grumbled, "Don't move. Stand right there." Then he turned and, still shaking his head, stalked off down a very short hall and knocked on a door to his left. When there was no answer, he knocked again. He looked back down the hall toward me and said, "He had a few, so . . . ." He let the unfinished sentence hang in the air.

I wasn't quite sure how to handle this. I didn't want to barge down there, open the door to Duffy's room and drag him out of bed unless I had to. For the time being, I decided on, "I'll wait." I took off my slicker, looked for a place to hang it, didn't see anyplace to do so, and said, "I'll put this in the kitchen, if that's okay," figuring it probably had a linoleum floor. The old man shrugged and walked over to his easy chair, picked up a magazine I guessed he'd been reading, and sat down.

I went over to the small kitchen area—actually, it was more a kitchenette—and looked behind the narrow island used as a room separator. The floor, in fact, was linoleum. Green and white nineteen fifties vintage. When I returned to his so-called living room area, I said, "I apologize for barging in here but it is very important."

"You already said that," the man said, uninterested.

Jamesy said he worked on the ferry system, but he looked too old for that. Who knows. Maybe he did. "Not watching the Weather Channel?"

The old man looked at me as if I was daft. "Can look out the damned window and see what the weather is," matter-of-fact.

I was about to sit on the end of the beat-up, old brown, cloth covered couch, farthest away from the grumpy ferry boat guy when I heard a noise from the back of the house. I jumped up and went to the front of the hall. There was Duffy, standing in the middle of the corridor looking confused. At least he was fully clothed.

When I called his name, he looked at me through squinty eyes, rubbed them, looked again and croaked out, "Webb? What are you doing here?" He wove front to back. Afraid he would fall down and injure himself, I moved toward him and grabbed his arm. "Is the hurricane over?" he asked.

While it was obvious Duffy had been drinking, at least he wasn't totally shit-faced.

"No Duffy. It's just getting cranked up."

"Really?" Then he asked again, "What are you doing here?"

"I need your help with something, Duff."

"Need my help?"

"Right, but first, you need to get sobered up."

"Sobered up?"

Rather than continue with our mimic-driven conversation, I guided him down the end of the hall where an open door led into a small bathroom. Inside was the basics: a sink, a toilet and a bathtub with a shower. I led him over to the tub and said. "You need to take off your clothes and take a shower, Duff. Then we can talk."

"Talk?"

"First shower, then talk."

"Shower," he repeated, looking into the tub. "Should I take my clothes off?"

"Yes, Duffy. Take off your clothes first. Then take a shower."

He gave me a funny look. "You're not gonna watch are you. I'm kinda funny about other guys watchin' me get nekit."

"I'm not going to watch, Duffy. I'll be waiting for you in the living room with your roommate."

"Roommate?"

"Shower," I ordered, pointing at the shower head.

About fifteen minutes later, Duffy came wandering out into the front room and into the kitchen. The whole time I'd waited, the old man didn't speak, keeping his head buried in a magazine. That was fine with me. I spent the time considering how I would convince Duffy to help me.

Duffy poured himself a large mug of coffee from what was left in their six cup brewer, put the mug in their tiny microwave that didn't look like it could hold more than a cup or a bowl. When it was ready, he got it out and took a big swig. When he turned around and set the mug down on the island, he looked into the living room and stared at me. He squinted, shook his head, looked again, then muttered my name, "Webb?" I got up to deal with him in the kitchen. When I was across the island from him he said, "I thought I was just dreaming that you were here."

"It's no dream, Duffy. When you think your head is clear, we need to have a talk."

"A talk? The last guy who said that to me arrested me for . . . somethin' or other," his hand making a half-assed wave. "Can't remember what."

I chuckled. "You remember us talking about my friend, Blythe Parsons, right?"

"Yeah, the writer girl in the wheelchair."

"Well, she was kidnapped, Duffy." No use beating around the bush about it.

"Kidnapped? No shit!"

"No shit, Duffy. The deal is, I think I know where she's at and I need your help to go get her."

Duffy took another long swig from his coffee mug. "Kidnapped. Damn!" He shrugged and said, "Sure, Webb. Where's she at?"

"I'm pretty sure she's over on Portsmouth Island. And the person who has her is an escaped mental patient. And I'm pretty sure her life is in danger. And since you're the only one I know who knows how to get across the channel and knows a little bit about the village there." Duffy didn't answer. He just stood there staring at me. "That's why I need your help, Duff."

Duffy continued looking at me with weary eyes. "Isn't there a hurricane goin' on?"

"Can't worry about that, Duff. We wait around and she could end up dead."

"Damn! Dead ain't good," he said, a serious look on his face.

I decided to cut right to the chase. "I can pilot a boat myself, Duffy, but I don't know my way across the channel and I don't have a boat. I need you to guide me over there, Duffy."

"What about Mr. Meads?"

"He won't do it. That leaves you, we can't wait around. We have to go right now, Duff."

"Right now?"

"Right now."

"Shit!"

I tried to give Duffy my sales pitch, but he'd already headed back to his room. I wasn't sure if he was in or out. Then, a few minutes later he came out wearing fishermen's foul weather gear, including red Guy Cotton hooded jacket, bib trousers and a pair of black Ultralite deck boots. *He certainly won't be inconspicuous in that get-up*, I thought.

He asked me, "Whatchoo gonna wear?"

I picked my slicker off the kitchen island. "This is it."

"Then let's rock and roll."

"You know this isn't going to be a picnic," I warned him.

"No problem. I got me a waterproof Sakaq gear bag. I can pack us up some sandwiches and—"

Holding up my hand, I interrupted with, "That's okay, Duffy. I just meant in this weather it's going to be a rough ride going across the channel." I hadn't gotten around to discussing the probable danger on the other side.

As we were leaving, the old man offered his sage advice, saying, "You two ain't got the sense God gave yah."

He was probably right.

Chapter 28

ABOUT FIFTEEN MINUTES later we were at Silver Lake Harbor. Austin Meads' little office was on the wharf off the parking lot where the local grocery, ice cream shop and golf cart rentals, and a small boat ramp were located. I'd been there a few days earlier. On the way over, I'd asked Duffy if he knew a fisherman whose boat we could rent. He'd just laughed and said, "Austin's boat is the only one that knows the way."

"So we're gonna steal Austin Meads' boat?"

"We ain't stealin' it," Duffy said. "We're just borrowin' it for a rescue mission. They allow that sort of thing, yah know. The sheriff just borrowed it the other day to go after some druggies." I didn't bother telling him that it was Austin Meads I'd seen piloting the sheriff and his deputy up the sound, and that we weren't law enforcement who, emergency or otherwise, could just commandeer a vehicle, boat or whatever. When I'd asked the question, I'd already figured out that was our only choice. If Duffy wanted to call it "borrowin'," then that was fine by me.

Meads' rental shop was locked up, but Duffy knew where the key was—under the door mat at the back door. Go figure. We popped inside. Meads also kept a spare key to the boat in the office, just in case he lost or forgot his, or in case Duffy was making the charter run for him.

"So, see how it works. He ain't doing the run today, so I gotta make it for him, which means I gotta use this here key," holding up the spare key to Meads' charter boat. Duffy's logic.

"Good thinking, Duff," I said, pointing my right index finger to my temple. It would have been more accurate if I'd rotated my finger, indicating the insanity of our plan. Actually, my plan. Duffy was only the willing accomplice. I was sure the judge would take that into consideration.

And Nan would bail us both out.

"What about gas?" I asked.

"In the boat?"

I groaned, silently. "Yep, the boat."

"Was filled up ready for a charter that cancelled, so there yah go," he said, merrily, as if we were on a lark. This would be anything but a carefree escapade. I figured just getting out into the channel would be a chore, as the howling wind, even in the protected harbor, had whipped the water into three-foot waves.

We secured the door to Meads' rental place and jumped into the charter boat, which Meads had named *Channel Hopper*. The pilot house at the back of the boat was open, with only a roof on it to protect us from the elements, which wasn't much as the wind blew the rain sideways. Duffy started up the engine and took the helm.

Meads' charter business was deeper inside the harbor than the rest of the fishing docks, which were next to McShane's, which in turn was near the ferry terminal. The terminal building itself was at the west side of the entrance to the harbor, with the ferry docks on the channel side.

I thought getting out of the harbor was the first problem we'd have, but just pulling away from the mooring was a bitch. The waves came right at us and kept buffeting us back toward the dock, but finally we caught the swells just right and slid away from the pier and into the open waters of the harbor. Austin Meads' boat wasn't even near the best boat to try what we were doing, but it was what we had and we'd have to make the most of it. Bly's safety, maybe even her life was at stake.

While the wind blew hard—my guess was about 40 knots, which was at gale force—it hadn't reached the tropical storm level, but it was already picking up from just an hour earlier. Combined with the driving rain, visibility was a few hundred yards at best. I was thankful that it was still daytime, even though there was not a ray of sun to be seen. At night, an attempt at crossing the channel would be totally impossible instead of just nearly impossible.

Duffy had the wheel and guided us at a modest pace through the rough water. To his left, I held on to the aluminum pole, one of four that held the canvas roof in place. As we passed the fishermen's docks, a lone man was bent over, finishing up securing his fishing boat to the pier. Wondering what he heard, he stood up and peered out in our direction, a hand shielding his eyes from the driving rain. I could only imagine what went through his mind. I also expected that he would contact Sheriff Caswell about what he saw. Every local boater and fisherman knew each and every boat docked in the harbor, and certainly knew Austin Meads' charter craft. Caswell would know it was me. At this point it didn't matter. By the time he would find out, there would be nothing he or anyone else could do about it.

We were being buffeted around pretty good. So we wouldn't be pushed into the rocks on the west side as we approached the opening to the harbor, Duffy eased the boat over to the left. Just as the wind ramped up into what felt like a fifty knot gust, we pushed through the cut. Immediately, we were thrown to the right, and Duffy gunned the engine just enough to carry us past the ferry terminal breakwater and out into the open water. I was impressed with his boat handling. I hoped it would hold up.

Once out into the channel it felt as if we were nothing more than a buoy without a tether. Ocracoke Inlet was only about a mile across, but in a storm it was the longest mile you'd ever boat across. There were maps that charted the channel; however, there were ever-changing sandy shoals, deep channels, small, marsh islands, and desolate sandbars that appeared, disappeared and reappeared with every incoming tide, not to mention nor'easters, tropical storms and hurricanes.

Maps were only as good as the day they were charted. By the time they were printed they were obsolete. The standard procedure was to follow the buoy markers, but in the howling wind, driving rain and high seas, we'd be lucky to even find the reds and greens. As for the shoaling, in normal conditions it would be easy to see the wave breaking over them. Not today. I was lucky Duffy had run charters across the inlet and knew the best route to take. The trick would be keeping us on course.

It wasn't long before Duffy steered southeast, cutting at an angle across the heavy surf. However, he couldn't hold that course for long, and had to turn directly east into the waves then run again at an angle. Sometimes he just opened the throttle and ran parallel to the surf when there was a short break between larger swells. A couple of times he miscalculated and we were almost overturned before he recovered and turned back into the waves.

Seeing the look on my face, he shouted, "I gotta do it this way, otherwise we're going to be pushed too far west and end up out in the sound. Or run up on some shoals. If that happens we're French toast."

French toast?

"We gotta keep easing southeast down Teach's Hole afore we cross over to Bird Island, then around Bird for the final run to the village."

Bly and I usually fished the sound, as her boat was too small for deep sea fishing but, once on a clear and calm day, we'd cut through the channel and out to sea, passing both Teach's Hole and Bird Island. It was the day she and I hooked, fought, brought in and released what we figured was a six-hundred pound marlin. It was a great day for the story-telling that ensued, until we ran out of people who were tired of hearing about it. It was a new story for fresh victims; one I hoped we'd both be alive to tell again.

Teach's Hole was an open bay just inside and to the north of the Ocracoke Inlet and the southernmost tip of the island. It was one of the places where Edward Teach, the pirate commonly known as Blackbeard, and his crew would hole up and watch for unsuspecting ships to raid as they passed nearby out at sea.

Bird Island was a shoal that over time had built up enough to actually be given a name. Originally, on marine maps, it was known as Beacon Island. Some locals called it Pelican Island. Whatever name it went by, who knew how long the shoal would actually last. Could be this storm, could be the next one, or the one after that, before it will be a memory on an old maritime map. For now, it was a place pelicans used to nest and roost, although I was sure that they had long since headed for higher ground.

"Should be nearing Blackbeard's place of business," Duffy shouted.

"He was a pirate, Duff," I reminded him.

"Yeah, I know. That was his business."

Duffy was captain, partner-in-crime and one-man entertainment package on our insane adventure.

I hoped to hell Duffy knew what he was doing, because I had no clue where we were in relation to anything. For now, my only ray of hope was that the boat was still upright and the deck's scupper holes were handling the heavy rain and the water spilling over the gunwales.

We continued to make slow progress against the wind and surf, with Duffy shouting out his not-so-reassuring patter with statements like, "I seen waves bigger'n this on a TV show and they kilt the people in the boat, so we got nothin' to worry about," (I thought about *The Perfect Storm*) and, referring to the named storm we were churning through, "I once took out a girl named Angela, twice. The first time she paid for the McBurgers, the second time I don't know who paid 'cause half way through she told me to get lost. I took the burger, fries and a drink with me and left faster than a found-out cheat in a craps game." Duffy was serious about it all. He never once laughed. I was contemplating his Duffyisms when the next thing I knew I lost my balance, was thrown into Duffy. Then the deck went out from under us and we were both flying through the air.

I landed on my back in the water, was swept up in a wave and thrown into the middle of what I later decided must have been a pelican's nest. I made a feeble attempt at grabbing on to the brush, but before I could another wave hit me and I tumbled over backwards. I rolled up against a piece of scrub brush and this time I grabbed onto a small branch and hung on. I quickly got my feet planted into solid ground, found another branch that felt reasonably sturdy and tried to get my bearings. Duffy was nowhere in sight but Meads' *Channel Hopper* was about a hundred feet in front of me and a little to the left. It was still upright but being pushed around like a toy.

"Duffy!" I shouted, hanging on for dear life, I did a quick surveil of my surroundings. There was no sign of him. I did a three-sixty, first looking left then behind, then right and behind. Nothing.

"Duuuffeee!"

Then, a glimpse of something coming at me from the left. "Crap!" I had no choice. I released my hold on the scrub brush and with my right foot tried to push myself off to the right. It wasn't in time. Something hit my left hip, hard, and I found myself spinning around like a windmill. I was on my hands and knees on the ground, but under water. When I tried to stand, my left side felt as if I'd been hit by a two-by-four. My head broke water and I gasped for breath. I took in one gulp of air before another wave crashed down on me, pushing me off my feet and backwards.

The last thing I remembered was a thump in the back of my head and everything went dark.

Chapter 29

I FOUND MYSELF on solid ground. Water sloshed around me as if I sat in the surf on a hard packed beach. Confused about where I was and what happened. I tried planting my feet and hands to push myself up, when I discovered I was restrained around the chest—I wasn't sure by what. At the same time, I was being thrown around like I was a sack of potatoes. A sopping wet sack of potatoes. Then Duffy Duffner's voice rang in my ears and I realized I was back on the boat. How had that happened?

"Don't worry Webb!" He shouted in order to be heard over the howling wind and pounding waves. "You're safe as a pickle in a jar!"

Whatever that meant. Maybe it was an obscure reference to the brine the pickles were immersed in, as in "the briny sea," although I didn't believe Duffy had the capacity to make that kind of connection. All I knew for sure was that the back of my head felt as if someone had hit me with a lead pipe.

"What happened? Why am I tied up?" I shouted back. I got the questions out just as a large overwash slapped me in the face.

". . . pulled you back on board!" I heard him yell. "Had to take my belt off my britches and tie you there so you wouldn't wash back overboard." Then, "Damn!"

I'd have to find out later how he'd managed to get back on the *Channel Hopper*. The last I knew, Duffy had been washed off Meads' boat with me following him. And somehow he'd managed to get himself and me back on deck. And secure me. Jesus! I owed the man my life.

"Once I get us past this damned island and in front of the shoals near the point . . ."

I presumed he meant Portsmouth.

". . . the waves won't be too bad."

Maybe it was best I couldn't see what was going on outside of the boat. Watching Duffy struggle at the helm was scary enough. It wasn't that I was afraid of being out in a roiling sea that could, and almost did, send me to a watery grave. My fear was that if I didn't make it to the other side of the inlet in once piece, I would be letting down my friend, Blythe Parsons.

Life is strange. Just a few days ago I thought Duffy Duffner was nothing more than a buffoon. When he called me a friend, I laughed to myself.

Now, he was my only hope to reach Bly.

Another thought hit me. What if I was wrong, and Duffy and I went through all this for nothing? What if Bly wasn't on Portsmouth Island after all? What if . . . ? I couldn't even think of that possibility. That was my last thought before things went blank again.

When I regained my senses, I was still secured to the aluminum pole in the open wheelhouse. The wind still raged and rain blasted us like a giant fire hose on full throttle. I looked up at Duffy. Even though Meads' boat wasn't being tossed around quite as much as before, Duffy was still fighting the wheel to keep us upright.

"Where are we?" I shouted up at him. I paid for my utterance when a spasm of pain shot through my head.

"Almost at the pier," Duffy shouted back.

I remembered from Meads' map that the pier was just around the northwest tip of Portsmouth Island. The docks led to a walking trail that took visitors into the heart of the old abandoned village. "No! No!" I shouted, paying with more throbbing head pain. "Gotta go further down to Egret's Cove!"

"Egret's Cove? Where the hell is that?"

Damn! I thought I had this conversation with Duffy before we left Silver Lake Harbor, but maybe I hadn't. "It's the second inlet down from the pier!" I told him. "Unbuckle me. I'll help you find it!" even though I really didn't know what it looked like. I only knew the location as it showed on the aerial view of the map.

Duffy took a quick look down at me, unsure about what to do. When he saw me try to push myself to my feet, he relented. Still hanging on to the steering wheel with his right hand, he squatted down, reached behind me, did a quick yank and pull with his left hand, and I was free. Unfortunately, when he stood back up, the belt flew out of his hand and disappeared over the leeward side of the boat and into the water.

I struggled to pull myself to my feet and tried my best to get my bearings. The landing dock was just off to our port side. I hung on to the pole like a frightened kid on a roller coaster. "Keep going south along the shore line," I leaned toward Duffy so I wouldn't have to shout. I was light-headed and felt like throwing up. As they say, "Discretion being the better part of valor," I eased myself back onto the deck, "Let me know when you get to the second inlet," I groaned.

The next thing I knew, I felt a hand shaking my shoulder. I opened my eyes and looked up at Duffy. "I think I found your cove," he said.

While the water in Egret's Cove wasn't tranquil, it wasn't a roiling mess like it was off shore; and, compared to crossing the inlet, it was almost dead calm. When I pulled myself up, there it was. The *Lady Bryn*, bobbing around, anchor in the water and secured by line to the trunk of nearby scrub brush.

"I was right. She's here," I said to myself.

Bringing me back to reality, Duffy said, "Gonna be hell trying to find your friend in this weather." Then, he put his hand on my shoulder, "And I'm thinkin' you got yourself a percussion in your head goin' on."

Oddly enough, that's exactly what it felt like. He was probably right. I'd sustained a concussion. Hopefully a mild one, because I refused to let it hold me in check for long.

It took Duffy some doing to maneuver the *Channel Hopper* around behind Bly's *Lady Bryn*. To avoid the two boats being thrown into each other, Duffy pointed the prow of Meads' boat into the entrance of a small stream and moved it in as far as it would go before it grounded itself. Then he grabbed two mooring lines and jumped off the boat. First, he tied off around a scrub tree on the right, then ran around and did the same with a hefty-looking scrub brush on the other side.

"That should do 'er!" he shouted as I hung over the aft gunwale and puked over the side.

Once I regained my faculties, I turned my head and said. "We gotta find the old Tolson house."

By then, Duffy was back on board, behind me. "And where would that be? I been over here a few times, but don't remember hearin' about no Toltsoy house." I didn't bother correcting him. "'Course, I ain't never been this far down in the village afore, neither." He moved around the boat, checking the tie lines, then returned and said, "I'll tell you what, though. If there's a house down here, I can find it."

"We can find it," I reminded him.

"You gotta stay here and stay quiet," he said. "I'll go find it and scope it out. See what's what. Then I'll come back and tell you. I'm good at finding things that are lost."

I wanted to tell him that the house wasn't lost. We just didn't know exactly where it was. I relented. "Go find it and check it out, I'll stay here and wait for you." While I desperately wanted to go, I realized that I just didn't have it in me.

Duffy didn't reply. I watched him fumble around under the wheel and realized he was looking for a stow cabinet. Apparently, he found it, because soon he had a good-sized tarp in his hands. He held it up. "Just thought about looking for something like this. Grab this corner," he said. And fought against the wind to open it up. He held one side of it on the deck and told me to get down on top of it. I knew it was the best thing for me to do—at least for the moment. Once it was under me, he drew the rest of it over me and I helped him tuck it under my other side. "I'll be bock," he said, in a poor imitation of Arnold Schwarzenegger as the Terminator. Then he pulled the rest of the tarp over my head and was gone.

I don't know how long I was out, but when I groaned my way awake, I felt and heard the rain pounding against the tarp. I pushed myself into a sitting position and pulled the tarp off my head. The wind had abated, but it was still howling. "Duffy?" There was no reply. I laid back down and pulled the tarp back over my head.

* * *

The next time I woke up, all was quiet. I fought my way out of the tarp, got to my knees and, to my surprise, discovered it was dark. Were we in the eye of the hurricane or had I been out so long it had passed? "Duffy?" I called out. Nothing. I used the gunwale to pull myself to my feet. "Duffy?" I called out again, this time louder." Once again, my head throbbed from the exertion.

"Hey, Webb! Over here."

Simply turning my head toward Duffy's voice was a chore. All I could see was the outline of his body, standing on the deck of the *Lady Bryn*. I didn't think it was worth the pain to shout over to him, so I just watched as he moved around looking for . . . whatever he was looking for. As if reading my thoughts, he shouted, "Looking for anything we can use."

Suddenly, my head started to spin. I turned around and slid down the gunwale and sat on the deck. Duffy could give me his report when he returned to our boat. I had to laugh at that. Our boat! The boat we'd commandeered. That was a nice way to put it.

I must have drifted off when the sound of Duffy's voice woke me. ". . . find a real weapon of some kind, but no luck. But I did find a box of Ritz crackers in your friend's locker. I guess the kidnapper didn't see it there. Want some?" he asked, holding the box out to me, top opened. I could barely see him in the gloom and mist.

"Thanks but no thanks, Duff. I already up-chucked once and I'm not in the mood for doing it again."

"Yeah I can dig it." Then, "And this ain't all I found on the boat, neither," rattling the box of crackers. He reached into his back pocket and pulled out a four-by-six inch green plastic box. He opened it and, leaning over, almost bowing, showed me the contents. "Hooks," he said. "And big ones too. I can straighten 'em out some and we can use 'em as weapons. You know, put 'em between your fingers like, what do they call 'em? Fast knuckles," making a fist and jabbing it toward me.

Fast knuckles. Interesting. I just nodded, then said, "I thought you didn't find anything we could use for a weapon."

"I said a real weapon, like a knife or a gun or something."

"Or a bazooka."

"Oh, man. Wouldn't that a been good," not blinking an eye. "But . . . I also found us a nice long screwdriver." He reached back and pulled that out of his back pocket and waved it in the air. "Stick him with it."

"Her," I reminded him.

"Right. Her, too. And I found me a nice heavy-duty claw hammer."

"You got that in your back pocket, too?"

"Oh, no, I got it hung here on the wheel." He stepped aside and showed me. "So he better not mess with us or he's a gonner."

"She," I reminded him again.

"Yeah, her too."

I couldn't help but smile. "There's only one of them, Duff, and she's some piece-of-work skinny chick posing as a boy. And she's just a wee bit nuts." Before he replied, I asked, "So, you find the house or what?"

"What was left of it," he said. "I mean, I guess it was this Toltsoy house you said. There weren't no other houses anywhere around, so that had to be it, right?"

"What do you mean, what was left of it?"

"It's kinda like a pig in a poke. Just plumb caved in on itself," Duffy said.

I almost asked if there was any sign they'd been there, but that would have been something Duffy would have mentioned. Of course there'd be no sign. Any trace of their presence would have been washed away. And my guess was they had been there; that the crazy broad kidnapper would have gone there and found the place was no longer inhabitable. The question was, where would she take Bly next? They'd have to find shelter from the storm.

"You know the main part of the village well enough, don't you?" I asked Duffy.

"Yeah, pretty well, I guess," he said.

"Then where do you think she'd take Bly?" I knew Austin Meads had pointed out all the non-residential village structures, but with my banged up head and scrambled mind, I coudn't think of any of them.

"Huh, let me think on it." While he thought, he started taking the hooks out of the case. One at a time, he placed them on the deck, then used the hammer to turn them from curved fish hooks into straight—or at least as straight as he could get them—potential deadly weapons. When he finished, he looked up at the sky.

"I'm thinkin' we're on the west edge of this eye," Duffy said, putting the hooks back into their case. "Which means the worst part of this here storm is to the east. So's I don't think we got much time before it's back on us. So's we need to get going."

"Get going where?" I asked.

"There's an equipment shed up near the first cove. They got like golf carts that park rangers use to bop around the village. Will cut down the walkin' time and we can get around faster. Check out different places. I bet she used one for herself. You know, to haul your friend around and such."

Duffy finally got the gender correct. At any rate, he was probably right. Pushing a wheelchair through this mess would be a chore.

"We could take the boat up there before the storm starts back and tie up there, or leave it here and walk."

"How far a walk?"

"Take us about ten minutes," he said.

"Leave the boat here," I said.

He nodded. "You think you can make it?"

The pain in my head was down to a dull ache. I figured I could do ten minutes. "Sure. Let's get crackin'."

"Get crackin'," he laughed. "That's a good one, Webb. You sure have some funny sayin's."

While Duffy rounded up our makeshift weapons, I dragged myself to my feet and said, "Lead on Jeeves."

"There you go again with the funny stuff."

The pot calling the kettle black, I thought.

Chapter 30

WE SAW THE equipment shed from the south side of the cove when the rain and wind started up again. Not strong yet, but once again, building. As we slogged along, the dull ache in my head remained steady. I wished Duffy had found a first aid kit with some aspirin or some other form of pain killer. Maybe we could find some in one of the village buildings. Surely the rangers left something behind when they evacuated for the storm. Some mosquito repellant would be nice, too, but Duffy told me that once the wind and rain picked up enough, the "nasty little blood sucking leaches," as he called them, wouldn't be a problem. Grand choice. Hurricane or mosquitoes.

Finally, when we reached the shed and walked out of ankle deep water and up the ramp to the wide double doors, Duffy announced, "He's been here for sure. The lock's been busted." He showed me the broken padlock. I'd seen stronger locks on school lockers. Duffy threw open the door on the right and we went inside, out of the wind and rain. There were two golf carts on the right, with an empty space where one had apparently been appropriated, and two commercial-grade Toro zero-turn riding mowers. A variety of tools, everything from axes and machetes to weed-eaters and chain saws hung from hooks on the walls. Duffy grabbed an axe and a machete, held them up and said, "These 'll do 'er in good. Mince meat."

I didn't reply. I was thinking, if the kidnapper took one of the carts, where was Bly's wheelchair? "You see a wheelchair on Bly's boat?" I asked Duffy.

"Bly? Oh, you mean Miss Parsons." When I didn't reply he said, "Nope. And there weren't no place to hide one neither."

Curious, I thought. *If he didn't leave it, where was it?* As *I'd said before, there was no way he could have pushed the wheelchair around in this mess with Bly in it.* I didn't like where this thought was going.

I didn't know bo-diddly about golf carts. Only played the game once and I'd walked the course. By the time I was done I wanted to break every club, every iron and the putter, and throw them in one of the water hazards. "Are the carts electric or gas?" I asked.

"Gas, but they fill 'em up when they're finished with 'em. But them Toros are much faster."

"And louder. Even with the wind, they'd hear us coming a mile away." I didn't think my head could stand the noise. "Besides, only one of us can fit on them and we'd have to take two, and I don't think I'm up for that. Also, they're more likely to get stuck in the muddy ground. The golf carts sit higher and have a roof on 'em."

"Sounds like a plan," Duffy said.

"And you can be my chauffeur, Duff. I still feel pretty woozy."

"Now there's a funny word."

"Huh?"

"Woozy. It's a funny word."

Before we rode away from the equipment shed, Duffy laid the axe and machete at our feet on the floorboard of our transport, then closed the doors and secured them with the broken padlock. The eye of the storm was moving past and the hurricane was once again building quickly. I was glad Duffy seemed to know his way, because with water around us everywhere, it looked as if we were riding through a lake. Fortunately, it was only a few inches deep.

Once we reached the main north-south trail, we were only moving through soggy and soppy ground. The trouble with the golf cart was, it felt as if any moment we could be blown over. Twice, stronger gusts brought the driver side wheels up off the ground, but Duffy managed to maintain control.

"Told ya this cane was moving away out to sea." When I didn't reply, he said, "Wind blowing from the northwest. That's the ass end of Angela." Then he laughed. "I had a girlfriend named Angela once. She used to blow a lot out of her ass end, too." Then Duffy let out a hysterical outburst that took us up over a short wooden, arched bridge that went over a raging creek. He lasted another fifty yards up the lane before he ran out of steam. The dancing bears in my head precluded any jovial response.

A few minutes later we went over a second arched bridge. Off to the left was a house with yellow trim. "The Salter house!" Duffy shouted. Up ahead I saw several buildings and, further away, more structures outlined in the driving rain.

Soon, Duffy turned left and pulled in front of a small one-story structure with a steep roof. "Post office and general store type place," he said. He turned off the cart, got out and ambled up to the deck as if on a Sunday stroll. I got out of the cart and followed. I wasn't in any shape to run, so I slogged along behind. I'd never felt so wet, uncomfortable and totally miserable since the time Dave The Wave Meekins and I were holed up in a bombed out building in Mogadishu during a summer downpour. When you think of Somalia, the word "rain" doesn't come to mind, but during the rainy season, it's total crap.

"Been here, too," Duffy said, pointing to the door, where the lock, such as it was, had been jimmied. "I mean, a ten-year-old could get into this place." Even though the latch had held the door closed against the storm, when he turned the handle, the wind caught the door and slammed open. We quickly stepped inside. It took me some effort to shut the door behind me and set the latch. The door rattled from the wind bearing down from the northwest. I doubted the door would stay closed for long.

Even though we were wet through-and-through, it was nice to be inside and out of the elements. As we stood there, water poured off us and puddled on the hardwood floor.

We studied the inside of the building, as if we might notice something that would give us a clue as to where they went from here. The place was pretty darn small. It had what I assumed was the original wood floor. It had a mixture of rough hewn eight- to twelve-inch wide boards with either water or spill stains here and there. To the left on the counter were, for lack of a better description, a couple of curved glass pastry covers. The back wall held a large black and white picture of who I guessed was an early proprietor, sitting on a wooden cask. Behind the counter hung empty shelves and postal cubbies for the village inhabitants to receive their mail—no delivery. To the right was a wooden stand bearing information about the building's history and purpose. The place was now set up for tourist visits, not for daily use.

"I don't know what the person thought they'd get from here," Duffy said.

"Maybe she was remembering it from her grandparents' stories, when it was still in use. Is this the only place where she thought food might be stored?" I asked.

Duffy shrugged. "We can check the ranger station."

"Do they have beds there?"

"Yeah, they do."

"Then they might be there," thinking if they were, they probably knew we were here.

"Didn't notice a golf cart there," Duffy said, which meant he'd already checked as we drove up here. Then again, she could have parked it out of sight. "We can check there next."

"Are there any other buildings with beds still in them?"

Again Duffy shrugged. "I never actually looked inside any of the houses, but I don't think there's furniture in 'em."

I waited.

Finally, he said, "The Coast Guard Station building has eight or ten cots on the second floor, but," he hesitated. "I don't know. They could be anywhere. You think she knew the grandparents house had fallen down?" Duffy asked.

"Hmm. Maybe. Maybe not, You gotta remember, Duff. The kidnapper knows this village. Visited here after her grandparents relocated. The woman from the mental facility said the mother used to bring her here when she was a kid, so . . . ," I shrugged.

"I'd bet on the Coast Guard place," Duffy said. "But we can check the schoolhouse and the church first, unless you want to go straight there."

"Let's check the ranger station, then the school and church. I'm assuming they're along the way to the Coast Guard Station, right?"

"Kind of. The schoolhouse is that way," pointing east, "and the church is that way," pointing north.

"Which way is the Coast Guard Station?"

"At the end of the trail, past the church."

"Ok. Ranger Station, first, then the school, the church and the Coastie's. Before we go, I got one question to ask you, Duffy."

"What's that?"

"When you pulled me back onto the *Channel Hopper*, how'd you get back aboard?"

Duffy chuckled. "It was weird. First I was thrown off, like you. Then I was splashing around, trying to get my bearings. Then, all of a sudden, a big-ass wave just picked me up and the next thing I knew, I was back aboard on my ass. Then, the boat tips up and I grab onto the side to keep from falling back out. When it flattens out, I look down and there you were. I reached out, but you were too far away. Then, another wave comes along and washes you up against the side of the boat, and I reached down and hauled you in. Then I dragged you over to the wheelhouse, tied you down, grabbed the wheel and got the boat turned into the waves. The weird thing was, the engine was still running."

"Webb and Duffy one, Hurricane Angela zero," I replied.

"Hey, that's a good one, Webb."

"We get back, I'll think of some way to give you a proper thank you."

Duffy Duffner got a big grin on his face. "Shit, Webb. I don't know about you, but I'm having fun."

Me, not so much, I thought.

Chapter 31

OUR RESPITE AT the Post Office/General Store was short-lived. It was blowing and raining as hard as before. Fortunately, the Ranger Station was only a minute's drive and we were soon under the covered front porch. Unfortunately, the wind still drove the rain on us as Duffy did his magic on the front door with his pilfered screwdriver.

As before, once inside and the door closed behind us, we stood there dripping onto the floor. "I have to sit down for a few minutes," I said.

"Head hurting?" he asked.

"Light-headed," I replied.

While Duffy went through the building, I plopped down in a nearby chair. I must have dozed off. Duffy's hand on my shoulder woke me up. "You okay, Webb?"

Not really! "Yeah. Find anything useful?"

"They have a pantry back here. There's some canned stuff shoved way in the back of the shelf. I don't know about you, but I'm as hungry as a hunter with a pea shooter."

In a weird kind of way, that one actually made sense.

"Small fridge, too, but she took all of that with her. Guess she couldn't see what I'd found in the back of the cabinet. Anyway, I'll fix something for you. Unless you're going to puke it up," he said.

I hoped not. "Got any cans of chicken?"

"Got tuna."

Who in the hell would have canned tuna in a fishing village, inhabited or not? "Crackers?" Duffy nodded. "Water?" Again he nodded. I started to get up when he told me to sit still.

It wasn't long before he was back with a couple of plastic dishes, one for him, one for me, both with round blocks of tuna, a dozen or so Saltine crackers and a plastic fork. Duffy set a bottle of water on a small table, then helped me move the chair to be near enough to reach it. I ate two crackers with chunks of tuna. I was hungry but didn't want to overdo it. Besides, the taste . . . . I had a couple more crackers and washed it all down with water.

"That's all you're going to eat?" Duffy asked.

"I'll take the water with me," I replied.

He finished my meal before we left.

We went back out into Hurricane Angela. She's was a real bitch. The next stop was the schoolhouse. "Don't see them staying there, but it'll only take a few minutes," Duffy said. Actually it took more than that to get there, even though it wasn't that far down a lane going east. The building was about the size of an average shotgun house, but sturdy. I stayed in the cart while Duff ran up and checked the door, which was locked, then looked in the window. He turned, looked at me, shook his head, then ran back to the cart. "Church next!" he shouted.

On the ride out to the schoolhouse, the wind and driving rain was at our back. On the way back to the main sand trail that went through the center of the village, we drove right into it. It was like being in a wind tunnel with a high-pressure fire hose blasting us straight in the face. My relief at turning north on the main throughway was short lived. As we traveled over a bridge, a extraordinary strong burst of wind hit the cart. Before I realized what happened, our golf cart was at a forty-five degree angle. I fell out of my seat. The next thing I knew, I was on all fours on the underside of the roof—we were upside down. Fortunately, I did not hit my head. Duffy, a dumb-found look on his face, hung there with his hands still on the wheel.

"Shit!" from Duffy. Then he struggled to climb out through his side of the cart. He reached out and grabbed the running board. Another gust of wind pushed him back inside. By then, I was on my haunches and caught him. On the second try, he got out. There was still a dull ache inside my skull, but if I was dizzy I didn't realize it. I guess my adrenalin had kicked in as I soon found myself with Duffy, outside the cart.

We both headed around the other side of our transport and, despite the wind, within a few seconds had pushed it upright. We hopped back in. "Engine cut out," Duffy said, then tried to start it. He tried again. Then a third time. "Shit!"

"Time for Plan B," I said.

"What's Plan B?"

"Walk," I replied.

Duffy looked for the axe and machete. When he couldn't find them, he put the golf cart in neutral and pushed it out of the way, hoping the axe and machete would be under it. They weren't. Then he went to the edge of the bridge and looked down. "Damn things probably went into the drink." Suddenly another extra strong gust came up and Duffy lost his balance. I stood behind him and grabbed the waist of the back of his pants and pulled him back.

"That were a close one!" he shouted. "Guess we're even now!"

"Hardly!" I shouted back. "Come on," and began trudging toward the church, which was ahead and off to the left, about a hundred yards away. Unfortunately, the front door didn't have a roof or overhang of any kind. There were three concrete steps up to the entrance. It was helpful that the front of the long, narrow church faced south-east, and blocked the northwest wind. Duffy was correct. We were getting the wrap-around of the weak side of the storm. Even though it was moving away from us now, we still had several hours before it passed.

Duffy and his magic screwdriver quickly got us into the foyer, once again out of the wind and rain. It was dim inside. The foyer was small. To the right as we entered was an off-white painted wood wall made with four-inch wide strips, nailed to the studs at forty-five degree angles. If my memory was correct, it was beadboard done in a herringbone pattern. It reminded me of the old lathe and plaster walls, except here I guessed the plaster was behind the wood-work. The foyer had opposing Gothic style windows with frosted glass. To the right of the door was a small wooden cross decorated with sea oats, sea shells and a cork bobber hanging from a metal ring.

I peered through the gloom, down the aisle toward the altar. The altar was a simple affair with a podium for the preacher to do his or her thing (I guessed the church was non-denominational Protestant). Against the altar's left wall was a piano. The right wall had a small semi-enclosed area with a sound system and what I presumed were items usually found in a vestry for the preacher's use during service. This church was a one room affair. There were chairs across the wall behind the altar, presumably for a choir, or maybe just church big-wigs—those in the community just a bit more holier than the pew-sitters. There were eight more windows matching the two in the foyer, three on each of the side walls and two behind the altar. Only a hint of the storm could be seen through the frosted glass, although the sound of the raging wind was obvious.

We moved into the aisle between the pews. The church had an intimate feel to it. I could almost imagine the inhabitants during the village heyday, gathering inside, praying for good catches, good weather for outdoor celebrations, for the well-being of a sick neighbor, enough rain to fill their cisterns, that storms like Hurricane Angela would steer out to sea and save them from its fury.

Do I pray? Not since I was a kid. Well, maybe not a kid. I think the last time I actually prayed was when I was eighteen, and that was for Stacy Meads to say yes when I asked her to go with me to the senior prom. She went with Arlen James and I ended up going stag.

Do I believe in God? The verdict was still out on that question. When I was a kid I thought I did. My parents were believers and, as most kids will, take in what the parents and extended family tells and teaches them and run with it. Go with the flow. Get with the program. Why not? It was an easy decision. What kid wants to rock the boat and become a pariah in their own clan? But the Army changed me. I'd seen too many things that didn't square with faith in an all knowing, all loving, creator of everything who has a master plan for everyone's lives. Where did people like Ghengis Khan, Hitler, Stalin, Pol Pot, Saddam Hussein Radovan Tadić and, on a more immediate and personal level, Elizabeth Traynor, fit into God's plan? There was no real answer. One either had faith or they didn't. The thoughts gave me an even greater headache than I already had.

"Son of a bitch!" Duffy spit out. Then, "Oops," looking around as if God or one of His emissaries might be hiding behind a pew ready to declare him a defiler of this holy structure.

"What, Duff?"

"The hammer. It must have gone in the drink, too." Then, "You okay, Webb?"

I had my hand on the back of one of the pews. "Feel—" That was the last thing I remembered trying to say.

My eyes opened. I found myself in total darkness, laid out on a pew. At least I presumed it was a pew. There was a pillow under my head. I swung my legs down and sat up. I still had a slight headache, but nothing like it had been since wacking it against the side of the boat. There was a strange sound from somewhere nearby.

Snoring?

I sat there for a few minutes, letting my eyes adjust to the lack of light. While I wasn't exactly dry, I wasn't sopping wet, either. Just damp and sticky. I cocked an ear. Besides the snoring, something else. The wind. It was still there, but not howling as it had been. Remaining seated, I slid my way to the left. When I reached the end of the pew, I stood up and moved toward what I presumed was the center aisle. Once in the walkway I was disoriented. I wasn't sure whether I had been in a pew to the left or right as you entered the church, or which way I had been facing while asleep. I ran my hand along the arm rest at the end of the pew. It took me another few moments to orient myself. I decided the altar was to my left and the entrance to my right. I eased my way across the aisle and bumped into more pews. Inching my way along, using the pews as my guide, I worked my way toward the entrance foyer and the double front doors. I felt around for the handle, turned it and cracked the door open.

It was dark inside because it was nighttime outside. The good news, besides that the dizziness had passed, was the storm beginning to pull out into the Atlantic. The wind seemed to be in the thirty mile-per-hour sustained range. Water still came down, but it was now more a steady shower than driving rain.

"You awake, Webb?" Duffy, from behind me.

"Storms winding down," I replied.

"Damn! It's as dark as a witch's tit in here."

"We're in a church," I reminded him.

"Oh, yeah. Right." Then, "But there ain't no one here to hear it."

"I heard it, Duff," having some fun with him. I didn't care one way or the other. I heard him mumble something. "What?"

"Saying a prayer," he said. "Just in case."

"You know a prayer?"

"Well," came the voice in the dark. "The only one I know is 'Now I lay me down to sleep, no bad words should I peep. If I die afore I wake, I won't get no pie or cake."

I let out a soft chuckle. "Where'd you learn that one?"

"My mother used to say it to me when I was a kid. Never forgot it neither."

"Good for you, Duffy." Then, "You take yourself a nap, too?"

"Yeah. Figured I could use some shut-eye afore we make the final assault. Nighttime's good for that. Sides, I was tired as a guy who ran one of them Marthacons. You know. Them long-ass races?"

"Yep, those Marthacons are brutal." Then, "I think we should go straight to the Coast Guard Station. I feel much better and the more time that goes by, the more worried I am for Bly."

Suddenly, Duffy was there next to me. "After you went and fainted, I laid you out in the pew, then found a pillow and put it under your head. It was on the piano seat. Probably been farted on a lot, but all them smells long gone by now I ' spect."

I laughed.

"So then, I went out in the storm and checked all the houses around the church and stuff. Just to be sure no one was in 'em, you know? Went inside to see if I could find a weapon we could use, but they're all empty. Cleaned out."

"Good thought," I said. "I appreciate what you're doing, Duffy. I really do." In the dim passive excuse for light that filtered in from outside, I saw a big smile creep across Duffy's face.

"Yeah, well you ain't heard the best, yet."

Chapter 32

DUFFY'S "BEST YET" was pretty good. But with it came new concerns.

While I slept off what I hoped was the last of my problems with the concussion, Duffy had not only made the rounds of nearby abandoned dwellings, but he'd hoofed it down to check out the Coast Guard Station.

"I stayed close to the tree line, so's I wouldn't be easy to spot, in case someone was looking out a window," he told me, then went on to say how the station was a two-story building with a lookout station on top. He called it a turret. "So's they can see what's what out to sea," he said.

"Then there's this small building just before you get to the Coast Guard place that I think is their storage building. Whatever. I forget. It's a pretty good size though," he related, then told me how he'd used that for cover. Then ran up to the station, keeping low, "like them special forces people," he said. "Then I crept up on the porch and started peeking through the windows. But that didn't do no good. You can't see shit from there. You'll see when we get there." Holding up a finger, he continued, "So's I go around to the back, which faces the water, and look in the windows there. And guess what I see?"

"Just tell me, Duff. I'm not in the mood for Q&A," I said.

"Kew and A?" When I glared at him, he said, "Well, anyways, I see this person in there rolling around in a wheelchair—"

"A wheelchair?" I interrupted.

'Yeah."

What the hell was going on? "You said rolling around. What did the wheelchair look like."

Duffy shrugged. "You know. Usual wheel chair. Black."

"Black? It wasn't red and white? Motorized?"

"No. Black. She was close enough to the window that I could see that. I got eyes like a night hawk, Webb."

"She didn't see you, did she?"

"No way," Duffy asserted. "I was peeking through the window at the bottom, in the corner. I'm not stupid about peeking in windows."

I wondered how many he'd peeked through. There was a lot about Duffy I didn't know, and it was probably best I didn't. "What'd she look like?"

"If it was a girl, she looked more like a sissy-looking boy. Skinny. Short hair. Light color. Might be blondish, but hard to tell in the shadows."

Elizabeth Traynor! "What was she wearing?"

"Hmm. T-shirt with a picture on the back. Might have been a girl with a sword and a dinosaur or something on the back. Pants that didn't fit right?"

"In what way?" It seemed I'd have to drag each detail out of him.

"Like, too short. The bottom of the legs only came down about half way between her knees and ankles. Could be the style, though. I seen girls wear pants called cuplots or something like that."

"Coulottes," I said. But I knew they weren't Coulottes. The shirt with the woman, the sword and the dragon on the back and the too short pants.

They were Bly's. Did that mean Traynor had already murdered Bly and taken her clothes? The only other answer was that Bly was stashed someplace, completely naked, exposed to the elements—to Hurricane Angela.

"Your face is all red, Webb. Are you feeling sick again?"

"No, Duff. I'm feeling fucking angry. Let's get over there now." I pulled the door open, ready to go.

"Do you want the hooks or the screwdriver?" Duffy asked.

"When we get there, give me the hooks. You'll need the screwdriver to get us in."

It took us about ten minutes to hoof it over to the station. Since it was night, we just followed the main trail, as if out for a nighttime stroll. Duffy told me that even if the crazy girl was looking out the windows, she would n't see us because it was too dark. He said once we got close we'd be hidden by the storage shed. When we arrived at the shed, I saw that he was correct. Duffy was a pro when it came to sneaking around.

Peeking around the corner of the building at the station's covered front porch, I asked, "Is there a back door?"

"No, but there's a door on the right side that leads to a concrete walkway that's like a ramp, then turns left and goes down to the dock area where their boats used to moor." When it came to boats and seamanship, Duffy usually had his Duffyisms under control. He was a good waterman and knew his stuff. He'd certainly proved that to me. Before I could comment, he added, "But it's better to go through the front door."

"But—"

"'Cause," he interrupted. "The front door leads into a display room where they have one of them old-time life saving boats with place for four oarsmen and two or three other guys. There are open doorways on both ends of the room, but unless someone is standing right in the openings, no one will see us come in."

"They won't hear us?"

"I'm like a cat bugler," he said.

I knew he meant burglar, but it was no time for joking around.

"I'll be quiet as a mouse."

"Got those fish hooks?"

"Oh, yeah." Duffy fished the plastic box with the three straightened fish hooks he called crass knuckles. He took them out, handed them to me and started to tell me how to place them between my four fingers, but I told him I'd already figured that out.

I held the hooks loosely in my left hand, then suggested he leave the box on the ground where we were standing. "The smaller hooks in there might rattle when you're moving around in there," I told him.

Duffy agreed. He closed the little box and laid it on the ground. "We'll have to buy your friend some new hooks," he said.

A lump formed in my throat. *If she's still alive,* I thought. A vision of me torturing Elizabeth Traynor to get her to tell me where Bly was and what she'd done with her flashed into my mind. Could I actually do that? I'd shot Radovan Tadić while he sat in his jail cell.

That was revenge.

This was different.

Maybe.

Duffy was, in fact, a cat burglar. If not, he should be. While he was a fumbler with verbal phrasing, he was slick with a common household tool. Have screwdriver, will travel. We slipped into the front room. We could just discern the outline of the lifeboat on display.

While on one hand, I was ramped up with the fact that we had actually tracked down and found the kidnapper. On the other hand, besides Elizabeth Traynor, I didn't know what else I would find inside. I couldn't think about it. It made me sick to my stomach.

First things first.

I eased the door shut behind us, then stooped down and listened. Nothing. From here on, I decided it was my time to take the lead. "I'll go left, you go right," I whispered. I watched Duffy disappear into the darkness as he duck-walked to the opening on the right that led to the back room. I stood up and used a rope barrier surrounding the boat display to find my way to the opening on the other side. Duffy moved like a cat. I didn't hear anything. I hoped I was half as stealthy.

The back room was dark and quiet. I moved slowly, hoping my eyes would adjust, since feeling my way around was risky. I could run into or touch something and either knock it over or make a telltale noise. Once I moved farther into the room, I heard muffled voices. I froze. Then I heard Duffy whisper something from the other side of the room but didn't understand what he'd said. I eased toward my right until my hand touched a wall, then continued to move forward.

Suddenly, from right in front of me, Duffy whispered, "They're upstairs." We continued to talk in hushed tones.

"Jesus, Duff, give a little warning that you're there," I whispered back. In a knee-jerk reaction I had balled up my fist.

"Sorry, but I heard voices from the bunk room upstairs."

"Where are the stairs?"

"Right next to us."

"Will she see us coming up the stairs?"

"No. The stairs are enclosed. They open to the second floor at the back of the room. Actually, it's the front of the room," Duffy corrected himself. "She can't see us, even when we get to the top of the stairs. The room has five cots on each side wall. Behind the staircase wall is a wood stove for heat. 'Course, they don't need no heat now. We'll have to peek around the corners. See what side they're on."

That was the most concise speech I'd heard out of Duffy since we'd arrived at Egret's Cove. Like when he took charge of the boat crossing the inlet, it was crunch time and, in his Duffy kind of way, he was all business. "So, when we get to the stairs, you take the right and I'll take the left," I told him.

"Gotcha. Might as well stand up," he said. "I'll lead the way. Keep your hand on me 'til we get there."

I stood up, found his shoulder and followed him to the stairs. Once there we each moved against the walls. There were no banisters. As we moved upward, the voices upstairs became more pronounced, but I couldn't understand what was being said. Definitely, two people. That was promising news, unless Traynor was talking to herself. And answering herself. I chose to believe there were two people up there. And, it didn't seem heated or frenetic. I had renewed hope that Bly was alive and only a few feet away.

We took our time moving up the stairs, stealth and quiet being the prime concern. The further up we got, the darker it became. There wasn't even a drop of ambient light finding its way to my eyes. The only way I knew I was at the top of the stairs was when my hand felt the wall end and my fingers curled around the corner. Voices suddenly became more audible. It sounded as if they were on my side of the room.

I was about to move my head to look around the edge, to peer into what Duffy had called the bunk room, when a shrill scream pierced the black.

Chapter 33

IT WAS STARTING to rain when he took Blythe Parsons out of the cart and staggered with her up a short flight of stairs onto what she guessed was a front porch. He set her down on what felt like a bench. It was all she could do to keep herself from falling over. She heard him tinkering with something—probably the front door. Then she heard him move back and forth between the cart and the building, moving things inside. Once he was done with that, she heard him restart their transportation and drive away. It wasn't long before he was back. She guessed he'd stashed it somewhere out of sight.

Before he could secure her back in his arms, he practically dragged her off the bench. Then he carried her inside the building. That he wasn't very big or very strong was something to consider. If she could figure out a way to subdue him. Maybe something she could hit him over the head with.

But then what?

What would her fictional heroine Lady Bryn do?

First things first.

Stay alert and alive.

He struggled greatly and even stumbled and dropped her once, jarring her whole body, knocking the breath out of her. It took him forever to get her up a long set of stairs and into a bed of some kind—there was a mattress, but it felt more like a cot mattress than a bed. "I need food and water," she told him. "Otherwise you might as well kill me now, because my body will shut down and I will die."

In response, he tied her hands to the head-railing behind her. For the next hour or so she heard him rummaging around the room, clinking and clanking around, opening and shutting doors and, finally, going back down the stairs, repeating his exploration on the first floor. At one point, she heard him laugh in his high-pitched voice and shout, "This is great!"

From downstairs she heard something squeaking and rolling around on a wood floor. Had he found a bicycle? Eventually, he returned upstairs and, without saying a word, spoon fed her what tasted like tuna fish from a can and water from a plastic bottle. This went on for a long time, days probably; she remained blindfolded and had no sense of how much time had passed. Once she'd awakened and heard him softly snoring from somewhere across the room.

The first time she soiled herself and the cot, he removed all of her clothing and moved her to another nearby cot. Afterwards, she sensed him standing there staring at her. She thought he would rape her, but he didn't touch her at all, and eventually returned downstairs.

At that moment, she felt more helpless then she'd ever felt in her life.

She awoke to the sound of rain pounding on the roof and window panes. The wind was howling. It had to be the hurricane that they thought was heading toward the Outer Banks. They hadn't traveled far after she'd been abducted, so they were still somewhere in its path.

She heard him coming up the stairs. She was both hungry and thirsty. Dependent on her kidnapper. At the same time, welcoming and fearing his return.

She felt him sit on the side of her cot, his body against hers. This time, however, she felt him place a finger on her forehead, then run it down the bridge of her nose, over her lips and chin, down her neck, between her breasts and stomach. Momentarily, the finger stopped. Then she felt him move in through her pubic hair and below.

"Why are you doing this to me?" Blythe asked.

He chuckled. "If I'm going to be you, I need to know all of you, inside and out." Then, "You do want to eat and drink don't you?" Without waiting for an answer, he said, "It's not free you know."

Then he took off her blindfold, stood up and slowly disrobed.

She gasped when she saw that her abuser was not who or what she had thought.

The storm and the physical encounters went on and on. How many times she couldn't remember. She hadn't kept track. Each time her abuser finished, Blythe would spend hours being interrogated before she was allowed food, although she was provided with sips of water if she was "a good girl."

She thought about refusing to answer the questions. To not get nourishment. Just to die and be done with it. But she didn't. She'd always been a fighter and couldn't stand the thought of giving up now . . . or ever.

Obviously, the person was deranged. Maybe she would be simply left behind and found before she faded away. Like the heroine in her books, maybe she would pass on into another world where she could walk and ride dragons and fight evil doers with her broadsword. This is the world her mind retreated to during her ordeals.

Blythe could see out the windows at the far end of the bunk room that the storm was abating. Once her blindfold had been removed she realized where she was. She had once taken a charter boat out of Silver Lake Harbor to Portsmouth Village for a four hour visit. The mosquitos had been terrible. A kind young man that had taken the trip with her had carried her up stairways where she couldn't take her motorized wheelchair. He had carried her up to the second floor of the Coast Guard Station to the bunk room. Knowing where she was didn't sooth her anxiety and ever-growing fear.

This time it was night when Blythe's kidnapper came up to the bunk room. Blythe had been shocked when she saw that her kidnapper and abuser was not a young man at all. He was a she. A young girl. Early twenties maybe. The girl stood there looking down at Blythe and said, "I am now Blythe Parsons. And I'm the winner of the contest. You are nobody," then giggled like a teenager at a slumber party talking about boys. "It will save on my food bill." She went from giggles to laughing hysterically. Suddenly, she broke it off. "Maybe one last playtime."

When the girl finished, she got off the cot and went to an old cast iron heating stove that was no longer in use, opened the door, pulled something out, and returned to Blythe. Still naked, she climbed back onto the cot and straddled Blythe's withered legs.

Without preamble the girl raised her right arm above her head and said calmly, "I'm going to kill you now,"

In the ambient light filtering through the windows at the far end of the room, Blythe Parsons could see the outline of a knife in her kidnapper's hand.

Blythe's scream echoed in the darkness.

Chapter 34

I THREW MY body around the corner and, for some reason I can't explain, I shouted, "Elizabeth Traynor! FBI! Drop your weapon!" It just flew out of my mouth. I didn't even know if she had a weapon. All I saw in front of me was the outline of one person, her hand in the air.

Her head turned toward me just as my shin hit something hard and I fell forward.

"Shit"

I realized right away that I'd fallen over one of the bunks. I planted my chin on my chest and tried to do a roll so's not to bang my head on the floor. One whack to the noggin was enough for the time being. As it turned out, my ass smacked up against the next bunk bed in the row and I found myself on my shoulders, eyes facing the ceiling, and my legs from the knees down on the top of the next cot. I heard the hooks Duffy had turned into weapons, and that I'd placed between my fingers, clinkety-clink on the floor. So much for them.

That's when I heard Duffy, following my lead with, "You heard him! FBI! Drop yer weapon!"

He sounded more like a bad actor in a B-grade movie than an FBI agent, but I guess it worked because I heard Traynor shout back, "Don't shoot. I've got the kidnapper! I've got the kidnapper!"

Then Bly shouted, "She's got a knife!"

I'd wished she remained quiet when Traynor turned her attention back to Bly and shouted, "Shut up, bitch or I'll slice your throat and save the FBI the trouble."

I scrambled to my feet and shouted, "Put down the knife, Miss Parsons. We'll take care of the little scumbag that did this to you." It sounded dumb, but I guessed it worked because Traynor said, "They got you now, bitch."

While Elizabeth Traynor's attention was drawn to me, I saw Duffy's shape move across the room. Once behind her, he reached for the knife, saying, "I'll just take the knife," expecting her to comply, but instead she swung her knife hand back toward him. Fortunately, it was the haft that hit him above his right eye and not the blade.

"I'm keeping the knife!" Traynor screamed.

By then, I'd reached the cot she was on. As Duffy staggered back, throwing out "Mother-fuckers, and shittin' bitches," instead of going for the knife as he had, I rammed my hands into her side, just below her right shoulder and she toppled off the bunk bed. My impression was that she had nothing on—at least very little. There was a thunk as she hit the floor.

From the cot, Bly asked, "Webb? Is that you?" Then, "But how—"

I glanced down at Bly, was startled that her hands were tied to the head rail behind her—and that she appeared naked, too.

Holy shit! What was that bitch doing to Bly?

Suddenly Traynor shot past Duffy, going around the other side of the room. "She's heading for the stairs," I shouted to Duffy. "Follow her. I'll go this way," meaning to the left side of the stairs.

Duffy and I met on the landing at the top of the stairs. We stopped and listened. "I think she's buck-ass nekit," Duffy said, then "Stairs go up to the lookout. Coulda gone up there."

"You go down, I'll go up," I said. Then, "Be careful. She could be waiting for us. She's still got the knife."

Duffy headed down the stairs and I headed up to the lookout. The stairs turned to the right, then turned again. As I hit the second turn and moved upwards, I saw the outline of Elizabeth Traynor's skinny little ass and legs disappearing straight above me. When I reached a landing I found out why. To reach the turret-lookout she had to climb a ladder against the wall that was totally vertical.

I had to be careful. She had the advantage. Could cut my throat as my head rose into the opening. Why do people always go up when they're fleeing? There was nowhere to go. She was trapped. That was the good news. The bad news was, we'd have to wait her out. Who knows how long a crazy person with a knife could hold out. The answer to that came as soon as the thought entered my mind.

There was a series of loud crashing and glass breaking. "Son-of-a-bitch! She's trying to break through one of the windows." I made an instant decision I hoped I wouldn't regret. I placed my right hand and left foot on the lower rungs and began a slow assent upward.

More crashing, and Traynor screaming obscenities. Shortly there was a loud grunt and a thump.

Halfway up the ladder, I stopped to listen. I strained my eyes, but all I saw was a dusky outline of the top of the lookout. Not a trace of the girl. Had she already made it out the window and onto the roof?

I quickly went up the remaining rungs, stuck my head into the opening, and did a quick recon. Wind and rain hit me in the face. She'd gone out onto the roof.

"Damn!"

I pulled myself into the turret and, keeping low, peered out through the broken window. I expected square, but the turret was rectangular shaped, with the long side running along the spine of the main roof. There were two windows on each of the four walls. The window Traynor had gone out was at the front of the building, just to the left of the spine.

Then, I saw her. She'd found her way down the steep pitch of the main roof onto the roof of a small dormer on the east side of the building. She was trying to hang on and work her way down the south side of the gable dormer. Was she going to try and get through the gable window and back into the second floor bunk room?

"Shit!"

I pulled back into the lookout and went back down the ladder, dropping the last few feet to the landing, then back down the winding stairs to the bunk room. If she came back inside, I'd be waiting for her.

When I got back into the bunk room, I heard Bly call out, "Is that you, Webb?"

"I'm looking for the dormer window," I said.

"Can you untie me?"

"In a sec, Bly. That crazy bitch is still on the loose and—"

"Webb?" from Duffy.

"She's on the damn roof, Duff. Where is the dormer?"

"Dormer? Huh! I think they open inside one of the closets on each side of the room," he said.

"Closets?"

"There's a door tween each bunk. First one."

I felt my way around the first bunk in line against the wall, then found the closet door handle. I pulled the door open and looked up. I could see the silhouette of the dormer window. The window appeared intact and there was no movement from outside. I was about to say something to Duffy when I heard the faint sound of an engine cranking.

"She's bookin'!" I shouted.

As Duffy and I went around the landing to the stairs and headed back down, I heard from behind, "Webb! What about—"

By the time we blew out the front door, Traynor, in a golf cart like the one we'd used, was half-way across the front lawn, heading toward the main trail that led back to the village. The rain had eased off to shower level and the sky had begun to break up. Slivers of moonlight found creases in the clouds, illuminating portions of the surroundings.

"She's going for the boat!" I shouted.

Duffy surprised me with his speed. By the time Traynor reached the trail, I was trailing behind, but Duffy had already caught up to her. He'd grabbed hold of one of the roof struts and his left leg was on the running board, his right leg dragging on the ground, as if trying to stop her progress.

Suddenly, she jerked the steering wheel to the left and Duffy went flying off into the sopping wet grass. I heard him shout out the words, "Shit-n-shiney hola!"

In the process of turning so quickly, the golf cart went up on its left wheels, hovered for a moment while she did the right thing by yanking the steering wheel all the way to the left. If she'd turned it to the right, she'd have turned over and we would have had her.

While Duffy scrambled to get to his feet, I charged straight at her cart. By the time I got to where she'd been, the cart was back on four wheels and she was headed into a wide field, bordered on both sides by thick stands of trees.

"Where does that go?" I shouted to Duffy.

"It's a landing field for small planes. At the end there's a path to the left that goes around the back way to the school."

It was obvious Duffy was faster afoot than I am, so I said, "You run up the trail and cut her off at the school path. I'll follow her and make sure she doesn't try to back-track." Before I finished, Duffy was already running back toward the center of the village.

I wanted to lope behind the girl's golf cart, but the best I could do was slog through the thick, hurricane-drenched field of grass. The whole scene was bizarre. Creepy moon sliding in and out of view behind scudding clouds. Showers that sometimes stopped, then suddenly a few seconds of downpour. A toned down steady twenty-five knot wind was now only a mere annoyance.

It sounded as if she had the engine running full out. It wasn't helping. I literally had to maintain a slower pace so she wouldn't panic and bail out of the cart and run into the trees. If Traynor did that, I'd never find her. Then a thought hit me. Did she even realize I was behind her? Whether she did or not, I followed along at a convenient distance.

When she reached the tree line at the far end of the landing field, she took the golf cart left, suddenly disappearing from view. I quickened my pace. When I got to where she'd turned, there was an open area that appeared to be a dead end enclosed by trees. According to Duffy, there was a path through the woods and I heard the cart in there, somewhere ahead.

It took me a minute to find the entrance to the path. When I entered, I realized the golf cart was now somewhere to my right. Duffy had said the path wound through the trees, so I had to trust in continuing through the open way, which fortunately was wide enough for me to find my way.

All of a sudden I could no longer hear the golf cart engine. Did it cut out? Did she turn it off on purpose? It didn't take me long to come up on the machine. Elizabeth Traynor was nowhere in sight. Was this a set up? An ambush?

I stopped and listened.

Then I heard the sound of someone crashing through the trees. *Shit! She's doubling back to the Coast Guard Station.*

I had three choices. My first choice was to try to start the golf cart, turn it around and give chase back through the path and down the airstrip. I instantly ruled that out. I could run faster than the cart on the soggy grass field. My second choice was pursue her through the trees. It was the shortest distance between two points—mine and hers. The problem is, it was hard enough to see in the open. In the trees, it would be impossible.

I took my third choice. I turned and ran back along the winding path through the trees.

When I broke out onto the open grass I ran to the opening at the back end of the landing field. I stopped briefly to listen. If she was still in the woods, I couldn't hear her. Then, a sliver of moonlight broke across the grassy field and, just as the light disappeared, I caught a glimpse of her running ahead of me. Without further thought I ran after her.

I couldn't tell whether I was gaining or losing ground. I couldn't stop to listen, and running, all I heard was my own labored breathing. With the earlier head trauma and my undernourished body, I wasn't anywhere near peak condition. All I had left was pure adrenalin. And the building anger that we had left Bly there alone, still tied to the bed, totally helpless and defenseless.

It wasn't long before I saw the outline of the Coast Guard Station, and when I broke free of the landing field I saw her. I was closer to her than I realized, but whether I could reach her before she got onto the porch and through the front door was the problem. There wasn't much left in the tank, but I put on the afterburners and gave my best end-of-race-kick.

I was almost close enough to grab her as she went up the steps and onto the porch. I couldn't see details, but I could tell that Duffy was correct. Elizabeth Traynor was buck-ass nekit. Just as that thought ran through my brain, she hit the top step, tripped, and fell forward.

She grunted and let out a curse.

I was on her in a flash.

I reached for her right arm, where she still clutched the knife and closed my hand around her wrist. I didn't see her left elbow. She caught me just above the left eye, right on the eyebrow. I didn't let go of her arm, but I loosened my grip just enough for her to yank her wrist free and, when I fell off her to my right, she rolled away from me. The good news was, now I was between her and the door. The bad news was, she still had the knife.

I'll give Elizabeth Traynor this much. She was not only fast, but she was quick. I was half way to my feet when her arm came out of the dark and I felt the tip of the knife go into the fleshy part of the bottom of my thigh, maybe an inch, half way between the back of my knee and my crotch. Even so, it hurt like a bitch. If I hadn't been moving backwards, I would have been down and totally incapacitated.

She tried to come in and finish me, but I saw it coming and crab walked backwards. I thought she'd come at me again. I was wrong. She went for the screen door. I lunged at her right ankle, but her skin was wet and she easily pulled out of my grasp. She yanked open the screen door and rushed inside. If only we'd shut the main door behind us when we ran after her, I'd've had her.

My left thigh hurt like a bitch. I put it out of my mind. I'd have time to enjoy the pain later. I leapt to my feet and went after her. I'd fought Al-Shabaab in Sudan and tracked down terrorist cells in Europe, and wasn't about to let some crazy, skinny, bare-assed girl get the best of me. This was personal and she was going to pay.

I remembered to watch out for the rescue boat display and the roping that set it off. I wasn't sure which way she went, since earlier I'd felt my way along both, coming and going. I went to the left.

When I got to the steps heading up to the bunk room, the sound of her pounding up them echoed in the darkness. I heard her yelp and shout out, "Shit!" She'd stumbled in the dark interior of the enclosed stairway. I figured it was my chance to jump on her, but I stumbled, too, and while I caught myself with my hands on a higher step, I didn't make up any distance between us.

When I reached the top of the stairs I found the end of the wall and practically swung myself around into the bunk room. It was reckless. If she'd been waiting for me there, she could have gutted me and that would have been that. But I had to take the chance. If she wasn't waiting, she'd get to Bly before I could stop her.

I saw her outline racing toward Bly's bunk. Knife hand in the air. She wasn't going to waste any time with threats or gotchas. She was going straight in for the kill. As I launched myself at Elizabeth Traynor, for the second time that night, I heard Bly scream.

The knife was plunging downward as I hit Traynor. My right arm caught her up under her armpit and I rolled to my left to pull her away from Bly. Traynor came with me and was on top of me when my back slammed against the foot rail of the next bunk just beyond Bly's.

When I hit, Traynor was thrown away from me. I heard her hit the floor with a thud. The sound of the knife skittering across the floor soon followed.

I rolled off the end of the bed railing and found myself on the floor on my hands and knees. I saw her outline moving around in the dark, looking for the knife. Staying on my hands and knees, I scrambled over to her, reached out, found one of her ankles and yanked her back toward me.

She spun around and came at me with her fingers. Later, when I thought about it, I truly believed she thought she could claw me to death. I drew up on my knees, pulled my right arm back, and punched her square in the face.

When my fist connected, I was in a state of rage. Elizabeth Traynor went down hard on her back and I was on her, straddling her, the same way she'd been straddling Bly when I first saw her. If I had been a few seconds slower, Bly would have been dead. I hadn't been that blinded by anger since the day I shot Radovan Tadić.

I hit Elizabeth Traynor in the face, again. Then again. I was about to pummel her to death when Bly's shout penetrated both the darkness of the room and the darkness of my mind.

"Stop, Webb! Stop!"

My fist froze at the apogee of my next strike.

"She's done, Webb. She's done," softer, crying.

Chapter 35

THE RETURN TRIP across the inlet was not smooth, but at least it was uneventful. It was still pretty breezy, but the sun was out and, although I didn't feel totally dry yet, it was glorious.

Even though we towed Austin Meads boat behind the *Lady Brynn,* I took the helm of Meads' *Channel Hopper* just to be sure the two boats didn't collide in the choppy water. Duffy piloted Bly's boat, with Bly in the borrowed wheelchair Elizabeth Traynor had found in one of the two downstairs storage closets at the Coast Guard Station.

Elizabeth Traynor lay on the deck, securely bound. After a bout of uncontrolled screaming and threats, and continual claims that she was the famous author Blythe Parsons and why was her kidnapper being treated like the victim, Duffy put a rolled up pair of panties in her mouth and secured them with a piece of his own shirt he'd ripped off. Besides securing her, Duffy also cleaned up Traynor's bloody face. I couldn't stand the thought of touching the crazy bitch again. Truth was, I thought I might just punch her a couple more times, just for the hell of it.

Before we departed Portsmouth Village, Duffy had stopped by the Ranger Station where he found a first aid kit. Before we went down to Egret's Cove, he treated my superficial stab wound with antiseptic, then bandaged it up with gauze and tape. I tried to ignore it, but it still smarted.

We had just gone around the eastern end of Bird Island when a private plane, probably out of Billy Mitchell Field south of Buxton and the Cape Hatteras Light House, flew over and circled around, obviously looking for us. Duffy waved and the pilot wing-waved back, then headed north, presumably back to his airfield.

When we came through the entrance to Silver Lake Harbor, Bly shouted back to me, "Looks like we have a welcoming committee!"

Neither Duffy nor I told Bly we'd "commandeered" Meads' charter boat for our rescue caper.

She'd soon find out when Sheriff Caswell slapped handcuffs on us and hauled us up to his holding cell for stealing the *Channel Hopper*. When I'd mentioned it to Duffy (Bly was out of hearing distance) he'd just laughed and said, "Hell, Webb. It was worth it. They can't fry us in the chair for it." I didn't bother telling him that while they didn't do electrocutions any longer, spending the next few years in jail wasn't my idea of a good time. That said, Duffy was right about one thing. Without a second thought, I'd do it again and, no matter how things turned out, it was worth the chance. If Campers was there on the dock, I'm sure he'd be smiling as he read off the charges.

In fact, when we pulled into the pier, Campers was the first one I saw. He seemed amused at the rousing ovation we got from the crowd. A great side show for the tourists and locals alike. And a forum for him to exercise his authority. I didn't think it would enamor him to the Ocracokians.

Duffy waved at the crowd as if we were conquering heros returning home from war. Sometimes, in retrospect, things are pretty damned funny. At the time, my only thought was, *this is going to piss off some people,* thinking mainly of Campers—this as we passed by the fishermen's docks and headed further up to Austin Meads' pier. When the waiters and watchers realized we weren't going to stop where they'd thought, most of them broke and began to run north up the side of Highway 12, anticipating our next choice of port.

When Duffy pulled Bly's *Lady Brynn* into Austin Meads' pier, I jumped out of Meads' *Channel Hopper* and tied the mooring line around the cleat hitch, then moved up to take the line from Duffy and tied off both boats. By then the front-runners of the gawkers were pouring into the little parking lot and heading towards Meads' little charter house.

Some fellow with a camera was the first to emerge from the crowd, a camera bag slung over his left shoulder with the video camera propped on his right shoulder.

"Oh, boy" to Duffy and Bly. "This is gonna be a pain in the ass."

The look on Bly's face was like the proverbial deer in the headlight. Duffy jumped off the boat, took one look at the guy with the camera and asked me, "You want me to throw his ass in the water?"

When the camera guy heard Duffy, he got a wild look in his eye, but I said, "I think we're already in enough trouble, Duff."

"Trouble? Hell, we're heroes."

Then, the cameraman, emboldened by the fact we hadn't attacked him, started to push past us, saying, “Is that the crippled writer girl?” pointing his camera toward Bly, who was still in the boat.

I stepped in front of him and said, as kindly as I could manage, “First of all, asshole, she’s disabled, she’s a published author, and she’s a woman, not a girl. And if you don’t back off, I’m gonna change my mind about throwing your sorry ass in the drink.”

The camera guy almost ran into me, came to a sudden halt, said, “Hey, man, take it easy. I’m with the Norfolk News. This is a big story.” When I just glared at him, he got nervous and backed away.

“Still too close,” I said, moving toward him. He took several more steps back.

“Maybe we should get back in the boat and go over to Miss Parsons’ house,” Duffy whispered.

“I don’t want this asshole to know where she lives,” I whispered back.

People were still arriving for the show and laughter rippled around the crowd at our set-to with Camera-Asshole.

Then, breaking through the pack of people was Campers, obviously enjoying himself. Before he reached us, he turned back toward the crowd and shouted, “Everybody just stand back and keep quiet. I’ll deal with this.” Nothing changed. The people didn’t move back or stay quiet.

Campers didn't seem to care. He turned his attention back to us . . . and the cameraman, who had turned his attention to the deputy. Campers, playing to the camera, said, "I want to be sure you get all this on tape." He paused, looked at Duffy and me, smiled, then added, I'll need it for evidence."

"Two assholes in one day," Duffy said without cracking a smile, loud enough for the deputy to hear.

"Truer words were never spoken." I replied.

"Real smart guys," Campers said. Then, "Turn around and put your hands behind you. Both of you." He said it loud enough for all to hear.

Then, from behind us, Bly shouted out, "What do you think you're doing?" It was actually more a hysterical screech than a shout. "These two men saved my life from her," pointing down to the deck of the *Lady Brynn*.

Duffy just stood there, defying the deputy's order. I turned around, but instead of presenting myself to Campers, I strolled over to the boat and pointed down at Elizabeth Traynor. "That's the person you need to arrest."

As if on cue, Camera Asshole rushed in and shouted, "Who is she? Who is she?"

By now, the crowd of people had swelled even larger and had become restless. A number of them followed Camera Asshole's lead, shouting, "Who's in the boat?" "Who is she?" Several shouted, "What's going on?" I guess some of them were just following the herd. Sometimes people are idiots. In fact, most of the time people *are* idiots.

"I said—" Campers started when Duffy walked away from him, came over, and got into Bly's boat.

"Why don't you do something useful, Campers, and call an ambulance, a doctor or somebody who can attend to Miss Parsons and the kidnapper." I didn't wait for him to answer. I joined Duffy on board. "Let's get Miss Parsons out of the boat and—"

"Resisting arrest!" Campers yelled. When I looked up at him, he had drawn his weapon and had it pointed straight at me. "Put your hands up, both of you!"

Duffy and I looked at each other, shrugged our shoulders, then proceeded to roll Bly and her borrowed wheelchair over the port side of the gunwale, then each grabbed the top of a wheel with one hand, and the back of the seat with the other. "On three," I said. "One—"

"I'm gonna add to theft of a boat, and all the other charges, failure to obey the commands of a police officer!"

I looked at Camera Asshole, who was still shooting away, and smiled. "Two—"

"I'm giving you one last warning!"

"Three—" As Duffy and I swung Bly and the wheelchair up over the gunwale, Campers discharged his weapon into the air. While the onlookers gasped and a few screamed, Duffy, Bly and I all flinched in reaction, but finished the motion and set the wheelchair down on the dock.

Since Campers was closest to Duffy, he moved toward him, pointing his weapon right at Duff's head.

"What in the name of all that's sane and sensible are you doing, Campers?"

From oui of the crowd at the end of Austin Meads' dock came Sheriff Randy Caswell with Austin Meads following right behind, storming up the dock toward us with the purpose and resolve of someone who was ready to do some public ass-chewing.

Campers held his arm out, pistol still pointing at Duffy for just a little too long for my liking. Finally, his face flushed with anger, lowered his arm and placed the weapon in his holster. He didn't bother to turn around, though—just continued to glare at Duffy and me. I could tell that Bly wanted to say something to him, but was holding it in. I patted her on the shoulder and said, "We'll get someone to check you out."

Her response was, "I just want to go home and take a long hot shower."

"Campers!" the sheriff shouted.

The deputy turned around and, between gritted teeth, said, "These two men are felons and need to be arrested." He then went through his litany of charges and may have even thrown in a couple of new ones. I actually wasn't listening all that well. I looked past the sheriff at Austin Meads, who had an amused look on his face.

"Oh shut up, Campers," Caswell growled. "Nobody is going to be arrested for anything."

"But—"

"But nothing. Mr. Meads is not going to press charges for anything regarding his boat."

"But they refused to obey my commands, and—"

"Get the hell off this dock and do some crowd control, Deputy Campers, and that's a God damned order."

"What's the matter with this fucking town," Campers grumbled as he walked away. "I need to get out of Mayberry and find a real police department."

“We can arrange for that,” from the sheriff to the deputy’s backside.

“And the sooner the better,” from Austin Meads.

Turning his attention to Blythe Parsons, the sheriff asked, “You okay, Miss Parsons?”

“I’m good,” unconvincing. Shaking.

“Actually, sheriff, there is someone you need to arrest.” I walked back to Bly’s boat and pointed down onto the deck. Elizabeth Traynor was up against the bulkhead, partially obscured.

Caswell walked over and looked down. Austin Meads followed him. He stood there looking for a long time. Eventually, “That Elizabeth Traynor?”

“Yep.”

“She as crazy as they say?”

“Yep.”

“You two are something else,” shaking his head.

“Sometimes you just have to do whatever is necessary,” was all I said.

“Looks like she had an accident,” Caswell said with a straight face.

“Fell down,” Duffy chimed in.

Then, "Look Mr. Meads," I said. "About your boat—"

"Forget it," he replied.

"I mean, if there are any repairs needed . . . ."

Meads walked over to the *Channel Hopper*. "Looks okay to me."

Anne Simmons, a nurse practitioner from the Ocracoke Medical Center, came out, interviewed and did a cursory exam of Blythe Parsons, suggested a topical for the chaffing on her wrists. She also examined my leg wound, told Duffy he'd done a good job with what he had to work with, then cleaned it up, applied fresh antiseptic, and asked me to drop by the medical center for a follow up as soon as I could. Finally, she did a cursory exam of Elizabeth Traynor, then did some clean-up of her face and applied some antiseptics and the like. The sheriff stood next to Simmons and Traynor while the nurse worked on the girl. Elizabeth Traynor didn't say a word when the gag was removed.

Caswell agreed to come by Bly's house in a few days and take her statement. He offered to get someone to stay with her, but she wouldn't have anything to do with that. After unhooking Austin

Meads' boat, Duffy piloted Bly's boat around to her house and redocked the boat for her.

I took Bly home, helped her get settled back in and asked if I could come back and fix her a late lunch after Duffy and I went up to the sheriff's office to give our statements. She reluctantly agreed, but said to give her a couple of hours.

Campers took Elizabeth Traynor over to the village medical center for further treatment before she was taken and placed in a holding cell at the sheriff's office.

Ms. Terwilliger was the only one there when Duffy and I arrived to give our accounts. "The sheriff will be back shortly," she'd said, then gave us forms and paper to start filling out and writing our statements. Apparently, Ms. Terwilliger was familiar with Duffy. It was obvious the way she turned her nose up at him. I'll have to admit, neither one of us smelled all that good, but with him, it wasn't just that.

I had to help Duffy with his paperwork. "Cornfusing," he called it. "Usually they just throw me in jail. The only form I sign is the one when I get my empty wallet back."

I had to laugh. I did laugh. Duffy laughed with me. The laughing went on for so long, Terwilliger, apparently embarrassed by it, took a moment to step outside.

When the sheriff turned up with Elizabeth Traynor in cuffs, he took her in back to their holding cell, then returned to look over Duffy and my statements. Traynor didn't look at us, nor did she let out a peep. Caswell was not only interested, but fascinated in the unofficial tale of our daring rescue, although he did record it for posterity. I'm sure Duffy's rendition was grounds for plenty of barnyard humor for years to come.

When we left, I took a rain check for dinner with Duff. He understood and I knew I would make good on my promise. When I finally got back to Bly's she had taken that hot shower she'd promised herself and was, to my surprise, sitting at her computer writing. She'd turned off the speaker to the elevator and had the place locked up tighter than a drum. I had to go around back, climb up on her deck and knock on her writing room door to get her attention. Bly gave me a big hug with a good cry attached.

We talked well into the night. By the time I left the next morning, I was as confused as she was about the whole affair. "I guess we just have to chalk it up to total and incontrovertible insanity," I'd said.

"I almost feel sorry for her," Bly had said.

She was kinder than I.

She always had been.

Epilogue

IT WAS A glorious day.

Pea Island.

Quiet. Peaceful.

No one but Nan and I and the sand and the dunes.

And the Atlantic Ocean. Today, flat and serene.

"So you want to get naked and take a swim?" Nan asked.

I was on my back, eyes shut behind a pair of cheap sunglasses (who needs Ray-Bans unless you're a celebrity) on a funky tie-dyed beach blanket that had been my mother's—why she'd had it was a curiosity. She'd only gone to the beach with us a couple of times when I was a kid and dad said after I left home, he couldn't remember the last time she'd walked or sat on the sand.

Nan had been smart enough to bring the blanket along. Left to my own devices, it would still be on the top shelf of the closet in my so-called guest room.

When I didn't answer right away, she asked, "Are you asleep?"

I chuckled. "If I was, I wouldn't hear you ask."

"Smart-ass!" smacking me on my left shoulder.

"And, to answer your very naughty question, I have no problem with getting more naked than I already am, but I have no interest in getting wet. I spent I don't know how many days out in the storm, not to mention in the water, and I'm just now feeling dry. Just taking a shower was traumatizing enough."

Nan laughed. "Good thing I was there with my wash cloth to keep you calm."

"Good thing."

"Well sorry to interrupt your not-really nap, but I've been wondering . . . you didn't say much about the guy who you saved your life and helped you find Blythe. The Duffy guy."

I chuckled. "Duffy Duffner. Actually, I was just thinking about him." I shook my head. "Saying he helped me is an understatement." I thought for a minute and Nan was patient enough to wait. Finally, I said, "You know about my theory on friendship."

Nan kinda chuckled. "Yeah. You're a real hard-ass."

"I don't think so," I shot back.

"You are," she said, matter-of-factly.

I gave a passive shoulder-shrug. "I'm just selective. But I'm reassessing."

"Because of Duffy?"

I nodded. "I mean, without a thought he just threw himself into the mix to help me go after Bly. I know he's impulsive and not all that . . ." I hesitated. I didn't want to offend Duffy, even in my thoughts. ". . . well, anyway, he's a big-hearted guy who means well."

"Good thing for me," Nan said. When I laughed, she said, "Seriously. It's taken me this long just to get you to realize you need me around . . . ."

I knew her unspoken words were, "all the time."

"Don't want to have to train your next victim, huh?"

"You know, Webb, you're getting to be a little too much of a smart ass," serious.

Lifting my sunglasses up, "Hey, I've just come back from the land of the dead. Cut me some slack."

Nan smiled. "Good thing, too, or I'd never have forgiven you." Then, "So, after all this you've decided Duffy has met your rigid expectations for being your friend?"

Rather than go into a long discussion or explanation, I just said, "Any man that did the things he did for me is gonna be my friend, whether I like it or not." After a few moments of silence, I said, "I also have a new appreciation for weirdness."

Nan frowned. "Meaning?"

I told her about Jenine Wahab, the quirky teenager, and how without her help I might not have discovered Bly's whereabouts. "I've asked Bly to give the girl signed copies of her books or take her out on the boat fishing or something."

"So, shirking your personal responsibilities, I see," Nan jibed.

"Yeah, right. Middle-aged man taking extra interest in a sixteen-year-old girl? I don't think so."

Shaking her head, "You're a strange man, Webb. A strange man."

"I agree."

After a short period of silence, "Another question," from Nan, who lay on her side, right elbow in the sand, her head, with her shoulder-length dark brown hair, with its hints of gray, propped on her open hand. She had a voluptuous body and felt self-conscious in a bikini, which was strange, as she had no problem parading around in front of me sans clothes. Today she had on a two-toned blue one-piece suit she called a tugless tank—whatever that meant.

"I'm all ears."

"About the crazy kidnapper. About what she did to Blythe." When I didn't answer, she said, "if you want to talk about it some other time, that's okay."

Translation. If you don't talk to me about it now, I'll keep bugging you until you give it up. She'd told me more than once that it wasn't healthy to keep things that were bugging me, pent up inside. Translation. I want to know what's going on inside that head of yours. She was probably correct. I was a private person about my mental gyrations. But I had learned to trust Nan. I knew she wasn't a gossip. That she was only interested in my well-being. So, she was the only one I'd talk to about personal thoughts, particularly ones about myself and, in this instance, about Bly.

"You know, I probably would have beat Elizabeth Traynor to death if Bly hadn't called me off." When Nan didn't respond, I said, "And here I am, telling Bly that she really should talk to a mental health professional about her experience. Maybe I'm the one who needs a shrink—again."

"Do you think she fell into the Stockholm Syndrome? You know, where the victim begins to identify with the kidnapper."

"You mean like Patty Hearst with the SLA?" referring to the daughter of the famous newspaper baron, William Randolph Hearst, who had been abducted back in the 1970s.

"Yep."

I shook my head. "No. Not In this case, Bly told me she knew Traynor was totally bonkers and knew she would probably kill her when she felt like it—which almost happened. It was the sexual abuse Traynor subjected her to. I don't want to get into details, but—"

"She gave you details?"

"Yes, she did, but—"

"Don't tell me. I don't even want to know."

"I wouldn't anyway because Bly asked me to tell no one. But I will tell you that Bly said after the first time, which shocked her, the second time, she began to like it. At first, she told herself it was because she was playing along so Traynor wouldn't hurt her. Afterwards, she said, she realized it was because she actually enjoyed." Now she's questioning her sexuality. That's why I suggested she talk to a professional about it. I told her it was a natural response, but, hell, what do I know. I just didn't want her laying a guilt trip on herself. Otherwise, that crazy bitch Traynor would be inside Bly's head for who knows how long."

"Hmm," from Nan.

"What?"

"I was just thinking that whether you know it or not, it probably was a natural response. Any woman with a strong sex drive has probably had fantasies about having a sexual encounter with another woman."

"You've had them? Fantasies, I mean?"

"Of course. I'd never act on them. I like this too much," sliding her left hand down the front of my shorts. I didn't have anything on underneath. I gave her a half-assed laugh. She didn't remove her hand and I responded, causing her to wiggle her eyebrows.

"So, did Bly take your advice?" Nan asked.

"About the psyche guy?"

"Mmm."

"Calm down there," I warned her. She laughed. "You want to hear the answer?" She nodded. "She promised she would."

"You think she'll follow through?"

I nodded. "I already had a person's name and she called her the next morning, before I left to come home."

"Too bad about the fishing trip. You re-schedule?"

"She said she'd get in touch when she was ready."

"That's good. I hope it's sooner than later."

"Trying to get rid of me?"

"Hard-ly not."

"Now she's the clever double-entendre lady."

Nan giggled. "Why else would a lady have her hand down a man's shorts?"

"Do you want to know what Sheriff Caswell told me about Elizabeth Traynor?"

"Sure."

I told Nan that, at the sheriff's request, I stopped by his office on the way out of town and he read me the report on Elizabeth Traynor. The crux of it was:

Elizabeth Traynor had always been a troubled child. When she was sixteen, her mother died. There was never a father in the picture. She had a good relationship with her grandparents who lived in the village on Portsmouth Island. She visited every summer and had fond memories of them. After they passed, with her mother gone, she ran away before she could be placed in the foster care system during the last two years she was eligible.

Eventually, she found her way to an aunt on her father's side. According to the aunt, while there, Elizabeth lost herself in video games and online gaming. She fancied herself a writer, and spent a lot of time writing stories that were never published, and hanging around fantasy conventions. Playing wanna-be. It wasn't long before Elizabeth became so withdrawn into her fantasy worlds that the aunt couldn't deal with her. The aunt claimed she'd become afraid of her niece, although she could never quite articulate exactly why. Since the aunt had the financial resources to buy her way out of the problem, she had Elizabeth committed to the Harrow-Martin Psychiatric Hospital near Asheville, North Carolina.

"While she was there, she became obsessed with Bly and decided her life would be much better if she, in fact, was Blythe Parsons." I said.

"And this Elizabeth Traynor thought she could accomplish that by kidnapping her?"

"And after finding out what she could about Bly, then getting rid of her. In Elizabeth Traynor's sick mind, she thought she would take over writing Bly's novels and that people would actually believe she was Bly."

"Wow! How do people get so fucked up in the mind?"

"That's what the Army wondered about me after I shot that fuck, Tadić."

I was taken off guard when Nan leaned over and kissed me on the lips. She didn't take her hand out of my pants though. "It's a good thing General Tillman intervened. Otherwise, you'd be breaking rocks in Leavenworth."

"He saved my ass, that's for sure."

"What are they going to do with Elizabeth Traynor?" Nan asked.

I shrugged. "That's up to the courts. But my guess is they'll send her to a secure facility for the criminally insane."

"I guess we should feel sorry for the girl."

"Hmmph. You can. I don't. She tried to kill my friend."

"I still hope the next place she goes can help her find some peace."

"Mmm," non-committal.

"What about that deputy who gave you such a hard time?"

"Campers. The thing is, he was pretty good at the forensics stuff, but a real jack-off at on-the-street police work and community relations. He needs to either find another career or at the very least be kept away from the general public. Maybe stick him in a lab where the only people he pisses off are his co-workers."

Nan laughed. "I'll bet he felt like Barney Fife after making an ass of himself."

"All I know is, Caswell gave him two weeks leave to, quote, 'decide what he wants to do.' It was a polite way of saying, 'you have two weeks to find another job.' He's a real asshole."

Again, Nan laughed. "You know what you need," pulling her hand out of my pants and rolling over to her left.

"You going to *present* yourself to me?"

"Not yet. First you have to maintain, you know what." She had opened the cooler and was fishing around inside. Shortly, she pulled out two plastic cups, one blue, one red, and a thermos.

"What do you expect, talking about that fool Campers," I complained. Then, looking at the thermos, "Coffee?"

"Frozen whiskey sours, you silly-mon. Made with only the best. Jack Daniels Black Label," filling both cups to the brim.

"You're wasting good Kentucky whiskey by putting lemonade in it?" rolling my eyes.

"I'm told it's a sure way to get the blood flowing back into the joy stick," handing me the red cup.

I looked at it with distaste, shrugged, then, to humor her, I tipped up the cup and downed it in three gulps.

Big mistake!

"Geeze!"

"Brain freeze. I coulda told ya."

"Just for that . . . ." I stripped off my shorts and pulled myself up on my knees.

Sipping on the contents of her blue cup, like a sane person would, Nan's eyes got real big, and she said, "Oh my!"

Douglas Quinn
Presents

Yellow Bird

The next book in the
Webb Sawyer Mystery Series
Turn the page for a preview of

Yellow Bird . . .

Prologue

ERSKINE WEEKS HAD a dental appointment at one that afternoon, so he'd only booked two of James Nixon's fields for spraying, totaling 200 acres. Truth was, the tooth ached and he'd wished he'd put the jobs off until tomorrow. Too late for that now. He'd committed. Besides, it was a perfect day to fly. And he needed the extra money, if for nothing else, to pay for the new filling and cap. He had no coverage and Betty's plan didn't include dental.

Always something.

He went through his routine. It began with coffee, black, a banana and an Entenmann's chocolate covered donut. Just enough to keep him going without setting too heavy on his stomach. Betty had been on his ass about his gut. She'd thrown out the last box of Entenmann's he'd bought. This time he found a hiding place. And he didn't have to worry about her catching him with them. She was up and out of there early every morning for a workout with her trainer at the Elizabeth City YMCA. She'd been on this working out kick for the past three months. One day, she just got up and said, "I'm gonna get my body looking good again." Hell, he'd been satisfied with it how it was. She had lost about twenty pounds though. He'd give her that.

Once Erskine was finished with his breakfast, he collected his aerial maps, which he'd already marked. A farmer may have several fields, but may only want a certain field or fields sprayed. Sometimes, he just wanted a particular section of a field done.

Erskine studied the maps, then folded them up and headed out to the hangar, which was really just a open-faced metal building with an office and connecting storage room. He had a four-wheeler parked near the side door, but that was primarily for his teenaged son's use. Erskine preferred a leisurely walk up the field road out to the shed.

Five minutes later he was unlocking the office door. Once inside, he stood there and collected his thoughts. He went through his morning, step by step, one, two, three . . . .

Once the schedule was organized in his mind, he stepped into the storage room next to the office and went straight to the mixer, where he filled it with water in preparation for adding the Asana, the insecticide.

The Asana AX, a Dupont product with an emulsive concentrate of .66 pounds of active ingredient per gallon was delivered to him in 30 gallon drums. He was currently well stocked. Erskine connected the pump to one of the drums, which he used to pump and meter the insecticide into the mixer. As he added it, the mixer kept the water moving, agitating the 50 gallons of Asana into the plain water. For the 200 acres he needed to do this morning, he needed two loads, which used about six ounces per acre.

Before he loaded up with insecticide and fuel, Erskine did his pre-flight walk-around. His little yellow crop duster with blue striped trim and a closed cockpit was an Air Tractor, designed and manufactured in Texas by a man named Leland Snow. Erskine gave it a name. He called it Yellow Bird. As part of pre-flight routine, he checked the oil and gas tank and the prop for nicks, as well as the rest of the plane for anything loose. Once that was done, he hit the fuel drain, bleeding some fuel into a plastic cup to check for water. When he was sure there was no water in the fuel tank, he filled both 84-gallon tanks with 170 gallons each of Jet-A fuel—a fancy name for kerosene—from his 2,000 gallon storage tank. Finally, he filled the spray tanks with the insecticide from the mixer.

Once Yellow Bird was ready, Erskine got his ear plugs, his ag pilot's helmet, given to him by his father before he died, his Ray-Ban sunglasses, because his son said he had to be cool when he was flying, and his maps, then crawled into the Air Tractor. Inside and seated, he set the maps in the open glove compartment, then did a quick look at the gauges, including the torque meter, alternator, and temperature gauge. Everything looked normal. Even though the land was actually about twelve feet above sea level, there were enough topographic fluctuations that it worked best to set it at zero, which he did.

Everything was a go. He flipped the ignitor switch, hit the starter, introduced fuel into the carburetor, and cranked up the Lycoming Radial 9-cycle piston engine. He listened closely to the whine to be sure it was running smooth. It was.

He taxied out onto the air strip, which was a two hundred yard mowed area cut into the crop field, rolled down to the west end, closest to the hangar, then turned the plane around. He rotated the props from level to a slight pitch to assure oil was moving to them, then feathered them as flat as possible so the engine could get more horsepower for take off.

Since he didn't have a heavy load, he set the flaps at ten degrees, then powered up and began rolling down the runway. While he monitored the torque and heat gauge, he pushed the speed for take off up to 2,500 rpms. On a hot day Erskine's take-off speed was about 90 mph; on a cool day, between 70 and 80 mph. Today was somewhere in between and he lifted off at about 85 mph. Once he was off the ground, he pulled back to about 2,000 rpms.

Like his father, who taught him how to fly, Erskine was old school. He'd flown without communications in the plane for many years. Finally, he broke down and got his first radio in the cockpit. That said, he refused to use it unless there was an emergency. If he was flying near the Coast Guard Station or over the Pasquotank River, he'd call the Base air control tower before take-off and let them know his schedule, but this day he wasn't doing either.

James Nixon's farm was right next to Tabby Talmadge's place on Union Church Road. While they were still alive, John and Erskine's dad, Clayton, had been best friends. Erskine liked Tabby, but while she was a kind-hearted woman, she was a non-stop gabber and he avoided her when possible.

Erskine flew straight to Nixon's fields. Even though he was very familiar with them, he double-checked his maps to be sure he sprayed the correct sections. Once he was sure, he began his runs over the spray sites. As a precaution, he always did three passes to be sure there were no new obstructions that would hinder or endanger his runs. When satisfied that all was well, he began his run, although if something didn't "feel" right, he would abort and make another pass.

This morning was particularly calm. Even so, that could quickly change. His first pass was to check the wind drift. There were two reasons for this. One, he didn't want to fly back into the spray on the next pass. Two, he wanted to avoid having the spray drift into the owner's or his neighbor's house and yard. To do this safely, he engaged his smokers by flipping the switch to inject Corus oil, a paraffin-based substance, close to the end of the exhaust pipe where it is extremely hot. This creates smoke, which is expelled out the rear of the plane, mimicking the actual insecticide spray run.

From above, Erskine watched the smoke settle pretty much straight down. That was good. If the breeze had been blowing right to left, on his first run he would have had to release the spray over Tabby's side yard to let it drift onto that edge of the field of soybeans. If that happened, he knew he'd get a call. Not that she would bust his chops for it, but there would be an excuse for her to say, "I saw you flying over my yard this morning," and on and on it would go. If he let the call go to voice mail, she would fill up the space, then call back later anyway. Betty always checked caller ID, never picked up when it was Tabby, and always acted as if she didn't get or hear her messages.

He remembered the time, not long after he'd taken over the business from his father, when he'd either misjudged his tailwind, or an unexpected gust had come up—he never had determined exactly what had happened—and caught him at the end of a pass, just as he was beginning to pull up. His heart almost blew up when he saw the oak tree at the back of Tabby's yard looming in front of him. On pure reflex, he yanked the stick all the way back and just made it over the top of the tree, but not without several terrifying seconds of bumping and scrapping as he passed over. Later, he had to call her and ask if she minded him coming over and looking for the expensive nozzles that had been torn off the end of the booms. It had not only been a frightening ordeal, but embarrassing as hell.

With his right hand on the stick and his left hand working what crop-dusters called working the money handle, which opened and closed the valve under the plane to move the spray from the pump to the booms and out the nozzles, he began his first pass. With no appreciable wind, he didn't have to worry about kicking the rudder to keep level.

On the first spraying run, he used his GPS system to mark the A/B line, which is the set-up for the rest of the run, then set the GPS at three feet for the vertical. Each pass he would check the light bar in front of him on the outside of the cockpit, which had three red vertical lights with a horizontal amber light on each end, to be sure the plane remained as level as possible during the passes.

At the end of the first pass, he pulled up and turned to his right, being sure to go around the north end of Tabby's house and yard. If she was home, she'd make it a point to come out on her front porch while he was spraying and wave at him as he came in for this runs. This too, of course, would prompt a phone call later. When he came around for the second pass, sure enough, there she was, hand in the air, waving away. As always, he groaned and waved back.

Sometimes, by the third pass, she'd have returned inside, but she was still there. As he pulled out of his fourth pass, Erskine Weeks was thinking ahead to the coming ordeal in the dentist chair. He was at the top of his climb and had just turned to the right when he heard a distinct POP. "What the—" The words died in his mouth as the stick went dead in his right hand. Erskine wasn't a man who used profanity, but the words, "Son of a bitch, this isn't fuckin' good," came roiling out like water over a falls.

The Air Tractor continued up and forward for a short period of time while Erskine tried to think of something he could do. The thoughts were useless. The last thing that went through his mind was something his father had told him when Erskine was first leaning how to fly. "If the stick goes, you'll lose total control of the plane and you will come down like a shot turkey buzzard."

Fortunately, Erskine Weeks had passed out before he hit the ground.

21205104R00262

Made in the USA
Middletown, DE
21 June 2015